CONTACT: ECHOES IN THE DARK

JOSHUA T. CALVERT

PART I

LIFE

1

My eyes are closed as the first thought forces its way into my consciousness. It is not lofty or profound, but raw and unformed.

I am.

This is followed by a whole cascade of further thoughts that draw concentric circles around this first point of contact with myself.

Who am I? Where am I? Why am I not breathing?

These thoughts turn into emotions that fight a brief, brutal battle in my heart.

In the end, fear wins.

I want to inhale – my whole body is crying out for oxygen – but it's like I'm trying to climb an invisible cable to escape an invisible fire. It's burning hotter and hotter. The impulse is there, but nothing is here to fill my lungs.

A weight compresses my chest, squeezing harder and harder while the breathing reflex becomes stronger, driving me almost mad. Fear turns into basic survival instinct and removes reason from the equation of my short life. My body takes control, twisting and convulsing, trying to force its survival at any cost.

I open my eyes so wide that they hurt.

The world is murky, dark blue and grainy, shapeless, as though it cannot decide what it wants to be, life or death?

It happens suddenly. I was warm a moment ago, but now I feel cold because something is separating from me. I didn't know it was around me until becoming aware of losing it. The pressure grows worse. My skin tingles, my arms and legs feel heavy. I'm still looking into darkness, but I can see outlines that weren't there a moment ago.

I see a bright surface moving away from me. Red light above me. The warmth leaves along with the support I'd had and I fall forward. My hands and knees react without my doing anything and I land painfully on the cold and unyielding floor.

It doesn't matter because death has taken up residence in my chest and is now spreading even faster.

Pain shoots like liquid fire from my fingers and kneecaps through my entire body. I tremble as I raise both hands to my mouth in a last, desperate attempt to halt the end.

Breathe. I must breathe!

Cold fingers feel a warm resistance in front of my lips. They don't stop to find out what it is, but tear at it, roughly and driven by sheer panic. A snake twists in my gut, resisting its awakening and biting into my windpipe.

I scream within my mind because the black edges that were pulsating a moment ago are approaching from the sides of my vision, like curtains closing and ending my brief, terrible existence.

End of show.

No!

My hands find strength that I cannot feel and tug at the snake, tearing it from my body. The fight is short but brutal. It takes revenge with biting pain.

I make out its outline as it falls to the floor in front of me, hissing. I gasp a breath and a scream tears out of my throat, I

AM HERE. Guttural and wet, yet liberating, it is my primal message to a cold world.

I live.

I greedily breathe in dry air and fall back onto my hands. I inhale again, once, twice, three times. New life finds its way into my organs as an unpleasant tingling sensation, spreading as though streetlamps are being lit one after the other. It's wonderful because there's no room for thoughts. The fear is gone, too, and for a moment there is only a deep, all-encompassing sense of relief, perhaps even joy, in being alive – in breathing.

But it doesn't last long because I feel nauseous. A volcano in the middle of my body threatens to erupt. I start to shake all over. Cold sweat breaks out of every pore of my skin. A feeling of finality sets in. Then the eruption follows and I vomit multiple times. The cramps come in waves, and each wave brings a gush of stinking liquid that pours out between my lips onto the floor. It tastes sweet on my tongue and metallic at the same time.

When it's over and nothing more comes, I fall to one side, powerless, and pull my legs up to my body as if I were being controlled by someone else. My mind is far away, seeming condemned to watch. I close my eyes that have yet to see very much. The world is blurry and the red flickering is unpleasant.

I lie curled up on the cold floor and start to cry. I am too exhausted for grief or fear. They find no home in me because there are no doors or windows. My body seems to have an intelligence of its own and I surrender to it because I no longer have the strength to think for myself. The tears flow for a while, freeing me from part of the burden that has been weighing me down the whole time, something I only realize now as it leaves me.

After a while I scan my surroundings. Behind me is a wall that is a little warmer. I notice I am shivering. Cold.

I pull myself up to sitting and lean against the warmth,

drawing my knees up close to my chest. My ears pick up something, but the sounds are muffled and distant, as if I were deep under water.

Once I've rubbed some life back into my fingers, I use them to clear my eyes of whatever is blurring my vision. It feels sticky and slimy. I blink a few times and flinch when I spot a creature in front of me.

It is small and has four arms that it uses to support itself on the floor. Its contours are jagged like a reptile's and its color is a deep blue. I can't see much because my eyes hurt and I have to keep closing them. But I can see a bright area on its head that is constantly changing.

A flight reflex awakens in me, but dies somewhere halfway into my consciousness because of my lack of strength.

The creature isn't moving, so it doesn't seem to want to eat me. I take that as good news. I don't feel particularly tasty with all that vomit, either. Besides, there can't be much flesh on me, the way I feel.

I look up and see a lamp that flashes red in a steady rhythm. Red is not good, I know. But *why* do I know that?

Blink. Keep blinking, I remind myself, because blinking helps. The image my eyes are creating for me is slowly clearing. I am in a corridor. The walls are brilliant white with an octagonal pattern that looks strangely familiar. The floor is dark blue, which is due to a huge puddle that has spread out around me. I look down at myself and see bare breasts, dark brown skin smeared with blue liquid, and small hands.

A bright light in front of me vies for my attention.

The creature!

I flinch, bang my head on the wall, and groan. As the adrenaline subsides and the pounding in my ears lessens, I realize that I have been covering my face with my hands.

Extremely effective protection against a monster, I think mockingly, but I don't pull them away. Instead, I spread my middle and ring fingers and look through the gaps.

The creature is not in fact a creature, but a robot. Part of me is curious how I know this. The point is, I do know it.

What had looked like the blurry scales of a reptile are blue-green squares that surround his small torso and keep raising and lowering themselves. Like mechanical plumage. The four arms are identical and long compared to his torso. He is sitting on two of them. In one he is holding a bowl with things that send shivers down my spine, and he has stretched the other one toward me, the mechanical hand with its five fingers flat, like he wants to 'high-five' me.

And then there's the 'face,' a curved, oval display with a simple smiley face that looks so out of place that a laugh works its way from my stomach and over my lips. Suddenly, the flashing warning symbol on its forehead is extremely funny too. I don't know why, but I laugh and can't stop. I find myself reaching out my right hand and high-fiving the robot, whose simple pixel face suddenly looks confused.

My laughter doesn't sound healthy, and it doesn't feel funny, but it has taken on a life of its own and I can't stop.

At some point I suddenly fall silent because I notice that one of the robot hands is resting on my shoulder. It feels neither warm nor cold, spectacularly unspectacular, and yet so significant that a whole torrent of feelings rises up inside me. They sit like an unformed, constantly moving lump in my gut, a lump that has to come out, because if it bursts inside me, I will burst with it. I can feel that.

For some reason, my body wants to cry, so I let it happen, even though I don't understand it, because I feel warm. Not on my skin, but around my heart. The feeling becomes even stronger when the smiley smile returns to the robot's display. The warning symbol flashing on his forehead makes me feel sorry for him.

Then he reaches into the bowl he is holding with his other hand and pulls out a syringe. I wipe the tears from my eyes.

"You don't want to put that in my body, do you?" I ask,

coughing violently a few times as the remaining mucus comes out of my windpipe. My voice sounds bright and somehow beautiful. Like proof of my existence, it's devastating and uplifting at the same time.

I am so caught up in my own sounds that I am briefly confused when I notice that the robot is pulling the syringe out of my upper arm and its 'face' looks concentrated before it notices that I am looking at it. Then it turns back into a smiley face. Two eyes, a mouth. And again and again that intrusive warning symbol.

"What did you do?" I'm a little outraged.

He doesn't answer, but he keeps smiling. It feels like he's betrayed me. Instead of protesting, I rub the puncture site. It hurts, but the pain in my chest subsides a little and fresh energy flows through my limbs.

I stand up, straighten my back, and move my hands to my face to make sure they are mine and working. Then I poke a finger in each of my clogged ears. Viscous fluid runs down my cheeks. Only now do I hear the alarm siren that has been blaring the whole time, as though it were begging for my attention with increasing intensity. It no longer sounds like I am underwater, but now the noise hurts my ears.

My gaze returns to the little robot, which has raised itself up on two of its arms and is standing upright like me. It doesn't even reach up to my chest. With an outstretched finger he points behind me.

I turn around and stagger as if I were hit by an invisible blow.

2

I see ten oval windows, nine of them curved outward and filled with dark blue liquid. Four on the left, one in front of me, five on the right. The one in front is open, raised up like the wing of an insect, and between it and me is the large pool of the sweet-smelling substance in which I was kneeling a moment ago. The empty chamber is just big enough for me, and a kind of umbilical cord hangs out of the back, shiny pink and smeared with blood. I look down at myself and see the same blood in a small hole at the middle of my belly.

My fingers automatically move toward the hole, but I recoil before touching the wound.

I know that my life began in this chamber. I also know that it is called a bionic torpor capsule. What I don't know is, why do I know these facts?

Or why I am here, I add.

My eyes fall on the robot, and when it raises two fingers and smiles, I gather that it is a positive gesture and means 'it's okay.' I return it reflexively and walk along the other pods. In each of them I see others like me. Most are still babies, others a little older. Two of them, on the far right, are almost fully grown. At least I guess they are. Their faces look peaceful, eyes closed, lips closed around fist-sized mouthpieces of dark cables.

The snake.

Hope begins to grow within me and, ironically, with it comes worry, like a kind of dark counterpart. What if I had been alone? All alone?

"We have to wake them up," I hear myself saying. "These two."

I look at the robot and point to the two capsules to my right.

His display shows a sad smile and the outstretched index finger of his right hand points to lights above the two oval windows. I have somehow overlooked them until now. They are very small and part of identical control panels.

And they glow red.

Something inside me tightens. I know that red is not good. With growing unease, I go to the left and look at the next light. Also red. The one next to it, as well. Then my open capsule. Through the glass I can see that mine is flashing green. I walk faster as I move past the other capsules. Every single one flashes red at me, as if it were imitating the alarm light above me.

My forehead sinks against the glass of the last torpor capsule. It feels warm, but the warmth offers me no comfort. I close my eyes for a moment. The robot nudges me, but I raise a hand to tell it to leave me alone.

"Give me a minute," I say, taking a few deep breaths. I don't want to cry again. When I reopen my eyes, I'm staring at the outline of the infant on the other side, floating in the dark blue liquid, held in place by the umbilical cord attached to his belly and the snake in his mouth. His tiny chest doesn't rise or fall.

"I'm alone." It's a simple statement, but it hits me hard and I slump down. The robot nudges me. I want to reprimand him, but my desperation is not his fault. So I take another deep breath and turn to him.

He gesticulates excitedly.

With one hand he points to himself, with the other to the warning symbol on his forehead. Then he points with some vehemence to the blaring alarm on the ceiling. His face now shows a sad smile with crosses instead of eyes.

"You need my help, don't you?" I ask weakly.

The robot nods.

"Okay. But I'm afraid you'll have to tell me what to do."

Instead of answering, he flops forward, catches himself with his hands, and starts walking down the corridor on all fours like a dog. I follow him and only now realize that the floor is not flat, but curved. It seems to be constantly going uphill, like being on the inside of a treadmill.

Once we're past the torpor capsules, we pass through two doors and enter a large room containing a long table and chairs, surrounded by waist-high cabinets and work surfaces. On the left, a ladder protrudes from a narrow hole in the ceiling.

My little robot companion runs toward it, jumps up nimbly, and grabs the rungs with all four hands to pull himself up. Shortly afterward he disappears into the hole. I quickly follow him. To be honest, I do so mainly out of fear of being alone.

The sudden movement stimulates my blood flow and distracts me from the emptiness I have felt ever since I saw my dead comrades. Were they ever alive?

The higher we climb, the queasier my stomach feels. It's not as bad as before, when the nutrient fluid was trying to get out of me as quickly as possible, as though I'd eaten something gone bad. Gravity is easing and I understand that it's the centrifugal force that's decreasing the closer I get to the center of the rotating frame of reference I'm in.

How do I know this?

My body becomes lighter and lighter, and when I come out of the ladder tube, I am floating.

I find myself in a long corridor. Unlike below, it is round like a tunnel, and instead of octagonal patterning, the walls here are smooth, but just as white. The robot skillfully makes its way along by using handholds to the right while heading toward a hatch. I follow it, my movements fluid.

Apparently I've done this before. At any rate, it's easy for me. The weightlessness is pleasant but every impulse needs to be carefully measured so that I don't shoot forward and crash into the hatch.

I bring my legs forward and support myself on the plain metal. The robot puts a hand on the display on the right side and looks at me expectantly. At least that's how I interpret it. His face shows a smile, then he moves back a little.

"Should I?" I ask myself, putting my hand on the control panel. The hatch opens like magic, revealing the bridge of my spaceship. I recognize it immediately when I see the network of stars through the windows and the two large armchairs with the curved displays in front of them. Something in my head clicks into place and another mental door opens.

How do I know all this? I ask myself as I slide into the cockpit. It is cramped and dark, as though the metal fittings here were sucking out all the light from the surroundings and turning it into deep shadows.

As though controlled by someone else, I sit down in the right-hand chair, knowing that it is the commander's and not mine.

"If I'm alone, at least I can be the boss, right?"

The robot climbs onto the seat next to me and holds out two fingers in agreement. The red flashing warning symbol above his smile looks like a small fire – like his head is smoldering. That's how I feel every time I look at him.

I return the gesture and tap the display in front of me. It takes up almost my entire field of vision and blocks out the windows with the stars. It seems to be getting a little darker around me, but maybe I'm just imagining it. An image comes to life, showing me complex trajectory data and the orbital mechanical relationships of an alien solar system that consists of several planets and a central star. And a green dot in the outer system.

"That's probably both of us," I say and the robot holds up its two fingers.

A keyboard with complex symbols and numbers appears in front of my stomach. It is made of light, transparent and yet clear enough to see everything. I understand the hieroglyphs, telling me yet more puzzle pieces are miraculously falling into place in my head.

The star map decodes itself and I watch it reveal its secrets. Cryptic data becomes a mathematical language, and from this, clear insights emerge.

I zoom out with my fingers, letting them fly over the holokeyboard and display the previous flight route.

"Twenty light years," I say in awe. "We've been traveling for eighty years. This is our destination system. Or so it seems. But I'm getting a lot of error messages here."

My gaze slides to the bar on the left side of the display – 30 different dots, flashing red, vie for my attention. With a bad feeling in my stomach, I press the first one.

"Damage report," I mumble.

The robot beside me wears a sad face.

"That's okay," I say. "I'll take care of it."

The drooping corners of the mouth revert to a smile.

I call up the plan of my spaceship and look at the schematic. It looks like an arrow made of composite materials, a little thicker at the rear, where a powerful drive nacelle is attached. Block-like modules are arranged around the shaft in the central corridor, and I know that most of them are cargo containers. On the starboard side, three of six are missing, as if a monster had bitten into them and feasted on them. Just behind the bow, which includes the bridge where I am currently located, a large ring circles the ship, connected to the rotating base by four spokes. Pale light shimmers from small windows. I see deep, black scars on the shell of the wheel, as though it had burned – which I know is not possible in a vacuum.

Several sections of the ship flash red and form dashed lines that connect them to the damage reports on the left side and can thus be assigned.

"Three of twelve cargo modules are gone, six are damaged and have lost their atmosphere," I read.

The robot looks like it is listening to me and it somehow feels good to speak out loud.

No signs of life in the torpor capsules. I gulp and move on to the next report. "Critical course deviation. Energy matrix cells almost discharged."

I skim through the rest of the reports and then look at the robot sitting beside me.

"If a summary is enough for you, we are screwed."

3

First I seal the damaged cargo modules and decouple them from the rest of the ship. After that, the life support system stabilizes. At least a little. The readings for remaining thermal energy and oxygen don't look good, but at least they're no longer in freefall. Next I turn off the alarm because I realize that it's stressing me out, and if there's one thing I don't need more of, it's stress.

I scroll through the torpor capsule logs. It's like a glimpse into my own past. For 30 years, my body has been growing in a torpor capsule that doesn't even deserve its name because I didn't hibernate in it, I grew up in it. I see that the on-board AI, which has been offline since an apparent solar event, initiated my 'birth' after 50 years of flight. Apparently that was its last action before the main computer and memory redundancies were destroyed. Before that, I was a frozen embryo in a small vial that lay like a cartridge in the back of the torpor capsule. My vital data developed normally, as did my brain, which was indoctrinated via a kind of memory implantation system. It apparently functions via a chemical exchange whose substrate is the nutrient fluid.

But why did the AI initiate my development as its final

action and not that of one of the other nine crew members? I will probably never know the answer.

"Okay, I was born and raised here. I know everything, and I know that I'm on a spaceship. With this system as my destination. But I don't know why or how I was not born until I was thirty." I summarize my existential dilemma and wave it off. "It could be worse, right?"

I look at the robot. "I could have a warning symbol on my forehead and only communicate with smiles."

The robot sitting with me hangs his head and the corners of his mouth sink downward.

"Sorry, bad joke. But hey, the less you know the better you sleep."

Is that a saying? Did I remember it? Or is that an original thought that just came to me? I ponder, and shudder. Not knowing who or what I am feels terrible. But I don't have time for self-pity, which isn't likely to solve any of my many problems.

"One thing at a time," I say out loud and take a deep breath. "Since we both seem to be alone, you need a name first. I can't keep calling you robot."

He smiles wider and raises two fingers.

"Rofi," I say.

His head tilts to the side.

"Robot friend," I explain. "Not particularly creative, but you're a robot and my friend. Rofi works as short for it, I think. That's a bit easier to say, don't you think?"

His eyes become question marks.

"You brought me here. That was nice of you, and you're the only one here besides me. So it would be nice if we were friends, right?"

He nods and the smile returns to his display.

"Great. So, Rofi. First we need to find out where we came from and what our mission is. Why we are here," I summarize. "Then we'll see what happens next. Maybe we can call for help or something, although I fear we are stranded very far from home. Wherever that is. Once we have a picture of where we are, we may also find a solution to two of our most pressing problems, oxygen and energy."

I start by giving the onboard computer a sequence of commands, after which the ship's many sensors collect data from the alien system we are in.

"Okay, so what do we have? A central star that makes up more than ninety-nine percent of the system's mass. Normal nuclear fusion by fusing hydrogen nuclei into helium," I read aloud to my new friend. "Around it there are eight major bodies that orbit in a roughly flat plane. Four are terrestrial."

I lean a little toward Rofi, as if I were telling him a secret.

"That is, they are made mostly of silicate rock and metal. The innermost of them is interesting. Its surface shows signs of geological activity, despite its small size and lack of a dense atmosphere. The third planet has been marked by the computer. Maybe it's our target? It's in the habitable zone, where liquid water can exist. Not too close to the central star that it evaporates, and not too far away that it freezes. It's also the only one that has a dense, nitrogen-rich atmosphere and is mostly covered by water. I think that's our target planet, Rofi."

I quickly scan the rest of the system data. Another dusty rocky planet, lifeless and desolate, followed by a band of smaller, icy bodies – an asteroid belt. This region appears to be the result of the accumulation of leftover material from the formation of the system. After that come four gas giants, huge bodies that consist mainly of lighter elements such as hydrogen and helium. They have more or less pronounced ring systems and numerous moons. The second of these gas giants is notable for its strong magnetic field and intense radiation – and it is located in close proximity to my spaceship. *Our* spaceship.

"Do you see that one there?" I zoom it closer on the

display. It fills the monitor like a brown giant, surrounded by mighty rings of dust and ice. It reminds me vaguely of a very similar gas planet in my home system.

I push myself out of my seat and float toward the window. By now, I can see it with my naked eyes, almost the size of a thumbnail, standing out against the brilliant starfield of the Milky Way, which surrounds us with its gentle shimmer.

Rofi waves at me excitedly.

"I'm coming," I say soothingly, floating back through my holokeyboard and buckling myself back in. Rofi extends a finger and points to one of the gas giant's rings, where a red dot stands out against the gray. I imagine it's blinking.

A marker.

"Why does everything always have to flash red?" I ask with a sigh. I move my index finger to the mark and press it. A new section appears and zooms in several times. When I understand what my eyes see, they widen and I tense involuntarily. I immediately recognize the shape of one of the cargo modules arranged around the hull of my ship.

It is located in a kind of hollow in the middle of the many various sized ice chunks that form one of the unimaginably large rings in the middle of which the gas giant rotates with its mighty cloud bands of ammonia. The module looks badly battered with countless pockmarks and scratches that are visible even from this distance with the optical telescopes. And it is flashing – not red like the marking on the onboard computer, but white. A lamp on the top is purposefully and directly aimed at my ship and is blinking. It takes me a few moments to recognize the repeating pattern.

SOS. *Help.*

"There's someone in there!" I shout. The sudden excitement makes my skin tingle all over my body. "Someone survived, Rofi! Someone else is alive besides us two!"

Robi raises two fingers and displays his smiley face.

"Okay, calm down," I admonish myself. "One hundred

and fifty thousand kilometers away. That's a lot." I glance over the reactor data and do some calculations in my head. "We can still manage that with our remaining energy. Maybe we can even use the gas giant there to refuel a bit."

I know myself that the latter was more of an excuse, because it would be a tight squeeze to even get there. And the onboard computer, with its marking of the 'water planet,' left no doubt that it was the real destination of my 80-year journey.

But what if someone survived? Just the thought makes my heart soar. Someone has to be stuck in the cargo module. Otherwise they wouldn't be sending me light signals.

Rofi's eyes become exclamation marks.

"Yes, I know it's dangerous," I answer. "But we still have to save them."

My robot friend stretches out a hand and points to my display, more specifically to the symbol for the crew section. I click on it and see the overview of the torpor capsules. All but mine are marked in red with the sad message that the corresponding crew members have died.

I think about it and then I understand. "There is no empty capsule."

Rofi raises two fingers. *Correct.*

"Hmm," I say, rubbing my chin. "Maybe there's someone who didn't sleep and kept watch throughout the flight?"

Rofi doesn't respond.

"The cargo modules have no computer system of their own on board. Only the rudimentary heuristics of the internal systems. So how would we get a coded light signal that requires intelligence if not from someone with a mind?"

Since it's a rhetorical question, I don't wait for an answer and start to calculate a course. When someone like myself is out there alone and – even worse – in a tiny capsule, there's only one right decision. I have to launch a rescue mission.

And quickly.

"Apparently the module was blown off during the solar event that damaged my ship – sorry, Rofi – *our* ship," I muse as my fingers fly over the holokeyboard, calculating distances, the rotation speed of the rings, the ship's drift speed, and the exact position of the cargo module in the ice belt. "It must have been accelerated somehow, then crashed into the ring and was slowed down by the chunks. It's a miracle that it wasn't destroyed and that its hull is still intact."

At the end of my calculations, I arrive at a flight time of two hours without accelerating. I don't dare use up what little energy is left or there would be no remaining life support once I've rescued my comrade.

"Now we just have to think of a way to recover the module." My newly rekindled courage is about to sink, but I don't let it. I clap my hands to chase away the looming pessimism.

4

I have a problem.

My unknown and unfortunate comrade is stuck in his cargo module, about a meter deep in the ring. It is denser than expected, despite its gigantic size, with several moons that are barely noticeable within the sea of particles. In some places, the field of ice crystals and larger chunks is so dense that they cast shadows on their neighbors.

Of course, the module is in just such a shadow. Several house-sized objects made of water ice are rotating on their axes very close by – so close that it will be impossible to get to the module with my spaceship. In addition, the small container has no life support of its own. But as long as there are light signals, I am hopeful that he or she has found a way to be protected from the cold. I do not know how long the breathable air can last, not knowing when the module was blown away.

"In order not to endanger our habitat module, we have to keep a minimum distance of one hundred meters," I explain. Rofi looks sad. His eyes become crosses.

"Do we have something like a gripper arm on board?" I call up the blueprints of the ship, which is apparently called the *Ankh*, I realize now from an inconspicuous heading, and I search in vain for a corresponding device on the hull or in the inventory lists of the remaining cargo modules. "No, we don't. But we have an interferometer that can be extended and can be up to one hundred and twenty meters long."

Rofi's fingers are raised in an encouraging gesture.

"But that still doesn't give us a gripper arm," I mutter, clicking my tongue. "But we need one because the only thing we can attach anything to is the docking device on the cargo module."

Next, I pull up the field tool inventory and look at the various hooks and carabiners and compare them to the specifications of the retaining clips. None of their diameters is large enough.

"I won't allow us to get so close to our comrade and then not be able to save him," I say, frustration starting to spread through me again. I make no room for it because I need help right now and losing courage doesn't seem particularly helpful.

I glance sideways at Rofi. "I wish you could give me a little help, my little friend."

He points meaningfully to the warning triangle on his forehead.

"I see, you're damaged." I blink. "Do you think I can fix it?"

He shakes his head with a sad smile and I reflexively pat the side of his display.

"It's fine." I point to my work console. "I saw that you got me out of torpor. So, I'm indebted to you. You may keep quiet as much as you like. Maybe my friend knows how we can get you back on your feet. That would be something. But first we have to rescue him."

Ten minutes later, I am back in the habitat module, my still bare feet pressed to the floor by centrifugal force. On the way here, I noticed for the first time that I was cold, and I searched the closets for clothes. I found the living quarters, which consist of eight bunk beds, two stacked on top of each other. I wonder why there are only eight when there are ten torpor capsules. None of the bunks look used. Blankets, covers, and pillows are still sealed in transparent foil.

This surprises me even more. My crewmate must have been sleeping somewhere, because there is no 11th torpor capsule on board. I checked.

"It's all very mysterious," I say with a touch of fatalistic humor and a sigh.

Rofi has followed me and is looking at me with question marks for eyes.

"It would be too easy to despair because of fear, wouldn't it?" I justify myself with a shrug and finally find what I was looking for, an on-board overall that looks a bit small, but is made of a stretchy synthetic fabric that I hope will adapt to my contours. I slip into it and overlay the fasteners, which run diagonally from my collarbone on one side to my hip on the other. They merge together like magic, so that the juncture is barely visible. Only a thin line remains. The suit clings to me like a second skin and warms me enough that I return to the console next to the ladder and turn the temperature down even lower. I have to relieve the energy storage and stretch its remaining capacity for as long as possible.

"What do you say?" I ask Rofi. He smiles his trusty pixel smile and holds up two fingers. "White suits me, doesn't it?"

I don't wait for his answer and go to the small lounge that I have discovered behind the living module. There is an elliptical trainer and a complicated-looking exercise machine with rubber resistance bands that I definitely won't dare to use because it looks like an instrument of torture. There is also a table, a small seating area, and a kitchenette – lots of things in a small space, so it feels cramped. Right now, I just need something to eat.

In the refrigerator I find dozens of identical-looking packages that simply list the amount of macronutrients. Proteins – 30, fats – 30, carbohydrates – 40.

I choose one and put it in the **microwave**. It takes only a few seconds to inflate the package. When I take it out, I almost burn my fingers and let out a curse. After a short while, I find a plate and cutlery – a two-pronged fork and a knife. My stomach growls as it realizes that something will soon be done to address its hunger.

I tear open the packaging and look at the contents with interest.

"Rofi, I'll switch to batteries at the next opportunity," I announce.

In front of me is an indefinable concoction made of legumes and green leafy vegetables. Whether I simply don't know anything about food, or it looks so horrible that it's unidentifiable, I'll probably never find out. Unfortunately, it reminds me of my vomit. Nevertheless, I wolf down every bit of it, mechanically and quickly, so I can get back to work as soon as possible.

Two and a half hours of flight time isn't much if I still have to find a way to turn my idea into a plan by then. This without support, without a robotic arm, without a small spacecraft. What I'm planning would be quite a challenge even with a team of several astronauts.

For some reason, I know that the table behind me can be transformed into a digital work surface by moving my hand over it in a specific way. A monochromatic surface becomes a glowing display.

Rofi stands on his hind legs on the other side and looks over the edge with interest. At least that's what I imagine, because he's still smiling much the same as usual.

I draw a planet and several rings, the outermost one

thicker than the others. When I look up, a little embarrassed, I notice that Rofi's semicircle, which is supposed to represent a smile, has turned into a laughing mouth – thanks to a line that connects the ends of the semicircle.

"Really?" I ask him, feigning outrage, and point to my drawing. "Now can you think of a third emotion that can be portrayed?" I snort. "I was never meant to be an artist, that's for sure. But I'm good with numbers and physics. That's something."

I draw the module as a small gray block in the third ring of the gas giant.

"The particle density in this area of the ring is very high. According to our radar measurements so far, many of the larger chunks near this point are unevenly structured and rotate quite erratically. It is therefore difficult to calculate the safe distance for us. Our safety cables for external missions have a maximum length of one hundred and fifty meters. A little buffer is important, so we will approach within one hundred meters. That should still be safe. The maneuvering jets can bring us into the appropriate orbit around the planet so that we stay on a parallel course with the module. The gravitational forces of the gravity sink will do the rest."

I speak my thoughts aloud and scroll through the *Ankh's* inventory lists with my left hand.

"We need a device with which we can grab the crashed cargo module and pull it toward us. Weightlessness is all well and good, but mass still has inertia out here, which means it takes a certain amount of force to move it."

My thought is to use the extendable interferometer designed to measure gravitational waves. It's basically a simple extendable tube with a mirror in the end cap and a laser aimed at it on the other side.

"We're here because of the habitable planet, I assume, and not to measure gravitational waves. So we can use it for something else. The interferometer extends from the starboard side, so we have a telescopic arm. It can't be bent or swiveled, but if we position ourselves precisely, we don't need those options. We grab the cargo module and then pull the sensor rod back in. I do the rest by hand."

I nod, convinced of my own plan. But there is still one essential problem.

"But we don't have anything that can be used to grab." I point to the end of the interferometer, which is basically just an oversized extension rod. "Not quite what we need."

I'm just about to continue browsing the inventory list when the rotation suddenly stops, and with it the artificial gravity. Shortly afterward, I start to float, just like Rofi, who stretches out his four hands and just manages to hold on to the edge of the table. Since I had just started to lean back, the impulse remains and I hit my head on the kitchen counter directly behind me.

I see the remains of my food floating up on the ceiling, along with the cutlery. I should probably be tidier. Have I ever had parents who reprimanded me for something like this?

The alarm starts blaring, hammering unpleasant memories of my 'birth' into my mind, only to immediately fall silent again. Gravity abruptly returns.

I crash onto the floor on my back as I feel downness return. A blinding pain spreads through my core, burning hot and icy cold at the same time. When I look down, I see the knife from my meal sticking out of my belly with the handle pointing upward.

5

"Today is my lucky day, Rofi," I groan. "I get to visit the sickbay before I continue." I cough wetly, wipe my mouth, and to my relief there's no blood.

Suddenly everything around me starts moving. At first I think it's a dizzy spell but then I notice that Rofi has grabbed me under my arms and is pulling me behind him. He is surprisingly strong, despite his thin arms.

"Well, from the looks of it, I would have anticipated trouble from the food. Who would have guessed that cutlery would be my downfall?" I ask, in a somewhat desperate attempt to distract myself from the fact that there is a piece of metal stuck in my torso. It feels cold, like an icicle, but it doesn't hurt much.

So far.

I could permit myself to be angry about the bad luck, having the knife fall on me this way and having gravity return at the exact moment that the knife aligned to impale me. But if I don't survive this, I don't want to have wasted my last few minutes worrying about things I can't change.

"I bet you're smiling right now," I say. "If not, just shut up. I don't want to know."

The ceiling passes above me, white and covered with the octagonal patterns. What is behind it?

We turn. To the left, I think. The white around me seems to become even brighter, almost aseptic. This must be the sickbay. The pain comes when Rofi is suddenly above me and pulls me upward. My waist bends and puts pressure on the knife.

I gasp. Stars sparkle before my eyes.

When I look at his face, Rofi looks sad.

"It's okay, little one." I force the words out between my lips. Then the robot is gone.

I am lying on a treatment table that adapts perfectly to the contours of my body.

Maybe I should adopt the sickbay as my bunk.

The area above me is filled with shimmering analytical equipment and a surgical arm controlled by a medical robotic unit. It too has a display on which I see a happy face – animated and complex. Not as simple as Rofi's.

"It's nice that we're all in such a good mood," I say, feeling beads of cold sweat seeping through the pores on my forehead. Am I getting a fever, or am I just scared?

The medical unit, a complex network of sensors and processors embedded in a casing of brushed polymer compounds, begins its work. A female voice, synthetic yet soothing, patiently explains each step. Shouldn't she sound more focused?

"Patient stable. Starting local anesthesia," says the soft, soothing computer voice.

The delicate hand of the robot arm bends downward and two infusion devices emerge from a flap above it. They look like flattened pens and press against the skin around the injection site.

The pain subsides immediately, leaving a dull pressure as the mechanical fingers probe the same spots.

"Do you still feel pain?"

"No," I mumble.

"Starting by removing the foreign object."

The surgical arm, a sleek, flexible mechanism made of titanium – how do I know this? – moves with incredible precision. Yet I still feel like a piece of meat being chopped up on a countertop.

She approaches my abdomen, the knife in her sights. In the equivalent of her wrist sits a small, round device that opens to reveal a series of delicate surgical instruments.

Rofi grabs my hand. His head just reaches over the edge of the treatment table. When I glance at him out of the corner of my eye, his face changes from a sad smile to a cheerful one.

"I saw that!"

I feel a slight pressure as the instrument grips the knife.

"Foreign body is being removed," the voice informs me. There is a brief tug, and then the knife is gone. The dull pressure subsides, replaced by a heavy throbbing.

The medical unit continues, "Foreign body successfully removed. Beginning wound care." The surgical arm moves again, this time with what looks like a spray gun extending from a small compartment in the arm. With quick, precise movements, she sprays something into the wound. It's a strange feeling, but not unpleasant. The cut closes up as if by a miracle. Then follows a small brush that moves rapidly over the seam.

Another device, a flat, rectangular scanner, glides over the treated area and sends data to the medical unit. Finally, the sober diagnosis follows. "You have a minor abdominal laceration, specifically a perforation of the subcutaneous tissue and underlying muscles in the abdomen. There are no signs of injury to the internal organs or major blood vessels. The wound has been sterilized and sealed with bionic symbionts. It is expected to fully heal within six hours. Prophylactic antibiotic bionites have been administered to rule out the risk of infection. They will dissolve on their own within twelve hours and be excreted via the kidneys. Only minimal restrictions on movement are to be expected, which should improve as the wound heals. No permanent damage is to be expected."

I breathe a sigh of relief. Rofi's eyes alternate between circles and crosses.

"Yes, I'm glad, too." I sit up to check, let my legs dangle from the treatment table, and wait a few seconds while the medical unit retracts into its compartment in the ceiling.

"Stop," I say. "Extend the robot arm again."

The autonomous system obeys dutifully and the androgynous face on the display smiles at me expectantly. "Do you need further assistance?"

I wink at Rofi, who tilts his head.

"You know, I thought I had been so unlucky with the knife," I begin to explain with a smile. "It was a truly bad day. But I couldn't have been luckier." I point to the robot arm. "We found what we were missing, a gripper arm for the interferometer. If I manage to dismantle it and put it on the interferometer, we can use it to secure the cargo module, pull it toward us, and recover it. Our injured crew member would be saved and breakfast would have been worth all of the trouble. Can you do something for me?"

Rofi raises two fingers.

"Can you bring me some tools? I think I can do this."

The little robot nods and disappears from the sickbay. Until he comes back, I lie back down and instruct the medical unit to show me its structure in the form of schematics on its display, and to reveal the exact anchoring in the ceiling.

By the time Rofi returns with a well-organized toolbox, I have come up with a plan. With the precise details I learned from the medical unit, I begin to dismantle the surgical arm. Its titanium outer shell is secured with a series of microscopic screws, which I loosen with an electric screwdriver. A complex network of fine wires, sensors, and microscopic servo motors is revealed beneath the shell.

Thanks to narrow lenses that are part of the tool, I can see into most elements.

I study the inner mechanisms, following the paths of the wires and the electrical impulses that flow through them. I need to reprogram the arm to respond to radio waves, so I connect one of the relays to the display of the medical unit and enter the corresponding code. My hands move almost automatically. The relay is a small, flat piece of technology, a chip barely bigger than my fingernail, but it is able to interpret radio waves and convert them into commands the arm will understand.

I solder the chip in the correct place and connect it to the main control wires of the arm, a delicate job that demands steady hands and fierce concentration. But finally it is done. The chip is installed and the arm is ready to follow my commands.

I put the titanium shell back in place and secure it with its microscopic screws before picking up the medical unit controller, a small device that emits radio waves and is intended to enable manual control in the event of a failure of the autonomous system. I press the activation button. The arm twitches, moves, responds to my commands.

Rofi smiles and holds up two fingers. I return his gesture with a heart full of satisfaction just as gravity begins to lessen again. Not as abruptly as before, when the on-board computer actively slowed down the entire habitat. I hold on tight and it is over quickly, before I can float away. Fortunately, there are no knives lying around and I wisely stowed the tools as I finished with them.

"We have to get this done," I say, swallowing the sigh that tries to fight its way up my throat.

No time for frustration!

6

I tell Rofi to take the robotic arm to the starboard airlock, along with my spacesuit. Fortunately, he doesn't look sad, so I assume he knows what he's doing – and that there is in fact a spacesuit for me.

When I arrive on the bridge, I float to my seat and buckle myself in. My movements are so precise and routine that my head fills with questions. Have I been an astronaut before? Am I perhaps a clone of my real self, a copy that was bred during the long journey to an alien solar system and trained with *my* knowledge? I don't know a lot about the human brain, but I do know this much: neural connections are formed through learning and experiences that cannot be separated from the respective environmental influences. That's why you can't copy a brain. For it to be identical, a clone would have to have had the same exact experiences, have lived the same exact life.

That is certainly not the case with me. The way I see it, I only existed in the torpor capsule that transformed me from a frozen embryo into what I am today. So am I *me?* Or do I exist as the duplicate of the person whose genetic blueprint I am based upon?

These thoughts are so intrusive and unpleasant that I push them aside while I fire up the heuristic programs to investigate why the habitat module is suffering from errors.

I find over 600 bugs in the ring's control software, most of which have existed since the moment the onboard AI failed many years ago. It is responsible for constant bug monitoring. But it is no longer working. I think my skill set includes programming, but this is too advanced for me. So I check the software for the main and maneuvering engines and the starboard airlock. There are a few bug reports, but they relate to minor things like efficiency optimization with minimal energy input and are not relevant to my immediate plans.

My biggest problem remains the energy matrix cells. They are only five percent charged. That's just enough to reach the cargo module and maybe the gas giant to fill the graviton converter that serves as the *Ankh's* primary power source. But that would require us to stop at the cargo module and to be able to collect it without using the main engine – meaning nothing can go wrong.

"What could possibly go wrong?" I ask ironically into the silence of the bridge. "It's not like I have any reason to be pessimistic after everything that has happened so far."

I look at the sensor data one last time. The cargo module is still 30 minutes away. The trajectory data shows a precise approach to the orbital parking position above the third ring around the gas giant. Nevertheless, I recheck everything to make sure that the onboard computer is executing the correct commands. If I go out of the airlock, I have no chance of remotely controlling the *Ankh*. I have no AI to support me, and no comrades who can take over in here.

At least not yet, I remind myself, looking at the module and its constant SOS signals in the form of blinking light.

I check the approach vector and then start calculating the exact parking orbit, parallel to the piece of the *Ankh* that was lost. I plan the entire final phase of the rendezvous with hard numbers and calculate everything several times. Then I feed them into a simulation.

Orbital mechanics is a complex science, a mixture of speed, gravity, and time, all of which must be kept in a delicate balance. First, I need to get the spacecraft at the right speed. Too fast and we'll overtake the module. Too slow and we'll fall behind. I adjust the thrusters, letting them make a gentle hiss as they push us forward. On my display, I monitor our speed, making sure we're right on course.

Then comes alignment. The spacecraft must be aligned parallel to the cargo module in order to recover it safely. This requires incredible precision, as even the slightest difference in angle would throw us off course.

The gas giant's gravity also plays a role. Its massive gravitational pull will constantly be tugging at us, trying to drag us into its shimmering rings. I must factor that gravitational pull into my calculations, must balance it out to keep the *Ankh* on course.

Finally, there is the matter of time. In orbital mechanics, timing is everything. A few seconds too early or too late and our entire trajectory would be thrown off. I keep an eye on the time, counting the seconds until we are in the perfect position to retrieve the module.

The computer confirms that all calculations are correct. Only now do I give the order for the corresponding maneuvers to be carried out automatically after our arrival. I have to trust in myself for the rest.

With a gentle kick of my feet, I float down the central corridor to the starboard airlock. The doors slide apart as I place my hand on the control panel, and I slip into the cylindrical chamber that separates me from the infinity of space. My spacesuit, limp and empty, is clamped to a bracket on the left side. It looks so huge that I can't imagine how I'm going to fill it.

Maybe it was intended for one of the deceased comrades and I was never meant to carry out an outside mission? Do I lack the necessary skills?

I guess I'll find out soon.

Rofi is hanging like a monkey from a handrail on the other side. His blue-green scales shimmer in the cold white light of the lock. His display face shows a happy smile as he looks at me. He points to the spacesuit and then raises two fingers.

"Well done, Rofi. Thank you."

Putting on the spacesuit in zero gravity is a strange affair. It consists of several pieces that have to be caught before I can slip into it. One wrong touch and they drift away. Rofi with his four arms keeps holding me or the suit parts in place and is an invaluable help. I float my legs through the waist ring into the lower piece. We rotate around our axis a few times when my robot friend loses his handhold and only after several rotations can he catch one of his hands around a handrail.

The upper part of the suit is even trickier. It seems to have a life of its own and evades our grasps because the arms keep waving in opposite directions, giving the torso different impulses. After a few failed attempts, Rofi finally manages to catch it – and me. I push my arms into the sleeves and Rofi secures the wrist fasteners.

Finally, it's time for the helmet. With a deft movement, Rofi grabs it out of the air and puts it over my head. I secure the clasp and raise two fingers.

"Thank you," I say, simultaneously checking the radio. My voice echoes in my helmet. It sounds a little higher and hollower. When he also raises two fingers, I know he can hear me. "At least one of us can hear the other now."

I look him straight into his pixelated eyes and hold him by the shoulders with my stiff gloves. "Can you go out there? Without getting into danger?"

Rofi nods and raises two fingers again. I should have called him 'Two-Finger Bot.'

"Into the vacuum?"

Again he signals yes.

"Can you magnetize your hands or something?"

Two fingers.

"Good. Then I need you to bring the robot arm out and assist me with the tool. Otherwise there isn't enough time – I won't be able to do it alone." I wonder how long it would take me, or what would have happened if Rofi had said 'no.' In that case, I will have failed. My desire to be selected for spacewalks is almost non-existent or I probably wouldn't be so nervous. But I am the best qualified astronaut for the job, that much is certain.

"Secure yourself with one of the cables," I tell Rofi.

I wait for him to turn, then attach one of the safety cables to his torso where there are several carabiner hooks. After that, I hook myself to another one and double-check that it is secure, as are the winches beside the outside hatch.

Next, I press the virtual button on the forearm display of my spacesuit to evacuate the atmosphere from the airlock.

It only takes a few seconds before the light above the hatch changes from red to green. I take one last look at Rofi and then operate the opening mechanism.

The absence of air molecules causes the hatch in front of me to open in silence, and I step forward to the edge that marks the transition from the spaceship to space. I stop involuntarily and stare into the infinite blackness that stretches out before me. The silence is absolute, broken only by the low hum of my own life support systems. I hold my breath, realizing that I had not felt truly alone before. Only now, surrounded by nothing but darkness and starlight, does the loneliness feel all-encompassing.

A shimmering band stretches out beneath me, a dance of

ice and dust that catches the light of the nearby star and reflects it in a spectrum of colors ranging from pale pastels to deep, rich hues. It is a sight of breathtaking beauty and majesty that leaves me in awe. The rings turn in elegant arcs around the massive gas giant, as though painted by an unseen artist with a brush of light and shadow. They are so incomprehensibly vast in their extent that the *Ankh* is no more than another, slightly larger speck of dust near them.

Astrophysical concepts flow through my mind without my having to think about them, labeling the mystery before my eyes. It's a brutal reduction of this wonderful creation that is far too vast to name. But my mind ignores it and runs hot. The rings are made up of countless particles, from microscopic dust to chunks larger than mountains formed from frozen water, the result of the planet's gravitational forces pulling material out of its interior and spreading it around it in a flat, broad disk. The specific position and width of the ring I'm above is the result of complex resonances with the giant's moons, which force the particles into specific trajectories and proliferate them, in part, through cryovolcanism.

I have no idea how I know this, but apparently I know what I'm talking about. Maybe there's a similar gas giant where I come from?

I feel insignificant in the face of this vast scene, no bigger than one of the tiny ice crystals that make up the ring. The loneliness is overwhelming, a feeling of isolation so deep it is almost painful. And yet there is also a kind of peace amid this loneliness, a silence that penetrates deep within me.

I just stand there, high above the shimmering ring of a distant gas giant, and contemplate the wonder of space. The stars sparkle in the background like diamonds on black velvet, so far away and yet so close I almost think I can touch them. I feel small and insignificant and yet part of this incredible universe, a tiny dot of consciousness in the silent infinity.

A bright flicker reaches my eyes and tears me out of my reverent stupor. That must be the cargo module, my comrade in distress. By the time I can see its light signals with my own eyes, the *Ankh* is slowing down and I don't have much time left to prepare.

7

Rofi appears beside me. He holds the surgical robot arm in both hands like a trophy.

With him at my side, his remaining magnetic hands firmly attached to the spaceship's metallic surface, I step out of the airlock and onto the hull of the *Ankh*. My horizon tilts upward in a nauseating way due to the change in perspective. The gas giant spreads out before us like the ichor-filled eye of an angry god. Above us stretches the infinite darkness of space, crossed by a milky band of stars.

On my forearm display, I activate the interferometer, which consists of several telescopic segments that can be extended at different levels. With a quiet whirring sound that continues through the magnetizable boots of my spacesuit, creating the illusion of sound, the interferometer extends to the first stage. It is only about a meter long and as thick as a graviton tube. To get to it, we have to walk about ten steps diagonally across the *Ankh's* hull.

Intrusive thoughts disrupt my concentration. What if my boots lose their power and I drift away? How high will the radiation levels of the gas giant be?

Rofi has the robotic arm ready, his own arms moving with

a precision and skill that makes me jealous. I take the arm and guide it to the interferometer. With careful movements, I put it on the end cap of the interferometer and use my belt tool to apply the self-curing nano spray and an old-fashioned screw clamp. Then I secure the connection and check the data on my display.

The connections to the extension mechanism and the improvised gripper arm are in place. It now looks even more delicate than it did in the sickbay.

I look at my chronometer. According to my calculations, we will soon reach our parking spot above the cargo module. A tingling of excitement spreads through me at the thought that soon I will no longer be alone. I look down at the ring, which is slightly brighter than the others, and so wide that some of the planets of this system could swim in it and still look small.

Weightlessness creates a strange feeling. There is no up or down, just the gentle pull of the magnetic boots that keep me on the spaceship's hull. Every move has to be considered, every action carefully planned. One wrong step could send me flying into space, away from the safety of the spaceship – the only place far and wide where life is possible.

At least for now.

Close to me, the ship's habitat ring rotates, a constant swirl of light and movement. It's a calming sight, a sign of life and activity in the otherwise silent vastness of space. At the same time, it's so big and its rotation so fast that it's simply too massive for my comprehension. My reptilian brain feels threatened, doesn't understand how something so complex can work.

"All right, Rofi. The installation is complete. Be ready in case you need to fix something," I radio to him. His face display is turned off and frozen, probably to protect it from the indescribable cold that prevails out here. But he holds up two fingers to signal that he has heard me.

I take a few more deep breaths, then grab the first stage of the interferometer and cut off the power to my boots. I immediately lose my grip and reflexively pull my arms together even more tightly. I know that a long umbilical cord connects me to the *Ankh*, but out here instinct counts more than any rational thought.

I pause for a few minutes and look at the scene through my helmet's molecularly bonded glass visor. The ring is now within reach, a seemingly infinite surface that stretches from one end of the universe to the other. From this perspective, cosmically speaking almost directly on its 'surface,' the structure looks like a scratched record. Even to my eyes it seems impenetrable, its particles are so densely arranged.

If I tilt my head slightly, I can see the cargo module, a slightly curved composite box, plain and ridged, as though a predator had scratched its hull trying to get to its contents. The small light that still flashes and fades in the steady pattern of the SOS signal is something I now recognize as a maintenance light used for zero-g work in space dock. Whoever was inside had to have exposed and manipulated what little wiring there was to turn the power on and off in the perfect SOS pattern. I don't think the simple electronics can be repurposed to automate the signal, so he or she most likely has been repeatedly pressing two wires together. For hours.

"I'm coming," I mumble into my helmet and lick a drop of sweat from my upper lip.

I keep my eyes on the cargo module until I realize we're no longer moving. I'm now directly over my target, 100 meters away – or at least I should be. It looks much farther, I think, but appearances can be deceiving because distances in this environment cannot be put into any context that my brain is familiar with.

One last look at the gas giant that consumes almost my entire field of vision, at the different colored rings that form a flat plane around me. Then I fixate on the cargo module and its blinking light before pressing my forearm display with my right index finger and activating the telescopic mechanism of the interferometer.

I am slowly being lowered onto the module – at least that's how it feels. It is getting closer and looking bigger. I feel like a celestial body as I dive into the ring, which is becoming increasingly more eerie. The majority of the particles are dust or ice crystals, but many of them are as big as the damaged cargo module, others bigger than the mighty *Ankh*, from which I am getting noticeably farther. They collide with each other, change their direction of movement and smash into neighboring chunks. Kinetic abrasion creates more dust and more ice, which flies off in all directions. The mighty gas giant's gravity will catch everything and force it into its orbit. Eventually.

It's a miracle that the module hasn't been crushed or thrown erratically through the ring.

When it is within reach, my movement stops. The interferometer is extended to its full length. I dare to loosen my grip and spread myself a little. My eyes glide over the cargo module. Two of the docking device's top retaining clips are damaged. But I only need one.

I mark one of the two remaining ones in my head-up display and send the data to the robot arm's control software before gently pushing off and gliding the last two meters toward the module. I catch myself on the connector located above the closed hatch, which should normally be accessible via the *Ankh's* central corridor.

My umbilical cord to the spaceship doesn't have much slack left and is approaching taut. I can hear my breaths in my helmet rushing faster than before. With my magnetic boots activated, I stand on the cargo module's hull, bend down, and tap my suit's wrist cuff against the composite mixture that I have brought with me.

Clank, clank, clank.

Shortly afterward the light signals stop.

"He's still alive!" I rejoice. "My comrade is still alive!"

Some of my deep loneliness dissolves into hope. With renewed enthusiasm I command the robotic arm to grab the left clamp. The elegant piece of technology moves almost as fluidly as it would under gravity in the sickbay, opening its six delicate fingers and wrapping itself around the metal brim.

I press the button for the Move command and look up with satisfaction. My head just barely protrudes above the edge of the ring that is moving around me. Here and there I have to dodge a leisurely lump of ice. The *Ankh* stands above us, huge and shining in the reflected light of the gas giant. It appears motionless against the background of the endless darkness, but of course it is not. Just like us, it races at unimaginable speed around the giant planet, which in this part of the solar system does not allow anything to escape its gravitational field.

My forearm displays 'Error.' I frown and look down at the robotic surgical arm. It moves its hand back and grabs again. And again, the error message flashes on the display above the wrist ring.

I tap it.

Traction force not sufficient.

Apparently the fingers of the robot hand are too short and cannot develop enough power to move the considerable mass of the cargo module.

"Wonderful," I murmur. "Do you know what would be nice, Rofi?"

Of course I get no answer. The little robot is 100 meters away on the *Ankh's* hull. I can barely make out its silhouette on the shaft of the interferometer, which looks like the spine of a sea urchin that has impaled the cargo module I am clamped onto.

"A little boredom," I finally answer myself.

As if on cue, I get another warning message, this time in

my semi-transparent head-up display on the inside of my visor. It comes from the *Ankh's* onboard computer.

I read the message. 'Coronal mass ejection of the central star detected. Plasma cloud to arrive in 50 minutes.'

Here is a simple schematic of the cosmic problem. The ultra-hot, high-energy plasma breaking free from the raging surface of the star is already racing toward my position at the speed of light and will have a diameter that encompasses the entire gas giant, rings included.

The preliminary measurements from the on-board sensors indicate a high dose of gamma radiation, so it would be best for me to be in the *Ankh's* radiation protection room when the time comes. Or, ideally, behind the gas giant, which would be next to impossible.

To be on the safe side, I set a timer five minutes shorter than the plasma cloud's expected time of arrival.

When I'm finished, I lean over the edge of the cargo module so I can see the docking area that should normally be attached to the *Ankh* using four clamps and a magnetic ring. The robotic surgical arm keeps retracting and, as programmed, stoically trying to grab hold again. But it fails each time.

"I don't have time for this." I order it to withdraw with a few quick inputs from my controller and think feverishly. Without it, there is no way to attach and retract the module. I am a scientist, perhaps also an engineer, which I realize at the very latest in my current refusal to classify my problem as unsolvable.

So think about it!

I could use my safety line, which has a winch. However, it is designed for a mass corresponding to an astronaut like me, not for a cargo module weighing many tons. It would not make it. But it will have a large tolerance range or it would not be a safety line. I could of course help it along and reduce the inertia somewhat by drilling a hole in the back of the module.

This would turn the atmosphere inside into a kind of miniature rocket engine and push the module toward the *Ankh*. But the subsequent acceleration is impossible to calculate and the risk is far too great that I will just create a kinetic energy projectile that destroys my spaceship, or at least significantly damages it.

An idea comes.

"Rofi, how strong are you?" I ask him via radio, remembering how the little robot pulled me through the habitat module and hoisted me onto the sickbay bed. "If you think, like me, that you're much stronger than you look, I could use your help with something. You need to go back into the airlock and use your arms to help the winch pull in the cargo module. We just need an initial impulse that's just strong enough to get it coming toward us. Once its mass is in motion, we'll accelerate it so much that we'll have enough time to get the *Ankh* under the ring to safety from the coronal mass ejection."

All I can do is hope that he has heard and understood me and is on his way.

I grab the edge of the cargo module with my left hand and one of the clamps with my right. I demagnetize my boots and realize in the same moment that I was too impatient. I have too much forward momentum and my feet swing over me. They force my body into a rotational movement so that my visor slams into one of the docking ports. The sound is ugly and sends a shock through my bones, but the molecularly bonded glass does not shatter. I instinctively let go of the edge of the cargo module and grab the clamp with my left hand before my elbows cross and I lose my grip completely. There is no time for accidents if I don't want to be cooked by the approaching radiation.

A sharp pain suddenly spreads through my shoulder and I know something is wrong.

Shortly afterward, my oxygen gauge proves me right. It

flashes in panic. I am losing air and therefore pressure from my suit. A schematic appears and marks my sore shoulder.

A leak.

I don't have any self-adhesive patches with me, and only now do I remember that such a thing exists and should be in my equipment.

I definitely wasn't planned for field operations, I think. With the current loss rate, I only have a few minutes of breathing air left.

The gas release causes me to spin around and I can only stop my uncontrolled spinning motion by involuntarily getting tangled up in the robot arm and hitting my leg. The leg part of my spacesuit that was supposed to be inflated has already become so soft that it feels as if someone had hit me with an iron bar.

I have an idea. I use the brief moment of no movement and quickly type a series of commands for the surgical robot arm into my forearm display. I only sip the air that I have left so as to use as little oxygen as possible and not increase the carbon dioxide level too much.

"I hope that's more your thing," I finally say, and press the confirmation button for the sequence of commands. The arm dutifully begins to implement the command, which – except for the working environment – corresponds to its area of application. It feels my shoulder and locates the air leak, recognizable by a thin veil of freezing gas molecules. Then it uses its delicate fingers to pull the special material together and pressure seal it.

I am relieved to see that the oxygen levels are no longer dropping and the pressure is stabilizing. I only have enough air to breathe for 40 minutes now, but I can't stay out here that long anyway.

With my next command, I detach the robot hand from the joint behind it, so that it is now attached to my shoulder like a screw clamp and the arm retracts. To be on the safe side,

I also order the interferometer to retract. If the safety line gets tangled up with it, the entire rescue mission and the *Ankh* would be in danger.

And I am not prepared to abandon my unknown comrade. I know how it feels to be alone.

8

The interferometer quickly retracts into its telescope base and now all that's left is my safety line, which suddenly looks very thin and fragile. I know it's designed for a wide tolerance range, but it still seems far too delicate to be able to pull the bulky module.

I can think of no better alternative. With my left hand I hold the retaining clip, and with my right hand I feel for the carabiner on my waist ring that connects the line to my suit.

There are probably rules that say something like this should never be done, and that's precisely how I feel. In spite of it, I uncouple myself from the *Ankh* and suddenly feel naked and in mortal danger. I slowly move my hand upward, trying to stay focused and not make a mistake.

After I have wrapped the highly elastic material around the metal barrel of the retaining clip and I finally hook the carabiner around the cable, I am relieved.

But only a little, because now I have no safety net at all. If I lose contact with the module, I'm lost. I'll slide through the ring and either be crushed by chunks of ice or suffocate because my suit's oxygen supply is running low – whichever happens first.

I prefer to concentrate on saving my comrade.

I am just about to instruct Rofi to pull on the safety line, and activate the retractable winch at the same time, when once more a warning message demands my attention.

Will this never end? I ask myself. This message flashes right in my field of vision, so I can't ignore it.

"What do we have this time?" I inquire, my eyes widening as the visor tells me to look to the left. Whereas it was a very helpful piece of glass before, it is now demanding and strict.

I can just about see over the uneven surface of the ring. The gas giant fills the whole right side of my visual field. The particle disk seems endless, uniform in its unevenness like a landscape of dunes. But one of these dunes stands out, marked by the sensors on my helmet. The cameras zoom in optically 32 times and I see a cloud of ice crystals, several dozen meters in diameter, racing toward me. It is still many kilometers away, which is frighteningly close on the scales that apply out here.

Before I can ask myself how much bad luck can fit into such a short life, I take a closer look at the measurement data. The shower of micrometeorites rises about 30 meters above the ring, so it is unlikely to damage the *Ankh*.

At least there's that.

If it hits me, it will tear me apart, as well as the cargo module and my comrade.

Not good.

The chance of using the safety line to pull the module out of the danger zone within five minutes is zero – and that's about how much time I have before the shower reaches me. How it came about – through the passage of an asteroid or as a relic of the impact of the cargo module – is now of secondary importance.

My mind races, searching for a solution. My gaze darts feverishly back and forth, coming to rest on some of the chunks of ice that keep passing us.

"You're not that crazy," I say to myself, while thinking

about the specifications of a simple jet engine. Is that a memory? In principle, it's very simple to explain. What flies out the back accelerates the engine forward. Like a rocket. But in that sense, anything that ejects something in one direction to fly in the opposite direction is a rocket. I can't drill a hole in the cargo module because that would endanger my comrade. So I only have one solution left.

I have to throw stones.

Physics can sound so absurd.

I begin to implement my plan by moving to the back of the module, magnetic boots hip-width apart. As I straighten up, I feel like a fern in a breeze. I pray that there is no disruption to the power supply to my boots.

From here I can no longer see the *Ankh,* and there is nothing around me but an endless landscape of ice and dust. Smaller pieces keep hitting me, but they have hardly any kinetic force and do no damage. I ignore the sweat running down my forehead. Yes, I am anxious, but in my short life I have never been pulverized by a cloud of space ice – followed by a dose of gamma rays from the direction of the central star.

With deliberately calm breaths, I watch the ice chunks of the ring slowly drift past me, glittering fragments catching and reflecting the light of the nearby star. I grab the first one that is within my reach and throw it with all my might in the direction of the oncoming storm of micrometeorites. Then I take another, bigger than my head, and throw it after the other one.

Take that, primal force!

The cargo module starts moving with the two impulses. I pick up more with my gloves and throw them away one by one. Every now and then one slips out of my hands, but I have more success when I dare to use both hands. I feel the cold, rough ice in my gloves. The instinct-driven part of my brain doesn't understand how I can keep my grip on my boots with so much weight in my hands.

If only the slingers of my home world could see me, I

think triumphantly. In weightlessness there is no friction, nothing that could stop our movement. At first I think that the ice and dust around us are accelerating, then I realize that it is we who are moving, or rather, the module. It swings through the edge of the ring like a wrecking ball.

I throw a final chunk, almost the size of a full-grown man – which I would not have been able to move a millimeter in a gravity well – out into the darkness, whereupon the cargo module accelerates once again in the opposite direction to the throw and then slides out of the ring. It is the principle of conservation of momentum. Every action has an equal and opposite reaction, and without any form of friction, the result persists.

"Who would have thought," I murmur, excited by adrenaline and a small feeling of triumph, "that one day I would mutate into a jet engine?"

The module begins to rise farther out of the ring. There are no more chunks to collect and throw away now, for we are gliding now through empty space. Our movement looks slow, but I know appearances can be deceptive. I can see the particle shower with my naked eyes now, a glittering wave of material moving across the surface of the ring to my left. I only have a few seconds left.

I silently pray that the safety line won't break due to the tension generated by the module, and that I, and my companion, won't be lost forever. I can feel the centrifugal force pushing me outward, and I barely manage to press myself against the back of the cargo module with the help of my abdominal muscles, which are protesting with pain due to my injury.

My helmet is pressed against the edge, over which I can see both the particle shower and the *Ankh*. My hands each find something to grasp and I hold on, pulling myself as tightly against the module's surface as I can to offer as little surface area as possible.

Then the wave of ice and dust rushes in like a hailstorm, barely passing me. The fact that it happens in complete silence only makes it worse. I scream into my helmet. The storm rages longer than I expected and I keep closing my eyes as I hope I won't get hit. A single grain is enough to kill me at these speeds, either with enough force to rip me off the module, or by piercing my suit and causing me to suffocate or freeze to death.

My eyes fall on the line. I gasp when I see again how fragile and thin it looks. It is visibly vibrating under the weight of the module, which, through its movement, puts even more stress on the material and the winch.

"Hold on. Just a little longer."

I breathe a sigh of relief when the shower is over. I'm still alive and I'm not in pain. My fingers and toes still work, so I'm probably not in shock. I'd love to sleep for a year.

I have picked up two fist-sized chunks of ice, and they are clipped into tiny loops on my belt. With the help of my magnetic boots, I climb to the other side of the module and throw them in quick succession and with as much force as I can muster against the direction of flight to slow us down. It is still a risky maneuver, but I try to minimize the risks at least a little.

"So much for throwing ice cubes," I say into my helmet as I start to climb to the front side, facing the *Ankh*. The robotic surgical hand is still clamped to my shoulder, squeezing the fabric of the suit – a reminder of how fine a thread my life hangs by out here.

Arriving at my destination, I realize that we are in danger of wrapping around my spaceship by circling it.

"Rofi, now," I radio. I close my eyes, and give the winch control a command to retract the safety line at low power. "Slowly and in a controlled manner. We don't want it to break off."

9

We only have a few minutes left before the upcoming solar storm hits us. It feels like an eternity until we are close enough to the airlock. I gently push myself off and slide into the opening. Rofi catches me with two hands. His other two are firmly gripping handholds.

His screen is still off, but I think he's happy to see me. It's nice to think so, anyway.

The countdown on my HUD clock has expired, so I only have a few minutes left.

Rofi taps his wrist, uncouples the line from the winch, and pushes me back before pressing the emergency button for the outer hatch.

"NO!" I shout when I realize what he's planning. But it's too late.

The little robot glides out at lightning speed and then disappears behind the cold metal of the hatch, along with the cable. Air begins to flood the lock and quickly builds up an atmosphere. It takes 50 seconds for the inner door to open, which feels like an eternity, during which tears gather in my eyes. Because of the weightlessness, they have no chance to flow away until I rub them away and they float away in little balls.

Once the passage is open, I float into the central corridor and to one of the computer displays in the wall.

I connect to the control software on the bridge with a few quick inputs and give the order to ignite the dorsal maneuvering engines. Shortly afterward, on one of the external sensors, I see small fountains of cold gas shooting out of the *Ankh's* hull, causing it to swing in a rotational motion around its longitudinal axis, so that at least the pulling force to the side is eliminated and they are no longer in danger of wrapping around the hull until they crash into it.

I want to look for Rofi but don't have time. My timer has long since expired.

Breathing heavily, I push myself off toward one of the doors near the ladder shafts for the spokes. Panic spreads through my body because I don't know if the coronal mass ejection has reached us yet. The danger is invisible, but it has the potential to turn my DNA into boiled cellular garbage and me into a bleeding, whimpering mass in a matter of minutes.

I slide through the gap that opens in front of me to reach a tiny room with a seat on the opposite side. The door slams shut behind me before I've even sat down. A single light shines above my head, bathing the chamber in a pale light that flickers at regular intervals. Could it be from the mass ejection? I want to curl up in a protective reflex, but I'm still wearing the bulky spacesuit that makes any movement almost impossible.

I cry silently as I open the fasteners and peel off my helmet, gloves, and upper and lower parts one after the other. Underneath, I am drenched in sweat in my flexible overalls and immediately grow cold. The fact that I turned the temperature down to save energy could now be my downfall.

I don't care, I can only think about Rofi.

He's still out there. I instinctively knew the way to the

radiation protection room, but I don't know anything about Rofi's specifications, and that makes me feel guilty. Does he have highly effective shielding against radiation events? I hope so, but deep down I don't believe it. He looks too delicate, I think. Even if he survives, he could suffer damage that would prevent me from having the limited communication I've had with him, without which I would have lost my mind long ago.

Either way, it will be fatal for my comrade in the cargo module, whom I tried to save. I was so close. Now he is being cooked in his cold prison, so close to being rescued. My plan was doomed from the start. Too little time. I just didn't want to believe it.

I want to scream and I hear myself doing just that until my ears ring. It is a long, drawn-out sound, deafening and with a painful depth that makes me aware of what I have not allowed myself to experience. Raw, disordered emotions force their way out through my vocal cords, no longer able to be held back or rationalized. My body has taken control away from me and is releasing itself of everything that has been building up inside.

My life is so short. What does that say about my happiness?

Afterward I am exhausted, feeling like an empty vessel. I pull my knees up to my chest, wrap my arms around my shins, and don't move for a while.

At some point I notice thirst, my throat feels dry. I am forced to unfold my body and sip from my helmet's mouthpiece to drink some water. I put the helmet over my head long enough to see the time display in the HUD – 20 minutes have passed. Much longer than the six minutes predicted by the onboard sensors until the plasma cloud has passed the *Ankh*.

The feeling of remorse is deep as I put my hand on the door control and the massive hatch rises. Unbidden images of my unknown comrade play out in my head, showing him sitting in the confines of his cargo module and dying of acute radiation sickness.

Excruciating.

I wish I wasn't human, didn't have something as painful as empathy, and couldn't curse fate for constantly throwing obstacles in my path. It feels unfair that I take on so much only to end up being robbed of what I fought so hard for.

"Ten breaths," I say, my voice shaking, a contract with myself to allow myself ten breaths full of anger, despair, and everything that boils and simmers inside me and makes me curse everything. Next I hiss out all my breath and leave the radiation shelter. I float into the central corridor and pull my spacesuit after me.

With impatient movements I slip my legs into the lower part and then pull the torso piece over myself. I lock it into the waist ring and move on to gloves and finally the helmet. I feel exhausted, but I carry on and glide to the airlock. I wait patiently until the atmosphere has escaped and then open the outer hatch. With every command I give the system, a quiet feeling of relief mixes with awareness that the ship is apparently still intact and at least locally functional.

Although I cannot take away the pain of my failure nor the agonizing death of my comrade, whom I never knew, I still have a duty to carry on. Not to give up.

Solve one problem at a time, I tell myself. That's all you need to do.

I hook the second safety line, previously used by Rofi, onto my belt and magnetize my boots before I leave the *Ankh* and step out onto the hull. We are still above the gigantic rings of the gas giant, which still fills much of the background. The unimaginable primal forces that raged here are invisible to the naked eye and do not seem to have affected the universe in the slightest, as though they were all just a figment of my imagination. I look to my right and see Rofi behind the habitat ring.

When I notice he is moving, a weight lifts from my heart

and I cry again. But these tears come from relief. At least my worst fear has not come true.

I trudge toward him and only stop when I arrive in front of the rotating part of the ship's hull, which turns around its longitudinal axis. One of the mighty spokes, in which there is an access ladder, passes me like a gigantic clock hand. I can't go through with the cable because it would be torn away, so I gesture in Rofi's direction.

But he doesn't see me. The four-armed robot has apparently maneuvered the recovered module into place and is busy reconnecting it to the ship. I command my helmet sensors to zoom in until I see that he has folded his hands back at the wrists, and tools have extended from the joints to enable him to weld and turn screws.

"You little devil," I say, activating the radio, and his switched-off display turns in my direction. He pauses for a moment and then raises two fingers from one of his back-folded hands. I return the gesture with a smile, but when my eyes fall on the module, my smile dies. We have the cargo module back, but it is nothing more than a cold grave, and I will have to bury someone I desperately wanted to save.

10

Rofi and I are floating in the central corridor just before the reactor section. Directly in front of us is a round hatch with warning hieroglyphs indicating that we should pay attention to the pressure sensors.

If he were human, I would probably be a little embarrassed. I had given him a bit of a hug when he came in. His body, such as it is, felt hard, but I didn't care. He's probably wondering if people are clinically insane because I'm suddenly sad after my great relief and joy.

Opposite us is the cargo module. I think Rofi has sealed it up hermetically. He smiles at me with his display back on and keeps raising two fingers when I ask him if he's positively sure.

"He or she is dead," I say. Five words that hit me right in the stomach. "But we can't leave him or her in there. That's just not right."

Rofi's pixel mouth corners have turned downhill.

"I know, kid." I nod and pat his head. I'd like to forget that this module even exists, but running away from what is decent feels wrong. "We'll bury him or her in a vacuum. If we use one of the vacuum-sealable garbage bags, there might be enough space. Are you ready?"

He raises two fingers.

I place my hands on the control panel next to the hatch and unlock it, which triggers a slight hissing sound. I pull the manual lock wheel to open it.

It doesn't work.

I start to pull harder, but still nothing happens. Confused, I ask Rofi to help me and he puts his back arms next to the hatch and pulls on the wheel with the other two.

When something finally gives and the massive metal moves toward us, it hisses again and the hissing turns into a whistling sound, as though a hurricane were rushing through the central corridor.

"What...?" I blurt out until understanding comes. There is no atmosphere on the other side. The equalization happens within a few seconds, during which we must initially fight with all our strength against the unnaturally strong pull that tries to reclose the hatch. Then it gradually decreases as more air – and thus pressure – accumulates on the other side.

I frown in disbelief. Did the atmosphere escape from Rofi's annex? Did my comrade kill himself by initiating some kind of emergency escape? I probably would have done it to avoid the torments of radiation.

I swallow hard, afraid of what awaits me, and then I pull the hatch wide open with a jerk. It is dark inside the module until a red light comes on. Square cargo compartments with ring locks fill the walls, floor, and ceiling, leaving only a little space in the middle. The narrowness reminds me of the radiation protection room.

What's strange is that the light is shining right in the middle, as if it is floating in the darkness. Suddenly it changes and moves toward me.

I push myself back involuntarily and slide against the padded white wall of the central corridor. A robot floats out of the cargo module. It looks like Rofi, except that its display glows red and shows a much more complex face than the simple smile with two eyes and a semicircle. It is not that of a human, but it is a three-dimensional image with significantly more details.

"Hello," says the robot, clinging to the frame of the open hatch like a spider. He sounds somewhat mocking, but has a pleasant, androgynous voice.

"Uh, hello," I reply, puzzled. "Who are you?"

"My name is Ammit, like that one over there." Ammit points to his 'twin' with the white display, who suddenly looks sad. "Aren't you happy to see me, 48?"

Rofi hangs his head. Obviously not.

"Thanks for saving me. I won't forget that," he says in my direction. "Actually, I don't forget anything anyway, but that's what you're supposed to say, right?"

I'm perplexed by how human the robot's voice sounds. Apparently the best I can think of is, "You two are identical?"

"Almost. My name is Ammit and my identification number is 47. His is 48. So we're separate autonomous entities, but identical, if that's what you mean." His voice sounds a little hollow, like it's missing some important component that I can't quite put my finger on. It's probably just my imagination, but there seems to be a hint of cynicism in his words.

"I am…" I pause.

"The survivor," he interrupts. "The meatbag."

"The meatbag?"

"I'm amazed you survived. But thank you for saving me."

"What happened?"

"I'm not sure. I was in Cargo Module 4, getting heat exchangers to make repairs to the subdural vent panels when the alarm went off. Shortly afterward, the hatch closed on an automatic emergency command. Then everything spun and the module flew away – unfortunately with me inside, I might add," Ammit-47 explained, his face showing something like frustration. "I connected to the relays and used my mainframe as a data node to feed a distress signal into the maintenance lamp."

"That was clever. I saw it."

"Apparently."

"I thought you were..." I start to reply, but then I stop myself and shake my head.

"Another meatbag? I'm sorry." He doesn't sound even a little sorry. He points to Rofi. "What's wrong with him? Is he still broken?"

"I think so. He can't speak."

"This is the first good news in a long time – apart from my rescue, of course. A great service to our mission."

"Why is that good news?" I ask, realizing I'm getting a little angry that he's talking about my friend like that.

"He's annoying." Ammit-47 turns back toward me, his 'face' now looking intent. "I see that we have an energy problem."

"How can you see that?"

"I'm connected to the onboard computer. You should do that too." He points to my forearm. "There are forearm displays in the technical warehouse that should make your work easier. The onboard AI is apparently offline, so it's a bit more complicated, but it's still possible to control the individual systems."

"I had a busy schedule. Can you show me where I can find something like that?" I ask.

He looks at me confused. "Why do you not know that?"

"Some things I know intuitively, others I don't." I shrug. "Honestly, I have no idea. I don't even know my name or where I'm from, what kind of mission we're on, or why I'm the only one who survived."

"Apparently your indoctrination is not complete," says Ammit.

"Indoctrination?"

"During your growth phase, your brain was trained, fed

with knowledge, skills, memories. Including, among other things, about this ship and its functions and the reason for our journey."

"Do you know anything else about it?" I ask, my voice almost breaking. "Do my memories belong to someone else?"

"I have no idea. I'm just one of the two on-board robots. My programming is limited to my basic functions."

"And what are they?" My hope is not lost yet. At least I am having a conversation. A real conversation!

"Supporting the crew – that would be you – in carrying out the mission," replies Ammit-47.

"You have access to the onboard computer. Can you find out if there is any information about our target and the mission parameters?"

"I can, yes. Now, or do you want to have your forearm display first? Then we can communicate ship wide." He looks at his twin and gives him a condescending, regretful look. "At least those of us who can speak."

"He's my friend," I admonish him. "Be nice to him."

Ammit-47 sighs. It sounds almost human. "If that's an order." He releases one hand and pats Rofi's head. The gesture doesn't look the least bit friendly. At best, it's even more condescending.

I sigh and point forward to the bridge. "Bring me the portable computer, please, and then come to the cockpit. We need a plan to fill our energy matrix cells."

"Sure." The red robot skillfully climbs along the wall and pushes itself off toward the rear, where it catches itself on a handrail and wedges itself in front of another cargo module. I put a hand on Rofi's back.

His display shows a sad smile.

"You don't like him, do you?"

He shakes his head and holds two fingers down.

"Don't pay attention to his spiteful ways," I suggest. "I think he could be a great help to us."

At least I hope so.

11

Back on the bridge, I buckle myself in and ask Rofi to get me something to eat. After the field mission and all the adrenaline, I feel empty and worn out. When he returns, he has two hot food packs and a fresh pair of overalls with him.

I thank him profusely and slip into the dry clothes before greedily tackling the food. It is not easy to gobble down in zero gravity because too much can fly away, which the ventilation systems don't like. But in my hungry state I manage not to let a crumb escape.

Rofi leaves the bridge. I don't ask why, but I suspect it's because of Ammit-47, who comes in at almost the same moment. He skillfully climbs into the co-pilot's seat and holds up a wide cuff. "May I?"

I nod and he attaches the forearm display between the elbow and wrist of my left arm. It seems to work just like the one on my spacesuit.

"Thanks."

"This is my task."

"Can you access our reactor data?" I ask, pointing to the dark display in front of him.

"No."

"Why not?"

"Because 48 and I have access to the onboard computer, but limited to read-only, not command access. Only the human crew has that." He pauses and then continues, like he is speaking to a child. "That's you."

"But you know something about me? About the crew?"

"I know we've been maintaining your breeding tanks, 48 and I. Our job for many decades has been to change the nutrient fluid and make sure all the systems are working properly."

"But what happened then? Why did they all die?"

"I have no knowledge of that. Something hit us twenty years ago, perhaps an interstellar radiation event."

"Do you have any other theories?" I ask eagerly.

"I'm a maintenance robot, not an astrophysicist," he reminds me, and this time I'm sure I hear sarcasm.

"You seem somehow different from Rofi." It sounds more reproachful than I intended.

"We are also programmed very differently."

"What are the differences?"

"I don't know because I was programmed before we left and I didn't speak to my creators. He is far too gullible and simple-minded. I have no idea what the programmers were thinking."

"Can you remember the time before the trip?"

"No. I was only activated after ten years of travel, when the first maintenance cycle began," he replies.

"So you don't know anything about our mission," I say, disappointed.

Ammit-47 doesn't respond, which I take as confirmation.

"You should be nice to Rofi," I say, my hands sliding over the holokeyboard to find the reactor specifications. "Without him, you wouldn't be here now."

"You saved me."

"I did some of the work, but he docked the module when

I had to go to the radiation shelter. Without him, you'd be drifting away in space until your batteries died."

The robot in the seat beside me makes an indefinable sound. "This is totally ruining my day."

"You have to obey me, don't you?"

"Yes."

"Then treat him well," I order.

A sigh comes from his speakers. "You know we're robots, right?"

"Yes. Why do you ask?"

"We are programmed, we have no personality in that sense. Only to the extent that it has been programmed into us."

"Then what's the difference?" I reply. "I was programmed by nature – or some geneticist. Who knows? You're a computer. I don't see any relevant difference."

"Hmm," says Ammit-47.

"I'm now going to display the navigation data as a code overview on your display. You can read and interpret it, right?"

"I can do that."

"Good. Then please find out as much as you can about our journey while I come up with a plan to replenish our energy reserves before we die in here."

I send the image to his display and then start reading through the reactor specifications to get an understanding of what kind of heart beats in the *Ankh*. Little by little, a picture begins to emerge, although it takes me several hours. Apparently I understand enough about this kind of thing that my brain puts the information in the right places and makes the correct connections.

The ship's primary power source is a graviton energy converter, which is essentially an extremely powerful graviton detector capable of absorbing gravitons emitted by a massive body such as the gas giant near us and converting them into usable energy.

At the core of the converter is a superconducting sphere made of exotic material. This sphere is embedded in a complex of highly sensitive coils that can detect even the smallest changes in the gravitational field. They are made of a superconducting material that is able to maintain its functions within the artificial vacuum and the gravitational forces prevailing in the chamber. The sphere and coils are enclosed in a high vacuum to minimize heat radiation and magnetic interference that could disrupt the converter. The entire assembly is surrounded by a multi-layer protective shield that guards the interior from cosmic radiation, solar winds and other external disturbances.

Even as I read and interpret the specifications, a clear plan of what to do is forming in my head. I get the feeling that this kind of 'refueling' maneuver is part of the mission. We have arrived with little energy in a place that has plenty of it.

I turn on the ship-wide radio. "Rofi, strap yourself down somewhere. I'm turning off the rotation of the habitat module."

I wait five minutes, then I tell Ammit-47 that we're getting started.

First, I check the converter's control systems. They are functional and show no errors. The superconducting sphere of exotic material in the core of the reactor shows no anomalies – unlike the many thousands of kilometers of power cables in the ship, which suffer from the uneven and insufficient voltage distribution and are increasingly causing minor problems and failures. The coils in the converter, which can detect even the tiniest change in the gravitational field, are ready to convert the collected gravitons into electricity.

I align the *Ankh's* course with the gas giant. With precise control jet bursts, I use the spaceship's natural rotation to achieve the optimal alignment.

"That's very close," Ammit-47 commented regarding

what he saw on my display. "We're almost touching the atmosphere."

"I know, but we have to collect as many gravitons as possible in a short time or we won't have enough energy," I explain, while my fingers continue to fly over the holokeyboard.

We accelerate briefly but violently. I am pushed back into my chair as if a death guard had hit me with his fist. But it doesn't last long before we run out of energy and seem to be drifting straight toward the gas giant.

"Energy for what?" asks the robot.

"For a swing maneuver. We'll use the massive gravitational field of this planet to accelerate toward the inhabited world in the inner system. We can use that little push." In my mind, I add, because otherwise we won't make it.

The gas giant outside the window continues to grow until it dominates everything and seems to block out the universe. The maneuvering jets spit out their cold gas mixture and steer us on a course that takes us just past it. There is a cracking and creaking noise all around us and I shudder as the violent tidal forces kick in.

The graviton converter is starting to work, which I can tell from the readouts of the energy pattern and matrix cells.

With every moment that we get closer to the gas giant, the density of gravitons increases. This means more energy is channeled into the *Ankh's* storage clusters and accumulated there. I keep an eye on the energy display and watch as the bar rises faster and faster.

Now it becomes critical. I have to make sure that the spacecraft flies in an optimal trajectory around the gas giant in order to collect maximum energy without crashing into its atmosphere, bouncing off it, or leaving the exact trajectory of the swing maneuver. With carefully calculated jet impulses, I keep us on course to avoid getting too close.

Everything is vibrating now, my seat, the display, even the

holoimage seems to be shaking under the enormous strain that threatens to tear the ship apart.

The maneuver is a balancing act, a combination of astrophysical calculations and intuitive control. There is hardly any room for conscious thoughts. But it works.

After reaching maximum approach, we begin to move away from the gravitational center of local space. We move past the peak density point of the gravitons and energy production slows down. But I have collected enough energy to keep the ship on course and reach our next destination, the blue water planet in the inner system.

I switch the converter into working mode and sigh in relief.

12

For 12 hours I sleep with dreams of an army of scarabs bringing me the ingredients for a simple farmer's bread, but instead of a stone oven I only have a microwave at my disposal. I try to explain to the little beetles that any bread turns to mush in it, but it turns out that the microwave in my dream is a very special one. It doesn't heat water molecules, but yeast, and makes the dough rise wonderfully. When we want to eat the deliciously fragrant baked goods together at the foot of the pyramids, we realize that I forgot the salt. The scarabs apologize and tell me that they will have to eat me instead of the bread in order to maintain their electrolyte balance. They are very polite and little displays on their heads show sad smiles – which, in the end, doesn't stop them from eating me.

When I wake up, I'm very hungry. I peel myself from my bunk, brush my teeth, and wash up in the small bathroom that's adjacent to the kitchen-living room with the exercise equipment. I see Ammit-47 plugged into a charging station that's blinking green. It looks like the electric spike sticking out of the wall has impaled him. His display is offline and he's holding his arms wrapped around his small torso.

Rofi comes running from the direction of the workshop, his smiley face glowing at me from his display. I shudder at the memory of my fading dream.

"How long will it charge?" I ask, still a little dazed from the restless sleep of the last few hours. I suppress a yawn. Rofi holds up four fingers. "Four hours?"

Two fingers. *Yes.*

"That's quite a long time."

Two fingers again, and his smiley face turns into a laughing one.

"I know you don't like him." I wave him off and make myself a cup of tea. "Would you like something? Lubricating oil or something?"

Rofi's mouth corners sink downward.

"I was just kidding, little friend."

After a quick breakfast, I carefully clear away the remains – garbage in the recycler, dishes and cutlery in the dishwasher.

"I have a job for you," I say to Rofi, pointing down the corridor toward the workshop. I shudder just thinking about what else is there. "Can you seal it? The gate section, I mean?"

Rofi raises two fingers. He must have noticed the look on my face because the corners of his mouth turn down again. He walks toward me with short steps and puts one of his black metal hands on my knee.

"It's fine," I say, taking a deep breath. "I'll be fine. The whole section just scares me. But I'll have to go to the workshop more often, given the current state of the *Ankh*. And every time I have to go there…"

Rofi shows me two fingers, pats my knee, and shows them to me again.

"Thanks, kid. I'll take care of my dead comrades, but right now I need to concentrate on getting us to our destination safely." I smile at him and point to the ladder that leads over the spoke into the central corridor in the *Ankh's* hull. "I'm going to the bridge to make sure I get the sensor data down here onto the table display. Then we'll come up with a plan."

As quickly as I've said it, I climb up the spokes and into the narrow tube, where from halfway up it becomes easier to pull myself along, because my body loses weight. At the end I float out into the white corridor and remain in silence for a moment. Before I went to sleep, the rumbling of the engines had been piercing like a deep bass, but we are already in the drift phase and have not accelerated for a long time. I have to listen carefully. A gentle rushing sound, like sand brushing over a dune, comes from the life support air scrubbers. With lots of imagination I can hear the gurgling of the coolants in the walls that keep the superconductors close to zero temperature.

But the background against which all this takes place is silence.

For me, it's the melody of loneliness reminding me continually that I'm far away from everything. Everyone. Not just physically, but in my heart too. I don't even know where I came from, let alone where I'm going. But when I imagine that I have a husband and children who are now 20 light years away, I think I was better off being ignorant.

I float to the bridge and strap myself into the commander's seat.

"Very well," I say, rubbing my hands together. It's still quite cool on the ship, and that's a good thing. Rofi and Ammit's batteries will drain more slowly if they don't have to use as much power to cool down, and I've decided that too much comfort will make me inattentive. It also saves energy that the *Ankh* can use elsewhere. "What do we have?"

Before I went to sleep, all I did was check whether the planned course was being maintained and whether all trajectory data matched my plan.

Nothing has changed. We are still relatively close to the gas giant with its impressive rings, only it is now behind us and we have left its direct gravitational sphere of influence. A long journey into the interior of this alien system lies ahead of us. First, in 20 days, we must cross the orbit of another gas giant. It is even larger than the one whose sphere of influence we are currently leaving, but we will not see it because in a few days it will disappear behind the local sun from our position.

Ten days later, we pass through an asteroid belt, which, like most of its kind, looks different from what the human mind imagines – no regolith chunks that are so dense that I would have to employ daring maneuvers to avoid them. On the contrary, the distances between them are enormous, usually thousands of kilometers or considerably more.

No danger. What a nice concept.

After that, astronomically speaking, we are in the inner system, where four rocky planets are relatively close to each other. Two of them are on the other side of the central star for now, but the water planet, our target, has only just reached the side of its orbit that is facing us.

My current course takes me 1.5 million kilometers behind the target's satellite, to the second liberation point. There, the gravitational forces of the central star and the planet interact in such a way that the *Ankh* would orbit the star at the same speed as the planet. In its slipstream, we will be protected from radiation events – which I am sick and tired of, by the way – and we will need less energy to maintain our position.

It is an optimal observation point and therefore precisely what we need.

Over the last 12 hours, the sensor phalanx on the bow has collected a large amount of data about our target point, thanks to the telescopes having a clear view of the inner system. I make a few quick entries on the holokeyboard and give permanent permissions to the onboard computer so that it streams all relevant data from the bridge directly to the holotable in the kitchen-living room, saving me the trip up here. I want to spend as little time as possible in weightlessness. The more I spend in gravity, the less exercise I have to do – that fitness machine with the rubber bands looks sincerely scary. Plus, microgravity always reminds me of my torpor capsule, in which I almost suffocated.

I shudder.

Once I've finished my work, I return to the central corridor and slide down the ladder until I become too heavy and have to use the rungs to avoid falling.

Rofi hasn't returned yet and Ammit-47 is still charging on the wall, like a folded-up, battery-powered vacuum cleaner. I decide to wait until my little robot friend returns from his task. It takes almost an hour, during which I reluctantly use the elliptical trainer.

"Did everything work?" I ask, drying myself off with a microfiber towel. Rofi raises two fingers. "Very good, thank you."

I go to the table, activate the holofield using gesture control, and scroll through several menus until I find access to the ship's sensor data.

"Please wake up Ammit-47. We should all be present when we take a closer look at what we have learned about our target planet. Six eyes always see more than two," I say and wink at him. "The same goes for cameras, of course."

Rofi runs to his twin and presses a few buttons on the charging station. Ammit-47 then unfolds and his display turns on. The complex animated 3D face twists into a look of disapproval.

"My charging is not complete yet," he complains.

"I wanted you to be here," I say before he can get to work on Rofi. I feel a bit like a mother traveling with her two children and trying to make sure they don't fight. Fortunately that doesn't happen now. Maybe because I ordered Ammit-47 to behave nicely toward Rofi, or maybe – and I like to think this

– because they are just as curious as I am and want to know what awaits us at the end of our 50-day journey.

When the three of us are gathered around the table, I order the hologram to bring up a display of our target planet and its satellite with all the data collected by the sensors. It only takes a few seconds before my jaw drops.

13

When I first went to the bridge after waking up in the torpor capsule and sought out an overview of the system, many questions were swirling in my mind. Why here? Is the mysterious catastrophe 20 years ago the reason why we are stranded here? Do we no longer have enough reaction mass for our fusion drive to take us to our actual destination? Is this the only place we could still reach? Or was it planned from the beginning that this should be the end point of our journey?

When I saw the water planet in the habitable zone, I thought it was probably the latter, a mission to a nearby solar system, similar to ours, with a potentially habitable planet. Maybe I'm an explorer who is supposed to find out for future missions whether humanity can find a new home here. Or a second, third, fourth – I don't know.

Now that I look at the hologram, a second possible explanation for our mysterious venture crops up. First contact, because the water planet is inhabited.

I take a sharp breath because I am at a loss for words.

Ammit-47 states the obvious. "An alien civilization exists there." His face remains impassive.

Rofi smiles. As usual.

I rotate the image of the planet and its moon with my fingers. A space station is in orbit around the satellite. It is smaller than the *Ankh*, resembling a metallic sculpture – an elongated, cylindrical structure that shimmers silver in the sunlight reflected from the moon. Several dark spots along the module could indicate docking bays. Large sails grow out of its end caps, presumably to generate solar energy. I know that we humans did this a long time ago. What I don't know is why I know this. The sails are arranged like the petals of a flower, a bit crude, but beautiful to look at in its own way.

There are two other space stations orbiting the water planet, but they look different. One is of a similar size, the other much larger, about the size of the *Ankh*. Their solar sails are gigantic, unfolding into impressive wings that make the station's hull seem downright puny. The latter looks like it came into being by chance, with bulges and extensions along the central axis that do not reveal any clear system.

"Apparently they are a spacefaring civilization, the same as we are," I note.

"But they haven't gotten very far yet," replies Ammit-47.

"Well, they don't seem to be primitive, either." I point to the night side of the planet and the many lights on it, which indicate cities and settlements and an extensive electricity network. "They have energy and electricity, and they seem to inhabit the entire surface of the land masses. A young species, yes, but it's obvious they have a certain urge for discovery and exploration."

"An urge to expand."

"I'm sorry. What?"

"Exploration can also be interpreted as the urge for expansion," the robot repeats. "And expansion always has something to do with displacement."

"You think they're hostile?" I ask, surprised. I hadn't even thought of that.

"The space stations are filled with air – that's evident.

Only meatbags build thick tubes. Otherwise it would be cheaper to produce cuboids," he explains. "Robots don't need anything like that. They wouldn't need anything so heavily reinforced either because they don't have to have such extensive radiation protection. So it's not a machine civilization."

"You sound disappointed."

"I should be. Meatbags have emotions and have been conditioned by evolution to survive and preserve the species through proliferation. Talking to a machine civilization would be easier, because they would follow the laws of logic."

"Are you saying we're in danger?"

"Of course." His 3D face frowns and looks at me as if I were a little retarded. "What is foreign is seen as a threat because its intentions are unknown. I'm surprised you don't feel the same way when you look at that."

He points to the space stations and the lights on the dark side of the planet.

I think about it and reluctantly agree with him. I feel a little uneasy as my thoughts revolve around the realization that we are not stranded in an empty system, but in one inhabited by aliens. They may be technologically backward compared to humanity, but are obviously capable of flying into space. So it is not unlikely that they have mastered nuclear fission, perhaps even developed fusion and the basics of artificial intelligence. How will they react if they see an alien spaceship approaching them?

How would I react?

The answer is simpler than I want to admit. Fear, fear of the unknown, just as Ammit-47 predicted. I am worried about the unknown intentions of the aliens we are traveling toward. What do they look like? Slimy monsters with four arms? Reptilians? Are they bi- or even tri-symmetrical? Do they use language like I do, forming sounds using compressed air? How am I supposed to communicate with them? And even if that works in some manner, how aggressive or peaceful are they?

How do they react to a perceived threat from something unknown?

"You see," says Ammit-47. "You're just a meatbag."

"Why does that sound so derogatory?"

"Because it must be difficult to think rationally with this evolutionary burden. That's the long explanation."

"Let me guess. The short explanation would have been 'because it was a devaluation,'" I remark. "At least I can't rust."

"But *you* are compostable," he counters. "I, on the other hand, can brush off the rust."

I sigh and ask myself, not for the first time, why someone would program a maintenance robot to be cynical and quick-witted.

"How likely do you think it is that our mission from the beginning was to make first contact?" I ask.

Rofi tilts his head alternately to the right and left, his face showing a nearly flat mouth line.

"Is that your thoughtful expression?" I ask with a smile.

Rofi smiles and raises two fingers.

"It's difficult to say," Ammit-47 states, his display turning alternately between me and the holographic image. "We've been on the move for eighty years. For us, that's a fairly long period of time in which technology can advance a lot. But for the native species, it may be very different. They may live significantly shorter or longer than we do. If they have a very slow metabolic rate and think more slowly, they may need longer to do everything that we do quickly. Then we might have to listen for years to decipher one sentence from them. But they could also be hyperactive and we'll never understand them because we're too slow for them. By the time you have a thought, they've already been thinking for a lifetime."

"Is that your extended version of 'no idea'?"

"We have too little data to have the basis for a qualified assumption."

"Spoken like a robot."

Ammit-47 points to the hologram with one of his delicate-looking hands. "Have you taken a closer look at the engines?"

"No, why? They're working."

"So far."

I frown and bring up the reactor display. A schematic of the *Ankh* lights up between us, marking the reactor compartment at the rear and the connections to the four engines that culminate in the single, massive propulsion funnel.

"Helium-3 fusion reactor," I explain. "No malfunctions whatsoever, currently offline – as planned – because we are in the drift phase."

"What about the reaction mass?"

"There." I open the display for the helium-3 pellets and frown. "Supply at less than one percent."

"Yes," says Ammit-47, as if he had expected nothing else. "I'd bet the propellant mass indicator looks just as meager."

I check this too and find that the water reserves for the engines are only slightly higher. Two percent.

Both values are sobering. In a helium-3-helium-3 reactor, helium-3 atoms are fused to form helium-4 and two protons, generating enormous heat – and therefore energy. This heat is used to 'burn' the water as a propellant – yes, the water – and eject it from the back as ionized gas to accelerate the *Ankh* in the opposite, the desired, direction. In our case, to almost 25 percent of the speed of light.

But apparently only for the outward journey.

"Do you think the incident twenty years ago has something to do with this?" I ask hoarsely.

"I don't think so, no." Ammit-47 shakes his head and Rofi looks sad.

"So we're part of a one-way mission," I say.

A return flight was never planned. Unless we have equipment on board for the extraction of helium-3, which I didn't see in the inventory lists. An unpleasant coldness spreads through me. I feel used and thrown away like a disposable container. But there's nothing I can do about that now. "We're not here for first contact."

"What makes you so sure?" Ammit-47 sounds like he knows the answer, but for some reason he wants to hear it from me, giving me the impression that I am his subordinate, not the other way around.

"For a first contact, it seems more logical to have enough fuel for the return trip if things were to go wrong, or at least equipment for refueling. Besides, we have no weapons on board, and we would certainly have some if we were intended to make contact with an alien species whose motives we would have no way of predicting. I think we were sent here to explore."

With the index finger of my right hand, I poke the inhabited water planet after reactivating the holographic display.

"To explore this habitable planet right here. Our telescope images are always at least twenty years old, since our home is twenty light years away from this system. When we were sent off, eighty years ago, everything looked different. Perhaps these space stations didn't exist back then."

"It's all the more unfortunate that we have no weapons on board," says Ammit-47 calmly.

"How come?"

"Because we can't clear out the planet now," he replies.

When I look at him reproachfully, he raises his hands defensively.

"Just kidding."

14

It's late. Ammit-47 is on some sort of maintenance mission involving the cargo modules and Rofi is 'sleeping' peacefully at his charging station. I'm still sitting at the table between the kitchenette and the fitness equipment, scrolling through inventory lists and specification tables.

I can't shake the feeling that I'm not adequately prepared for what awaits me at our destination. The expectation of meeting aliens electrifies the scientist in me. We are not alone! There are others besides us! What can we learn from them? What can we teach them in return? Have they gained physical knowledge that is new to us? How is their society structured, and what values are central to their culture? Or are there many different cultures and peoples? The lack of answers to all these questions, however, electrifies the doubter in me.

So many imponderables that just the prospect of a few answers keeps me from sleeping.

But there is a dark side – the fear that things could go wrong and the whole thing could end in disaster. A misunderstanding could be enough to lead to a conflict. And then? What if they destroy the *Ankh* and us? What if my home world finds out? Will they send warships in retaliation? Or will they do it simply because it gives them a convenient excuse to 'liberate' the planet from those who occupy it, even though we have chosen it as a colony? Was that the plan for my mission all along? Am I just a tool to justify genocide?

Once again I miss my crewmates, even though I never got to know them. If only I could consult with them...

But I can't do that, so I focus on acquiring as much knowledge as I can. At best, I might be able to do some of the jobs they should have done. But I certainly won't do it by overthinking.

A while later – when I should have long since been in my bunk – I was working my way through the blueprints of the *Ankh* to expand my understanding of its structure. I really want to know what hit us 20 years ago and killed my comrades. An area just off the stern catches my attention. The doors as you go along the central corridor occur in sets of four, which are labeled and have fold-out windows on my display that explain what they are for. In the case of cargo modules, their inventory lists are available. So, there is a door or a hatch leading from the corridor in each of four directions.

Between the separated reactor section at the rear and the cargo section that adjoins it there is a small ring of four modules that serve as maintenance access for my two robot companions. One contains the maintenance ports for the cooling units, another for the extendable heat dissipation panels, and a third for life support. Because these are such important areas, they are significantly more heavily armored than the rest of the ship, as every single component is vital to survival. Without cooling, there are no energy matrix cells. Without heat dissipation panels, I would eventually be boiled in my own sweat. And without life support, I would suffocate to death.

But the fourth module has no name. I can't even select it when I press on it with my finger.

"This is strange," I mutter into the nighttime silence. The

lights are dimmed to simulate day and night cycles for me, the meatbag, and to ensure that my circadian rhythm is functioning optimally. I consider going to sleep and dealing with it tomorrow, but quickly dismiss the thought.

An unknown module with no function name? There is an ironclad rule on spaceships: No wasted space. Anything that has no function is left behind. I also have this knowledge, without being able to remember ever having actively learned it.

So why does this one room remain dark on the blueprint? And why is it one of the particularly robust ones with lots of armor and radiation shielding?

The whole thing looks so suspicious that I probably wouldn't be able to sleep a wink, so I might as well go and take an eyes-on look.

With soft breaths that can be heard clearly in the silent room, I walk to the ladder. Diffuse light reflecting off the white walls casts bizarre shadows that dance like ghostly figures across the octagon-patterned structure of the wall panels. If Ammit-47 saw me like this, he would surely have made some kind of comment about emotional meatbags.

Despite the continuous work of the air conditioning system keeping the air clean, I can still smell the slightly metallic odor of the spaceship mixed with the bitter note of ozone.

Does it only smell like this at night?

I climb rung by rung higher up the spoke of the habitat ring and finally plunge into the central corridor where the artificial gravity stops. My hands search for the handrail that spirals along the corridor walls and I let myself relax as I pull my body forward. Every muscle has adapted to the conditions in the area, every movement precise and controlled to avoid unnecessary drift. I wonder what technological wonders have led to me, as one developed from an embryo, having such good muscle memory. The delicate movements come naturally, as if I had never done anything else.

The silence here is almost oppressive, although I know that it must be a subjective impression caused by my latent excitement. The glow from the narrow ceiling lights plays over the sterile white surface of the walls, making them appear featureless and pale.

Why do I have a secret module on board? What is hidden inside it?

A faint red light flashes farther down the corridor. It is the only element that breaks the white colorlessness, as if intended to attract me.

I let the handrail guide me along and finally reach the wall at the end of the corridor. It leads to the rear, the reactor section. A radiation warning symbol reminds me that I should not go in there without a special suit.

Using the markings on the floor and ceiling, I orient myself to find the door to the module I'm looking for. It's easy to identify because it has no markings or labels, unlike the other three, which otherwise look identical. There's nothing to indicate the module's purpose or contents, just the blind eye of a camera trained on me and the silent blinking of the red light.

My hand runs over the smooth surface of the door, as if mere touch could reveal its secrets. A hint of cold seeps through my fingers, making me shiver. I stare at the impenetrable metal, feeling the silence of the corridor around me as though the ship were holding its breath in anticipation of disaster.

I am, at any rate.

It feels like the entire ship has fallen into a kind of morbid sleep, only this module seems to be like a ticking clock. Waiting. Lurking.

This is just a cargo hold, I remind myself, and place my hand on the control panel.

Access denied.

I try again with the same result. Once more, and a warning message appears: Code required.

"What kind of code?" I whisper. I can see that it is six digits long. I think about it, but nothing comes to mind. Finally, I type in random digits that pop into my head, and, to my surprise, something happens.

A new display appears. Activate manual opening?

I press YES.

The metallic click sounds unnaturally loud in the silence, followed by the hum of a magnetic field that soon dies away. The door does not slide up or down into its socket, it has to be opened manually. This is done using an old-fashioned twist lock that I have to turn clockwise multiple times. The mechanism squeaks as if it has never been used.

It takes some serious strength to open the door, which is almost as thick as my thigh and has several locking bolts as well as a magnetic latch.

I swallow, wishing it would moisten my dry throat, and pull the door the rest of the way open. Now it rises. The smell of solvent and ozone wafts toward me from inside, aseptic and too pure, like a freshly packaged computer circuit board. No wonder. As far as I know, this room has not been opened in 80 years.

As I slide into the small area, which measures less than two by two meters, I frown. Two identical black boxes with sides measuring half a meter each stand on the floor in front of me. Their walls are bare metal, which I assume is mono-bonded carbyne due to its characteristic structure, heavy and almost indestructible.

"What are they?" I murmur and float a little closer, but I hold on to the door frame because the walls are smooth and offer no grip. I know I do not want to touch the two boxes.

They lie before me like two impenetrable puzzles. Their perfect cubic shapes, the strict geometric precision, is strangely disturbing, as if they were measured *too* precisely. They stand unnaturally still directly on the floor, despite the weightlessness. Not even the ever-present, minimal vibrations of the *Ankh*, which is crisscrossed by thousands of kilometers of power cables and utility lines, seem to touch them. There are no visible means of restraint holding them in place, and yet they seem to refuse to obey microgravity and float.

Are they magnetically affixed?

The surface of the cubes is smooth, a black that allows no reflections. It is a darkness that seems to swallow light itself. Even the edges blur into mere illusion.

A chill runs down my spine. My gaze is caught by the strangeness of the substance and gets lost in it. I catch myself stretching out my hand toward the left box. Just before it gets to the box, it turns ice cold and I flinch as though I had been burned.

"Good idea to touch everything right away," I tell myself, licking my lips. Only now do I realize that it is very cold in here, and my shivering is not only due to the sinister nature of this cargo, which is apparently secret enough not to appear in the inventory lists – or in the blueprint of my ship. No seams or lines adorn the faces of the cubes, the edges appear razor-sharp and seamless, but can only be seen from the corner of the eye, where the image on the retina is sharper.

When I look directly at them, they seem to disappear into the featureless blackness. There are no visible openings, no switches or buttons, no signs of technology as I know it. And yet I can sense a kind of presence emanating from the boxes, a quiet authority that underscores the sophisticated nature of their origin. They are outside of time, seemingly without context or function, and yet I feel that they have a purpose beyond my imagination.

I find myself whispering and moving one hand above the boxes, a gentle plea for them to reveal their secrets. Of course, this is pretty stupid of me – and futile – but then I'm just a meatbag.

Who would have thought that Ammit-47's cynicism would rub off on me so quickly?

Finally, I can no longer control myself and touch the right box. I want to know if the surface is just shadows or solid. My hand gets so cold that I recoil, because at first I think I've burned myself. I try again and it's like touching icy metal. My palms leave no marks on the incomparably smooth material. It must be mono-bonded, perhaps only one atomic layer thick and thus virtually without even the smallest microscopic crack or imperfection. It feels hard, more solid than anything I know, and yet there is a pulsation underneath, an almost inaudible hum that runs through the box as though it were alive.

There's something in there.

It is this mixture of menace and fascination that captivates me. The boxes are strange and yet present in an unnaturally familiar way, as if I should know them and know what secrets they are hiding from me. But I just can't put my finger on their secrets, like when I can't remember a certain word that keeps eluding my memory. I know that the boxes belong here, in this spaceship, on my mission. But I don't know why. I don't know if they are dangerous, I don't know if they can help me.

I hover in the doorway for a while and ponder what I should do. Having cargo on board with a purpose unknown to me seems unacceptable. At the same time, I don't dare to touch it again because it seems dangerous and somehow wrong to do so.

But soon I will be in the vicinity of an alien civilization. Can I afford to undertake an endeavor potentially involving first contact without knowing what kind of cargo I will be bringing to the first interplanetary exchange between two species? What if they are bombs?

No, I can't do that. I answer my unspoken question in my mind and return to the corridor. I'll need tools if I want to unlock the boxes' secrets.

I'm just about to pull myself forward using the handrails when I stop and look at the open security door. I turn around and lock it.

Better safe than sorry.

I make my way to the small cargo hatch in front of the bridge, 30 meters ahead, and stock up on everything I can find there. I strap on a magnetic belt and clip two bags to it, which I would probably have had great difficulty even lifting in a gravity well.

Once I get back, I attach the belt to the door by applying the magnetic metal strips from the inside and then pick out several analysis tools one by one.

I use the multispectral scanner to examine a wide range of waves from gamma to radio to uncover possible hidden structures. The result is as sobering as expected. The boxes seem to absorb every beam and reflect nothing – absolutely nothing. The material seems to be a perfect cosmic black body that absorbs energy but doesn't emit any.

"Pretty selfish," I say, and try the soundwave scanner. Soundwaves would travel differently through hollow or liquid areas than through solid structures, but the echo is confusing, to say the least. Instead of providing clear results, the echo seems to return from an extreme depth, as though the interior is larger than it looks – which of course is not possible.

I proceed with a vibration and resonance test. The device for this looks like a gun, a fairly small one. Normal materials react to the gentle vibrations with some resonance or oscillation, these boxes simply absorb them, without any resonance pattern. They remain silent and unchanging.

Finally, I activate the magnetometer to check whether the foreign materials have any kind of magnetic field. But they don't. To the artificial field I created, they don't seem to exist. It is as if they are invisible, or nothing but imagination.

"I guess I'm lucky that my eyes can even see them," I grumble, and stare for a while at the enigmatic twins in front of me. These boxes are becoming creepier by the minute. But my curiosity is also growing. I am a scientist, in spite of everything.

With a mixture of defiance and persistence, I take the atomic force microscopy device out of the second toolbox. Its design is compact, maybe as big as my arm, but incredibly powerful.

The principle of atomic force microscopy is simple. A tiny, fine needle is passed over the surface of a material. Any atomic irregularity on the surface leads to tiny deviations in the position of the needle, which are detected by high-precision lasers and sensors. But the capabilities of this device go far beyond that. By using nanotechnology and extremely precise quantum sensors, it can identify and manipulate individual atoms.

I begin the process, placing the device on the left box, its four 'feet' spread apart. The probe arm begins its work by detecting the atomic structures. As expected, the surface is perfectly flat and shows no signs of wear or macroscopic features. But when it tries to manipulate the atomic bonds by poking between them, the box suddenly reacts.

It starts moving and vibrates so violently that the device bounces off its surface. This can't be possible! I just saw the device create vibrations in the box, which previously seemed immune to such energy transfers. Apparently it is not immune to physical manipulation if it is sharp and strong enough.

Before I can think any further, a bright light appears and fills the room. The box itself seems to transform into a dazzling source of photons. Instinctively, I close my eyes and push myself away from the box, hitting the back of my head against a wall and seeing bright afterimages on my retina. A white surface seems to dance in front of me, even though I have my eyelids tightly shut to protect my eyes.

When the light has gone out and I can finally see again, the box has stopped vibrating. The atomic force microscopy device is lying on the floor, smoldering.

Something about these boxes enabled retaliation when the device tried to tamper with them. Whatever is protecting them, it is powerful and highly active. I realize I am in danger and turn toward the door, only to find that I am on the opposite side of the room. I try to push myself toward the doorway when suddenly I can't breathe. The passage to the corridor is narrowing and the hatch slams shut as if by magic.

I'm trapped and feel like an invisible barrier is preventing me from breathing. My lungs won't fill and I start to suffocate. Panic spreads through me. I put my hand to my mouth, trying to remove something that isn't there, and start to kick my legs.

All in vain. My vision begins turning black from the edges and everything appears to be moving away from me.

Just when I'm sure I'm dying, I see a ray of light – is it coming from the door?

It all happens as if from far away, as though I had nothing to do with it. A red face appears, familiar but somehow alien. Hands grab me and pull my useless body with them. I notice that I can breathe again, and my inhalation sounds like a scream – only in reverse.

I live!

15

Ammit-47 drags me out of the heavily armored module like a piece of cargo – not to mention a meatbag – without hitting my shoulders, head, or legs against anything, which is a small miracle. I can't assist him because my body won't obey me yet. The breathing reflex has taken over and all I can do is gasp for air like a stranded fish.

A painful fire burns in my chest, as though every mucous membrane between my lungs and throat is aflame.

"T-T-Thank you," I stutter eventually, still short of breath. The robot shows a neutral expression and closes the door behind me. The button beside the door immediately shows that it has been magnetically locked and that access authorization is required.

"You're welcome," he finally says, and with a few quick, deft movements he 'lays' me across the central corridor. I float in the air and try to understand what just happened.

"How did you do that?"

"I grabbed you and pulled you out."

"I know that. But how did you know I was in there?"

"I was looking for the tool." Ammit-47 looks at me. The red face on his display looks like he feels sorry for me. He points to the locked door. "I hope we won't need it any time soon."

"I'm really glad," I say. "Thank you."

"I'm just following my orders," he replies, and I wish he would sound humble. Instead, he sounds like it's no big deal for a creature as superior as himself.

"How did you even get in there?"

"Into the module?"

"Yes. Did you have authorization?"

"No." Ammit-47 shakes his head. The servo motors in his neck joint make a whirring noise, just like Rofi's.

Suspicion creeps into my mind as I remember that my handprint – and I believe that includes an optical DNA scan – did not allow me to enter. Only the code that I somehow intuitively knew allowed me to enter in the first place. I also remember that the door slammed shut after the boxes started to glow. Otherwise the air would not have been able to escape so quickly.

So either this maintenance bot is lying to me, or the door was magically unlocked, which I cannot imagine, given the obvious security precautions to protect the two boxes. But I also find it unlikely that Ammit-47 has access rights and I don't. After all, as a robot, he doesn't even have write access to the on-board computer, can't formulate his own requests and commands, and can only passively receive information.

"So you don't have access?" I ask pointedly.

"No, I just said that."

"Would you try again?"

He twitches his shoulder joints in an almost-human shrug and puts his mechanical hand on the control panel. An error message appears. I tell him to repeat it until finally the prompt for the code appears.

Ammit-47 turns to face me and a very believable animated 'you see' expression appears on his display.

"You don't know the code?"

"No." Now he sounds like he's talking to a child who's slow on the uptake. "Your central brain organ has probably been affected by the lack of oxygen."

Then, I think silently, it is impossible that you could have saved me. The door was locked. I say nothing. It is obvious that he will not give me any other information.

"I understand," I say after a while, but I don't believe him. But I also don't understand why he would save me first, only to lie about it later. If he is hostile toward me, he could have simply let me die. Is he following his own agenda in which I play a role because he still needs me for something?

This idea is not so far-fetched, as I am the only one on the ship who can operate the on-board systems. He and Rofi can use some of the local subsystems, such as the maintenance access, the breeding area with the torpor capsules, and the habitat ring, but without control of the bridge, none of this is of much use to him. Is this where Rofi's dislike for his twin comes from? Does he distrust him, and was that why he was so depressed when we rescued him?

I don't want to think about all this, but I can't close my mind to it, either.

"What do you think they are?" I ask him, trying to change the subject. We've just been staring at each other for minutes while my head was spinning and spinning. A robot might not sense something like an awkward silence, but I certainly do.

"Those boxes?" He turns his display toward the door and back toward me. Then he twists his animated mouth. "I don't know. They don't resemble any of the other technology we have on board here. Much more advanced. I didn't have much time to look at them, though. One thing is certain. It's not hardware from the *Ankh*."

"You mean it's not of human origin?" I blink in surprise.

"I didn't say that. In any case, they don't match the rest of our equipment. There could be several explanations."

I grab the handrails above me and position myself directly opposite him, sort of sitting in the air with my legs slightly bent. My fingers and toes tingle. I felt the same sensation yesterday when I almost suffocated for the first time. I hope this doesn't become a daily ritual.

"Either the boxes were deposited here before departure, or someone smuggled them in there," I summarize. "I don't find either possibility particularly reassuring."

"Perhaps the event twenty years ago had something to do with it," suggests Ammit-47.

"I thought it was a solar event from the binary star system we passed through at the time."

"But a solar event shouldn't blow off our cargo modules, right?"

"No," I admit. "That's unlikely. But secondary events triggered by it could. Pressure losses, over-voltages, leaks in the coolant lines."

"Maybe." He doesn't sound convinced.

"Did you know about this cargo?"

"No."

"Did you know about the door?"

"Yes."

"But you never asked yourself what could be behind it?" I ask.

"No." Ammit-47 emits a sighing sound. "Unlike you meatbags, I follow my orders to the letter. I take care of the areas I am intended and trained for. If a door is not digitally signed and optically labeled, then it is none of my business. That also stops me from coming to your bunk at night, pulling back the curtain, and draining lubricant."

"You don't have any lubricant."

"No, fortunately not." The idea seems to disgust him. His face twists as if he had bitten into a lemon. But of course he doesn't even have a real mouth, which he's probably quite happy about. "At least I don't spend my time thinking about things that aren't relevant to my programming."

"Do you have *any* thoughts?"

"No. I'm very happy about that, too."

"I'm a little jealous," I say, not revealing that I'd like to get rid of any thought that he must have lied about the door.

16

After narrowly escaping the dark wings of death once again, I sleep for almost 11 hours straight. It is not a restful sleep. I am plagued by nightmares, confused images of black blocks that follow me everywhere and turn into shadowy demons with large beaks and terrible plumage as soon as I look at them. Turning away from them only makes it worse because I am afraid that they might come very close if I am not looking.

When I wake up, I still feel exhausted and decide to do a two-hour workout on the elliptical trainer. I need to clear my head.

After about an hour, Rofi leaves his charging station and runs over to me on all fours like a dog. He sits down in front of my training device and smiles at me.

"Good morning, Rofi," I say.

He holds up two fingers.

"Well charged?"

I wipe the fresh sweat from my forehead with the towel. I still don't enjoy exercise, but I'm slowly beginning to understand why it's good for me. The memories of last night are gradually peeling off like old skin cells making room for new ones. There's something liberating about the effort.

"Did Ammit-47 tell you what happened yesterday?" I ask.

Rofi shakes his head.

"Of course he didn't." I sigh. At the thought of his robot twin with the red display, I feel an unpleasant weight in my stomach. In my mind's eye I see his figure in the door to the secret cargo module, the lightning-fast movements and how he pulls me out. I know that I'm not in a good mental state, and the impressions were distorted by my death struggle, but one thing is clear. His lie is scaring me.

"There's a secret cargo module in front of the reactor section," I explain, breathing heavily. "It's in the same section as the maintenance entrances. The door that's not labeled. Do you know it?"

Rofi nods. His simple smile face now shows a neutral expression with a horizontal line for a mouth.

"Do you know what's behind it?"

A shake of the head.

"Two cubes made of an impenetrable, extremely smooth material. They are black and cannot be scanned with any sensor. When I tried to penetrate the surface of one of them, they resisted." My own words sound crazy to my ears. If the memories weren't so fresh and vivid, I would have doubted my sanity. "They tried to kill me."

Rofi's mouth corners point downward.

"Yes." I nod as I continue to exert myself on the elliptical trainer. "The bad thing is that whatever is in those boxes has to be connected to the module control. The alternative would be even more worrying, that it has access to the on-board computer. How else could it have sucked the atmosphere out of the interior? That can only be done with the approval of the internal control computer. Or the module is disconnected from the rest of the system."

Rofi raises a finger and points in the direction of the

ladder that disappears upward into the spoke that connects the kitchen-living room with the hull of the *Ankh*.

"Yeah, I should take a closer look," I say. "Can you do me a favor? Even if you don't like it?"

Rofi nods.

"Please assist Ammit-47 with his tasks for a few hours."

Rofi's 'eyes,' simple dots, turn into crosses and the corners of his mouth point downward. Then he suddenly smiles and raises two fingers. He obviously understands what I mean. I hope he doesn't feel like a secret agent now.

"Thanks, kid." I return his smile and climb down from the elliptical trainer.

Next, I take a shower and eat something that looks like vomit for breakfast, but according to the packaging, is supposed to be vegetable puree. It tastes surprisingly good. A few capsules of vitamins, minerals, and trace elements later, I put everything away carefully and double-check that I haven't left anything behind.

See? I am capable of learning.

Once I'm sure, I make my way to the bridge, climb through the spoke, and float forward toward the bow. At the very back of the corridor I see Ammit-47 and Rofi, who are just disappearing into one of the maintenance modules.

As soon as I'm in the pilot's seat, I close the door and rub my temples. A slight headache has been bothering me all morning. Maybe it's because of the lightning that flashed from the boxes, but it could also be because I almost suffocated again.

This is too close to becoming a habit.

For a moment I enjoy the silence and narrowness of the bridge, the unexciting environment with the dark fittings and displays. My gaze glides out to the band of stars that surrounds me outside the windows. It is beautiful and fills me with an indefinable longing.

I slowly turn away, forcing myself to focus my mind on the

problems before me. Sometimes I think that I am just a character in a stage production, insignificant and small compared to everything out there.

I imagine a neutron star, only about 20 kilometers in diameter, but so dense that a single sugar cube of its substance weighs more than the moon I'm heading to. A place where the laws of physics are turned upside down and a teaspoon of material weighs billions of tons. The strong gravitational pull there would even bend light rays and redirect them to the surface in a bizarre spectacle.

My gaze wanders to a distant galaxy that looks like a milky spot in the darkness. Somewhere there, a supernova could occur. A star 100 times larger than the central star here, whose life would end in a huge fireworks display so bright that it would outshine entire galaxies. The energy released would be so enormous it would equal what a star emits in its entire lifetime of several billion years.

I'm thinking of the cosmic jets ejected from the centers of active galaxies, of matter hurled into space at nearly the speed of light. They can extend for millions of light years, forming bridges between galaxies, and filling the dark void of space with their high-energy radiation.

Finally, I look at the shimmering bands of the Milky Way, a vast maelstrom of stars, gas and dust, rotating at unimaginable speeds around a supermassive black hole at its center, a place of such density and gravity that nothing, not even light, can escape.

And then there is me, a tiny creature in this gigantic universe, on a small ship gliding through the endless void. I feel small and insignificant. But then I remember that all these wonders, all these powers, all this beauty only exists because there are creatures like me who can observe them. Who, with our consciousness, help them to exist in the first place.

And with that thought I no longer feel small, knowing that significance has nothing to do with size and extent, but with the fact that nothing can have meaning without me. What is the greatest spectacle without an observer who makes it real through his experience?

It brings me back to my problems, grounds me for what I must do, and makes me realize that what I'm doing here is important. I'm responsible for two robots and a ship, and – as best I can tell – for establishing contact with an alien civilization.

And that's why I need to find out what's going on here.

First, I start my display and call up all the log files of the on-board computer. Next, I limit the window of time I want to view and get an endless list, even though it's only an hour in total. Not for the first time, I wish the on-board AI was working. Although I have no direct memories of working with it, I know how it works and what it should do and can imagine it. This state of knowing without having the corresponding memories associated with it is just plain weird. It's like baking a cake and knowing the list of ingredients, including the ratios in which I mix and process them to make a delicious confection. But if I had to say who taught me that or what the ingredients are all about, I wouldn't have the answer.

But wishing is useless. The onboard AI is broken and it looks like I cannot reactivate it. As a result, all I can do is go through these log files one by one and pick out the ones I want to look at. It takes hours, and it shows me how many things are happening every minute on the *Ankh* to keep the countless systems running smoothly.

But eventually I find what I'm looking for and lean forward in anticipation as the data spreads out before me like pages in a book of secrets that I've just dusted off.

First, I look at the signal connections between the mysterious cargo module and the *Ankh*. As soon as I put my hand on the door – I see myself in the surveillance camera footage – a signal goes from the module to the on-board computer. I cannot determine what it is, but I can tell they are communicating with each other. The bridge finally gives me clearance after the code is accepted. So I now know it was not just the control panel that decided that I could enter, but also the *Ankh* itself.

From there it gets even more interesting – or rather, more worrying. There are no surveillance sensors inside the module, but on the images showing the corridor in front of it I can pretty much pinpoint the moment when the boxes turn into dazzling flashes of light. At the same time, the amount of energy stored in the dorsal energy matrix cells drops by almost one percent.

"So, you two bastards are connected to my power supply," I mutter.

The question is whether this was planned from the beginning, or whether they came on board like two parasites that ate their way into the system. I expect to find that there was communication with the on-board computer for the sudden venting of the module, but I find I am mistaken. There must be a complex internal system that gives that specific cargo hold a high degree of autonomy from the rest of the ship, because the *Ankh* did not even register the extraction of the atmosphere. Normally, the escape of air immediately sets off a general alarm, because it is one of the most dangerous things that can happen in space. My near-death experience, however, seems to have never happened, if the log files are anything to go by.

I reopen the camera data. The optical sensors, which are installed in the form of tiny button optics all over the walls, create a three-dimensional image. I rewind to the very beginning and watch myself stopping in front of the unmarked door for the first time yesterday, putting my hand on the control panel next to it and hesitating before entering the code. Then I disappear from the picture and into the module before reappearing after much longer than I remember. I hustle my way to the front, get the two tool cases and return to the spooky cargo hold.

Nothing happens for a long time. The corridor is deserted and empty, until Ammit-47 appears. He makes his way to one of the maintenance rooms and doesn't even notice the open door – it looks as though it doesn't exist for him. Only when I see the flash of light shoot out of the opening does he appear in the central corridor as if on command and quickly pushes himself off with his rear arms toward the module.

I look at the door where he catches himself. It is locked, the LED on the side is flashing red, but it turns green the moment he pulls on the wheel and rips it open. Ammit-47 disappears inside and returns shortly afterward with me in tow.

"I've looked better," I say.

My violet eyes, normally my pride and joy when I view myself in the bathroom mirror, look frightened. If eyes are indeed the window to the soul, my soul is not looking particularly good right now.

My dark brown skin looks almost carbon-colored on the monitor. The contrast of the camera does not have enough dynamic range to do justice to my skin color – at least that's how I see it. Completely objectively, of course. My hair, or rather the many short, fine tentacles that grow out of my scalp and seem to have developed a life of their own, normally drapes gently downward like black jewelry. In the video, it looks like barbed wire, sticking out rigidly in all directions. The lack of oxygen has caused it to stand up, and the microgravity isn't helping things a bit.

My expression in the picture is... let's just say it's *not* an expression that would win me an intergalactic beauty prize. The corners of my mouth are drooping, my expression of despair says, 'Why does this always happen to me?' But then, upon closer inspection, I can see a hint of resilience in my crooked smile, a sort of 'you can't do this to me, universe' attitude. I'm almost a little proud of myself for this display of stubborn resilience.

I study my delicate nose, the soft, imperfect features of my face, and realize that I am not beautiful, but still somehow special. A face with character, yes. And even if my appearance at the moment resembles a frightened bird that has not yet fledged, I am still, with all my flaws and scars, myself, a product of my experiences. A child of the stars who, despite all setbacks, gets up and carries on. Like now.

I've had better days. But that's me. Still ready to fight, even if the universe sometimes disagrees with me.

I think for a while about what I saw. How Ammit-47 was able to open the door as if by magic, even though he shouldn't have been able to do so. And how he suddenly appeared when I needed him, but previously ignored the module as though it didn't exist.

In any case, I now know he didn't lie. At least not about opening the door without an access authorization or a code. Nevertheless, his behavior was more than simply strange.

Just like those two boxes.

I turn back to the onboard computer data and go back 20 years to the time of the event that damaged the *Ankh*. The camera footage from the central corridor looks the same as it does today – there is nothing to indicate that I have traveled back in time 20 years. The door is still there.

I rewind. It was there before the event, and the external sensors show me that the entire module is in its place. So unless the two boxes have defied the laws of physics, they have been on board since the beginning of the journey.

I take a closer look at the error messages at the time of the event. The general alarm goes off at 06:34 ship's time. Some of the sensors on the front sensor phalanx fail. Increased radiation levels are measured – at least that's what the log files say. But upon closer inspection, I see that the ionization chambers, scintillation, and semiconductor detectors are all offline at this time.

"That's strange." I frown. Either the time stamps are wrong because they're in the wrong order, or something else is wrong. According to the reports, the readings come from the seconds after the corresponding detectors failed, which logically should be impossible. Then come the various cargo modules blowing off from the starboard side and a whole cascade of problems – the failure of the ship's AI, problems with the power supply, short circuits, and finally the disaster with the torpor capsules.

I swallow hard as I watch the first two capsules fail after about a year because they were disconnected from the *Ankh's* power grid for too long due to malfunctions. Images of the two babies, pale and floating in the blue nutrient fluid, return to my mind. Their corpses haunt me in my sleep. I would like to simply erase all memories of them from my mind.

But that seems cowardly and unfair of me. I already feel guilty for avoiding the fact that they are still there. I will have to take care of them, even if that means going back to the place that I am even more afraid of than the mysterious module with the two boxes that do not seem to come from this universe.

I choose to set that task aside for now, even though I put it high on my mental to-do list. The radiation event continues to puzzle me. The measurement data clearly does not come from the corresponding sensors. Then something occurs to me. Rofi seems to have survived the coronal mass ejection pretty well, despite walking around on the hull to attach the module in which Ammit-47 was stranded.

With such a massive ejection of plasma particles and magnetic field energy, electrical and electronic disturbances would normally be expected, triggered by the charged particles of the central star. High-energy protons and electrons would cause computer parts to fail, perhaps even here in the shielded and protected ship. Since the coronal mass ejection would also have changed the pressure profile and plasma density in the ship's surroundings, it would be expected that heat management – at least of the unprotected Rofi – would have suffered greatly. And overheating in a vacuum, where heat can hardly, or even not at all, be dissipated, would have caused its systems to fail. At least partially. There was a reason why I thought he was lost. And I hadn't even taken into account that the particle streams could cause physical surface damage.

I massage my temples again. The headache has gotten worse. Before I force myself to drink something, I press a button on the ship's radio. I call the two robots over the ship's internal loudspeaker. "Rofi, Ammit-47, please come to the bridge."

I haven't even emptied half of my drinking tube when the door opens and the two bots, identical except for their displays, float in.

"You called us?" asks Ammit-47.

Rofi smiles happily.

"Yes. Is there a way to read your memories?"

"There is. We have to be docked to our charging stations for it to work." He points to my forearm display. "You can then submit a maintenance request."

Ten minutes later, we do just that. They are both hanging motionless on their charging hooks. Their displays show matching schematics of almost fully charged batteries, making them look like twins that I can no longer tell apart. Reading their memories takes less than two minutes, and then I have a complete report.

I sit down at the kitchen table and go through them. Ammit-47 shows no malfunctions, while Rofi's head memory shows several problems, including malfunctions in the central data processing system, which I quickly associate with his inability to generate speech output, even though his speakers themselves are fully functional. But I can't find what I'm looking for on either of them – damage from the coronal mass ejection that both were exposed to out there.

Either they are far more advanced than I've come to believe, and they are protected by technology of which I am unaware, or the *Ankh's* onboard computer has lied to me at least once and there was no coronal mass ejection from the central star.

I look up from my screen and stare out into space through the small window.

Both possible explanations make me shudder. There is something *wrong* about this ship.

17

Not much happens over the next 20 days. We pass the orbit of another gas giant and the asteroid belt, of which we notice hardly anything except for two days with the occasional radar contact. The celestial bodies are several tens of thousands of kilometers away and of different sizes. Nothing that could pose a threat to us.

I try to keep my days as consistent as possible to help against loneliness. This is what each day looks like: I get up, work out on the elliptical trainer for two hours – yes, me! – and then have breakfast. I've learned to like the ration packs even though they still don't look particularly tasty. Whoever was responsible for their appearance should be fired in my opinion. After that, I talk to Ammit-47 and Rofi, even though the latter doesn't have much to contribute. His smile is usually enough for me because it warms my heart a little.

The meetings basically consist of Ammit telling me what work he and Rofi have scheduled for that day. Most of it is repetitive maintenance, checking for micrometeorite damage, corrosion, material fatigue, and other structural irregularities. They begin by plugging into the maintenance network and reading sensor data.

Then there is a visual inspection of the ship and a visual inspection using the optical sensors on the *Ankh's* hull. Next is maintenance of the life support systems, which includes changing air filters, checking the water treatment system, the atmospheric composition, and the recyclers. Yes, recyclers. Everything that goes into the trash on the ship is recycled. Meaning everything organic, and that includes my waste.

When I eventually find out that the ration packs are produced and packaged by the automatic kitchen system – fed from the recyclers – I revise my opinion that those responsible should be fired. I would have nothing to eat. In spite of the feces and urine, it tastes damn good. At least I can justifiably say that this is the best human excrement I have ever eaten!

But back to Ammit-47 and Rofi.

The two hard-working robots read the energy matrix cells every day, look for fluctuations, and distribute digital stamps in the system when everything is correct. Normally they would also carry out software updates, but since the AI that was responsible for ongoing code optimizations of the firmware is offline, this task is no longer necessary.

Finally, and quite mundanely, they are also responsible for cleaning the *Ankh*. Whenever they move on to this part of the job, I can tell very reliably by the expressions on their displays. Rofi's mouth corners droop, his eyes formed into crosses, while Ammit-47's sour expression shows the complexity of animations his two-dimensional face is capable of.

I wonder if their programmer was just having fun when he implanted this response to cleaning into them, or if it indicates the extent to which they are independently operating, conscious beings.

Anyway, it amuses me every day to see two grumpy robots sweeping and vacuuming throughout the ship. It's even funnier when they catch me trying to hide my amusement – and no, I'm not trying very hard. Their mood sinks even lower every time.

These moments help to lift some of the never-ending burden from my shoulders. I still know nothing about the beginning of my mission. The onboard computer appears to have been wiped clean of all data from the time of takeoff and immediately thereafter. I can roughly make out my home solar system, but only by estimating it based on the speed and duration of the journey. I find some pictures of my – possible – starting point, Earth, a world not unlike the one I'm flying toward, which has a moon that looks slightly larger than ours, consists of almost 70 percent ocean, and is covered by bands of white clouds.

That's it. That's all I know. I can't find any information about the rest of humanity. There aren't even any entertainment programs, no theater performances, games, or anything else to pass the time. So I do what my two robot companions do and what the mission planners must have intended. I work a lot.

Most of my time is spent sifting through as much data from the onboard computer as I can. I want to know more about the strange 'event' that led to the deaths of my comrades and learn why I survived. But no matter how deep I dig, I can't find any clues that would help me.

And then there are the corpses in the nutrient solution. I find out that the nanonic liquid filled with highly effective microorganisms does not preserve the dead bodies, but keeps the tissue alive, even though they are all brain dead and have no heartbeats. So their cells are just lifeless flesh, clumps of cells in the shape of people of different ages. But they continue to be supplied with everything they need, even without metabolism.

The very thought is terrifying and I keep reminding myself that I must bury them. I must face my fear, return to my 'birthplace' and bid farewell to friends I have never met. I want to do it before we arrive behind the moon of the target planet so that I can concentrate on what lies ahead.

I've known for a while now that the best time to do this is 'tomorrow.' Always tomorrow.

In the evenings, I sit on the bridge, with Rofi and Ammit-47 taking turns as my companion, looking at the stars. At first, I had to order the latter to keep me company, but more recently he is often there before me. I don't know whether that's a sign that he likes it. He would never admit it, even if he did. Both robots have their advantages when it comes to spending time together. Rofi's forced indifferent nature leads to me having long monologues that help me keep my mind clear. It's amazing how many answers to your own questions come to you when you have a dialogue with yourself. Sometimes I even wonder whether it takes more than just stopping and listening to yourself.

Rofi thinks it's all great and gives me his cheerful smile and raised fingers. Over time, I even think I've decoded his reactions, because he does react to what I say. In any case, he is very supportive, just as I would like him to be, which makes my actual theory a little implausible. But that's okay, because I'm the commander.

Anyone who wants to challenge my position, come forward now!

On one of these evenings, Ammit-47 is already in the co-pilot's seat and wordlessly hands me a hydration pack as I float over the headrest and settle into my seat in one fluid motion. As the weeks go by, I've become much more adept and wish I could show it off to someone. At least a little.

"Good evening, 47," I say. We've reached nickname level now. At least that's what I've decided.

"Good evening. Do you prefer 'meat' or 'bag'?" replies the maintenance bot, looking at me with a neutral expression.

"How do you do that?"

"How do I do what?"

"Keep such a blank face while you say something like that," I explain.

"Are you jealous?"

"A little bit, yes."

"I can teach you," he suggests, folding his front hands in front of his face before turning it 90 degrees toward me via the neck joint.

"Let me guess," I interrupt before he can continue. "All I need is for you to cut off my head and replace it with a high-resolution display, and you'll coach me through the rest."

"Something like that." He nods. The joint under the base of his 'head' makes a whirring noise.

"I think I'm not ready quite yet," I say theatrically. "Maybe we should wait and see how things go once we get here. I have a feeling you're going to need my pretty face if you don't want to get blown up."

"Do you think that robots are not suitable for making contact with another species?" Ammit-47 sounds indignant. "We are superior creatures who do not sleep and do not get tired, who can think more rationally and are free of emotions."

"Are you sure?"

"Yes."

"Hello, meatbags, I'm Ammit-47 and I come in peace," I say in my best imitation of his androgynous voice with its typical cynicism, trying to keep my expression a complete blank.

"That's not bad at all," he praises me dryly.

"I had a good teacher." I sink back in my seat and look out at the stars. Even after so many evenings up here, the view has lost none of its breathtaking beauty. "I'm really glad you saved me," I say after a long silence. "Otherwise I would have missed all of this."

"Saved you?" he asks, furrows appearing on his animated forehead.

"From Module X." That's what I've been calling the secret cargo module for a while now. I think it's very apt.

"I don't understand."

I turn to him and look for mockery in his expression, or the typical twitch at the corners of his mouth that always lets me know he's making fun of me. But I don't see any of that.

"You got me out when I was almost suffocating."

"Are you not feeling well?" Ammit-47 sounds almost worried.

I fire up my screen and pull up the camera footage I've watched so many times. I play it back from the point where he comes out of Module X and pulls me into the central corridor, gasping like a fish, flushed and disheveled.

"Do you see?"

He looks at the display and back at me. "Is this a joke?"

"What do you think?"

"This is the empty central corridor." He points his finger in the direction of the image I paused, where I'm floating with him in microgravity. "There's nothing there."

Later, when I'm about to go to bed, I see Rofi, who is just disconnecting from his charging station. I ask him about Module X, but he just shows a neutral line instead of a smile, with question marks instead of eyes. Even when I get more specific and describe the position in the maintenance section, he seems to know what kind of door it is, but not what's behind it, nor that I almost died there. I also show him the camera footage of my rescue by Ammit-47, but he doesn't seem to understand either.

He doesn't see anything there.

18

Over the next ten days I observe them repeatedly. I take time away from poring over the on-board computer to watch them work via the internal cameras. They never exchange words when they meet, but perhaps they have another form of communication that does not rely on vocalization. No, I don't honestly believe that. After this much time, I would surely have found out about it.

Otherwise, however, they do not behave in an unusual or even strange way. They obediently carry out their tasks, repeatedly following the same patterns. Once a day, I watch the recordings of my rescue by Ammit-47 because I do not want to lose my mind. It is difficult to bear when you have memories that are questioned by the only other 'living beings' on board. It does not take long before you doubt your own mental health. But I view the images again and yet again, pixel by pixel, and know that they match what I have seen and experienced.

I'm not crazy. But maybe my ship is.

On the tenth day, when we are only a few days away from our destination, I start to have trouble sleeping. I am excited about the prospect of meeting aliens and at times I even forget that I am on a spaceship that seems to have a life of its own.

Before I can deal with that, however, I must finally face my dead comrades. I have made a contract with myself that I will not make first contact with literal corpses in my basement. It seems wrong on every level. My unknown friends deserve a proper farewell. Besides, what if the alien beings come on board with me and for some reason come across the breeding section?

How would I react if I were a guest of aliens and saw a corridor in which the corpses of babies, children, and adults were floating like in test tubes.

Like I'd been invited to tea with psychopaths.

No, I don't think that's a good idea, and so on the fifth day before our arrival I'm standing in front of the locked door to the breeding section, which hasn't been opened since I woke up. Ammit-47 and Rofi are flanking me. Their presence is a small comfort that gives me strength, even though I would prefer to run away. Rofi shifts his weight to his back hands and stands up like a human, almost reaching my shoulder, on which he puts a hand.

I look at him and he displays his smiley smile. I smile back and nod gratefully. Then I look at Ammit-47 and catch him rolling his pixel eyes.

"What is it?" I ask.

"You meatbags and your fear of death," he replies, letting out an electronic sigh. "That's just organic waste in there that needs to be taken away."

"Hey, that's disrespectful."

"To whom?"

"To the dead!"

"We can ask them whether they take offense at my statement," he replies laconically.

"They were my friends," I murmur, realizing that this thought is the result of a very deep desire.

"You're projecting something onto them. They were people who were never born. Clones, I think, just like you. But they didn't live and they certainly aren't living now."

"How can you say that so easily?"

"Because I can think rationally, unlike you meatbags. You can only do that depending on the situation, because your evolutionary heritage is constantly getting in the way," explains Ammit-47, sounding almost pitying. "The survival instinct is deeply woven into your DNA through millions of years of evolution. That's why you're so afraid of death."

"You make it sound like it's totally absurd."

"It is."

"Aren't you afraid of being destroyed?"

"No."

I frown and look at him, but his face has returned to its neutral state.

"Why should I be?" he continues. "I was *built*, and I do not have this reflexive desire to exist forever. Nor do I need psychological mechanisms to block out my inevitable end in order to function. I was created and I will follow my function until I no longer do so."

"That easy?"

"That easy."

"But you want to exist, don't you? Otherwise, you might as well just switch off."

"I exist, therefore I exist," he replies. "There's a difference. Just because I don't care about my end doesn't mean I want it to happen now. Only a meatbag thinks like that."

I do think about it, staring at the white bulkhead that separates us from the breeding section. My hands are sweaty as I look at the control panel on the right. I can't help but notice how utterly absurd this is. I've faced death several times in just a few weeks, outside in the cold vacuum, inside here with two eerie black boxes. But I was never as scared as I am now of confronting a few corpses. Is it because I was one of them?

Because they remind me that it could have been me, too, who will never wake up? Death before I was born?

Ammit-47 surprises me when he nudges me with his elbow to get my attention.

"I'm offline when I'm charging," he says. "When you sleep, you're offline too. At least in the sense of your personality, which is no longer active, right?"

"Something like that. What are you getting at?"

"Do you like to sleep?"

"Naturally."

"Even though you know that if you lie down you, your continuous personality will disappear – until you wake up?"

I'm confused. "Yes... And?"

"When you die, you're gone. You no longer look out of your eyes, you no longer think all that pile of ego thoughts that make you who you are and have no true substance. Just like when you sleep. The only difference is that before you sleep you have the thought that you'll wake up tomorrow and before you die you have the thought that you'll never wake up. But the same thing happens. Do you understand now how absurd you meatbags are?"

I think about it and have to smile. "I think so."

"And that, Meatbag, is true rationality," he replies triumphantly, but also a little compassionately. At least I think so. "Armed with it, we'll go in there and do our job. We'll clean up cellular waste, that's all it is. Your body does that all the time in the autophagy phase, by the way."

I look at Rofi, who smiles and holds out two fingers, and I put my hand on the control panel. The hatch moves upward into the wall – accompanied by a hissing sound.

The first thing that hits me is the smell, a mix of sweet and sour. A dark, furry patina has formed on the walls that wasn't there the last time. It's probably microorganisms that have spread in the leaked nutrient fluid from my capsule and eaten into the metal. The silence has taken on a heavy quality, almost suffocating in its intensity, and underlined by the odor of decay and putrefaction.

The ten capsules are set into the left wall like memorials to days gone by, and they bring back flashes of memories of my 'birth.' I flinch. The oval window that forms the front of each individual capsule now looks like a cold eye, watching me and following my steps. They seem to stare at me accusingly and spark pangs of survivor's guilt.

Why did I survive and not them?

The deep blue liquid in the capsules appears restless, as if reflecting the dark mood of the room, but it doesn't move.

The empty tank in the middle looks cold and lonely. The umbilical cord hangs limp and dry, its pink color having taken on a dull, lifeless quality. I think that much of the stench comes from it. The dried blood looks old and brittle. The liquid that had spilled on the floor has turned into sticky residue, smelling stale and sour.

Seeing the cradle of my short life like this frightens me. I was born from this filth?

My dead comrades, who never saw the light of the spaceship, seem less peaceful than before. The babies seem smaller, less developed, the older and larger ones more tense, their once relaxed faces now masklike. Their mouthpieces look like something that suffocated them, as though they are victims of a crime. Is the *Ankh* to blame for this too? An inexplicable malfunction?

The breeding section was supposed to be a place of growth and life. Hope and a spirit of discovery would have been produced if everything had gone according to plan. At least that's how I imagine it. People of different ages bringing life to the *Ankh* and each bringing their own perspective to the challenges and questions of such a journey. A team that is better as a whole than as its parts.

I know that these are the wishful thoughts of a woman who knows only loneliness and not her place in the universe, but I am not a robot. How simple Ammit-47 and Rofi's lives are. They know what they are to do every day and do not complain about monotony or possible dangers that may still come their way. They take care of one task at a time.

That's precisely what I'm going to do now, I think, squaring my shoulders. With both hands I grab the vacuum-sealable garbage bags from the kitchen and take a step forward.

"Okay," I say. "Let's get started. So, 47, you operate the controls on the capsules and drain the nutrient solution. Rofi, you start cleaning the floor and walls."

He raises two fingers.

"We need to make sure bacteria do not spread into the habitat module, so double-disinfect everything if possible."

Ammit-47 has already started operating the control panel of the first tank, and the liquid is running down from top to bottom, like a measuring cup with a hole drilled in the bottom. The infant inside floats down with the solution until the umbilical cord and breathing cable are stretched because they are attached higher up in the back wall of the capsule. Then he is lying dry, and a hissing sound tells me that the oval window has been unlocked. It flips up and the baby lies there much whiter than expected, his pale skin smeared with the viscous solution.

Now comes my task. I put on my gloves and take a deep breath.

19

When I'm very close, I hesitate. The tiny creature is so young that he's barely recognizable as a human. His skin is as pale as alabaster, against which the blue veins are starkly visible. His eyes, still tightly shut, hide the innocence they were never allowed to discover. The dark cable, which was supposed to give him the life that was taken from him before he had even begun, protrudes from his mouth.

With extreme caution, I remove the infant from the capsule, gently pulling the cord from his tiny lips. It's a silent moment, sadly reverent. The mouthpiece comes free with a soft smack, leaving a trail of fluid on his chin and trailing slimy threads behind it. I cut the umbilical cord with a surgical device attached to my magnetic tool belt. The small body feels unexpectedly heavy in my arms, a contrast to his tiny frame. It's cold and lifeless, yet strangely familiar. It could have been my brother, my son, a male version of my own younger self. I find it hard to believe I once looked like this.

I carefully place the body in one of the bags and run my hand over the seal. There is a quiet hissing sound as the air escapes from the bag. It continues to shrink, the shape of the small body becoming sharply visible through the transparent material. A tiny human being, captured in a moment of eternity.

I do the same with the next capsules. Some of the clones are older, their features having begun to form, a hint of individuality visible in their lifeless faces. Each bag I vacuum seal is like an echo of my own existence. Each silent witness of my lost brothers and sisters is a shadow of my own possibilities, of lives not lived aboard the *Ankh*.

Rofi comes near me, cleaning bucket and high-performance vacuum cleaner in his hands. He nudges me and looks up at me with question marks in his eyes.

What's going on? I mentally translate his unspoken question.

"I assumed all this time that we were clones because it would make sense," I explain quietly. "But what if we were conceived naturally? Had mothers and fathers who donated us as embryos for this mission? Maybe our genetic profiles were particularly promising? What if we left something behind that we don't even know about?"

Something valuable. Some *one* who loves us?

Rofi looks from me to the open second capsule and observes the five-year-old child inside. Then he nudges me again and smiles.

"It doesn't change anything," I agree. "At least it shouldn't."

"Change what is? You can't do that anyway," Ammit-47 remarks from farther to the right, without pausing in his work on the control panels. His mechanical fingers practically fly over the digital keys. "So you might as well just stop thinking about it."

In my head I agree with him and sigh before continuing with my work.

Over time, I almost fall into something like monotony or

routine. Cutting the umbilical cords, pulling out the cables, bagging the bodies. Each action becomes a little ritual that I keep performing, slowly and deliberately. Ammit-47 may think it's 'meatbag' sentimentality and irrational behavior, but I don't care. Dead or not, they deserve all the dignity I can give them.

It is all I can do.

Inside the capsule lies a person who looks like me. His body is fully grown, his features are soft, his age appears roughly the same as mine. It is as though I am looking into a distorted mirror that shows me an alternate reality in which I do not exist, but he does. Ammit-47 has not opened the window yet because he is helping Rofi to take away buckets of nutrient fluid that they have removed from the floor with their suction cups.

With a deep breath, I open the capsule and a gush of the sweet liquid spills out and spreads across the metal floor. It splashes onto my boots, but I barely notice as I reach for the man. He is heavy, his taut muscles a testament to the artificial maturation he has undergone in the capsule.

I hold him with one arm like holding a child, and with my free hand carefully pull the breathing cable out of his mouth, almost with a practiced movement after the many times before. But as I pull his body further from the capsule to reach his umbilical cord, he slips from my grasp. Before I can react, he falls to the floor, his head hitting the metal with a dull sound.

I recoil in shock. His head is lying in a rapidly spreading pool of white fluid that is running from a wound on his forehead.

White, not red!

Like spilled milk, it mixes with the midnight blue of the nutrient solution.

For a moment I am unable to move. He is not bleeding.

How is that possible? The gash on his forehead is finger-length and deep, and the white substance is continuously pouring out of it and puddling around my boots.

I touch my stomach, where the knife wound has long since healed. I remember lying in the sickbay, the warm red blood that flowed from my wound as the medical unit removed the blade. I remember the pain, the fear – and most of all, the red color.

My head is spinning. It was red, wasn't it?

My breath catches and I kneel down next to the corpse, carefully touching the white liquid and rubbing it between the fingers of my gloves. It is thick, almost gel like, and cool. It is something other than blood. Something foreign. Something that shouldn't be there.

With shaking hands, I activate the radio unit on my chest and call the robots to come. They arrive running on all fours, their efficient movements a sharp contrast to my dazedness. At my command, they pick up the body and carry it to the sickbay.

I follow them, watching as they place the body on the treatment table. His expression is peaceful, despite the white fluid continuing to run from his forehead, forming little rivers all over his face and running toward his neck.

I stare at it and don't understand what I see. But inside me the realization is growing that something is profoundly and fundamentally wrong here. I want to call for the robotic arm, but in the next moment I remember that I dismantled it and left it in space with the gas giant.

"Beginning examination of the patient," the medical unit purrs, and sensor bundles sprout from the ceiling, scanning the entire body. "Patient deceased."

"What? Why?" I ask impatiently.

"Starting cause of death investigation," the unit continues, followed by a rapid stream of data appearing on one of the displays. Small manipulators move out of the treatment table and work on the corpse like a piece of meat. There is nothing dignified about it. I feel a little sick.

"Pupillary response: Negative. Cardiovascular activity: Negative. Respiratory rate: Negative. Patient's condition: Deceased. Cause of death: Massive brain damage due to physical trauma and prolonged cerebral hypoxia. Cerebral activity has ceased. Massive cell degradation has been detected in the cerebral cortex and brain stem. Hypoxia due to lack of oxygen in the bloodstream and resulting damage to the central nervous system, probably due to a previous systemic malfunction."

"But he doesn't have any blood! Your diagnosis is wrong!" I feel pure anger rising within me. Everything on board seems to be habitually lying to me.

With a face twisted in disgust, I pick up a scalpel, hesitate for a moment, and then make the first cut below the ribs. Even the damn medical unit is playing tricks on me.

More of the strange white liquid comes out. It seems thick, almost syrupy, and has a strange, indefinable smell. It reminds me most closely of singed hair.

With a combination of fascination and disgust, I cut deeper into the body. It is surprisingly easy. I do not come across any tendons or dense tissue. After a while, I take a spreader out of a drawer, insert it into the wound, and open it wide. Instead of the muscle fibers of the diaphragm, I see a substance that looks like white foam. It is elastic and springy.

I cut deeper down to reach the ribs, flipping up the skin to expose them, and I turn my attention to the bones. When I press against them with my gloved fingers, I expect resistance, but whatever it is gives way and then springs back into shape. I cut into one of the 'bones' and instead of hard tissue, I find a porous, soft structure, almost like Styrofoam.

The realization can no longer be suppressed. This is not a

person in front of me. It is a mannequin, an empty replica, an illusion.

Questions swirl around in my head like a whirlwind. I drop the scalpel and sink to the floor, powerless. What does all this mean?

My stomach clenches and I close my eyes against the suddenly too-bright light of the sickbay.

20

In the evening, I sit at the kitchen table with Rofi and Ammit-47 and stare at the gray surface. Before that, I stood in the shower for an hour – until the *Ankh* turned off the water because the bathroom's treatment systems were overloading. I scrubbed the white liquid from my skin repetitively, even after it had long since disappeared.

I cut open every single corpse and examined each one. None of them had blood in their veins or muscles attached to their bones – not to mention that the skeletons also seemed to be made of an artificial material that was noticeably elastic. But the autopsies of the brains hit me the hardest. I don't know what I expected, maybe circuits instead of gray matter, but definitely not white jelly.

The sickbay looked like a monochromatic slaughterhouse when I was finished. But the sight didn't horrify me.

Because no one died there.

No one was treated with dignity after their death, because there is no such thing as death for mannequins. They were just a façade, the whole time. They never existed, so the malfunction in their torpor capsules couldn't have happened either.

Just another lie. Who does something like that? And why?

"That was... an experience," Ammit-47 remarks, and I would have liked to hit him for the sarcastic undertone in his voice. But I find this reaction in me primitive and weak. My horror is my own. It will not be lessened by expecting it from him or by taking out my anger on him.

"Tell me you saw that too," I say weakly instead of snapping at him.

"White stuff instead of blood, bodies that aren't human," Ammit-47 sums up, and Rofi also confirms this in the form of a sad smile and two hesitantly raised fingers. At least there's something good. This time they don't seem to be suffering from amnesia, like in Module X.

"But you thought they were humans all this time, didn't you?"

"Yes."

"What is the point of this? What is the point of putting fake corpses all around me? Just so I can mourn them when they never even existed?" I knock on the table and shake it without it moving even a millimeter. "Is all of this just a facade? A bad simulation?"

I stand up and walk around the room, looking in the directions where I know there are button cameras. "Is this a play? The last flight of the bird of death?"

Ammit-47 looks at me like I've lost my mind. He looks amused. Rofi looks worried in his own way.

"What?" I ask.

"If it were a play, they would have installed better cameras for me," Ammit-47 answers sarcastically. "I'd hope they wouldn't skimp on the equipment."

"This is no joke, 47."

"It depends."

"Oh yeah? On what?" I sigh and sit back down.

"On how seriously you want to take all this."

"This is my life!" I want to wring his neck, but I force myself to take a long breath. Finally, I spread my hands on the table in front of me. This robot will be my most unpleasant teacher. "Enlighten me."

"The onboard computer is faulty, and perhaps the mission planning is, too. Your comrades are just a facade, an act, and we have a secret cargo on board that is not listed in the inventories and looks much more advanced than our technology – that's what you say," he sums up. "Ammit-48 and I cannot confirm this because our programming obviously doesn't allow us to. All of this together is thoroughly strange."

"Thank you for seeing it that way," I reply equally sarcastically. As if there was any other way to see it. But it calms me down a little that he seems to believe me about the secret module and its cargo.

"Do you have a plan to undo all this?"

I look at him, confused. "*Undo?* How is *that* supposed to work?"

"Exactly. It's not possible. The facts are what they are. We can fly back and ask the mission leaders what they were thinking – please add my insufficient resolution cameras to the list. But to do that we need a lot of helium-3, and you need significantly more years of life than your genes allow."

"You're just saying that," I say dejectedly, and Ammit-47 sighs almost humanly.

"You meatbags and your thoughts. Sometimes I feel like you would make more sense if you turned each of your thoughts around." He sounds genuinely dismayed. "I shouldn't be alone, you think. But the fact is that you are alone. If you turn that thought around, it comes out, I should be alone. You have plenty of proof that this thought is correct, because you are alone."

I bite back my knee-jerk protest and think about his concept. And I remain silent for a moment.

"A robot that teaches me wisdom?" I think out loud. What irony.

Rofi comes close and points in the direction of the

corridor that leads to the breeding section. Then he shakes his head and pulls down the corners of his mouth. He points there again, wiggles a finger, and the corners of his mouth return to form his smile.

"Excuse me?" I ask, irritated. "I'm afraid I don't understand you, little one."

"He says it makes no difference whether there were nine dead comrades in there or nine dead mannequins," Ammit-47 translates. "Of course."

Rofi raises two fingers.

I want to ask how he can say something like that, but then I understand.

"First you mourn for people you never knew, for what they could have experienced or didn't experience," Ammit-47 continues. "And then it turns out that they weren't people at all, and thus no one died. Logically, that should calm you down, but you seem even more agitated because it's suddenly worse that no one is dead, but you believed something that turned out to be a lie. And then someone asks me why meatbags are so crazy."

I can't help but laugh. It's not a happy sound, but one of astonishment. He's right, and I can see my mind resisting it, which I find even more absurd. Ammit-47 and Rofi look at me with expressions that I translate as discomfort. After so many days, I've become good at reading them like open books. But I don't let it bother me, and I rid myself of the lump in my throat by laughing it out along with all the absurdities of my situation.

Eventually I calmed down a bit.

"Strictly speaking, it's not even a lie," says Ammit-47. "Nobody ever said there were other people in the torpor capsules. You just assumed it was true without verifying."

"You're right," I admit. Maybe I shouldn't make so many assumptions. What things do I honestly know are the way my head interprets them? That might be difficult, but maybe I'll be able to stop taking them so seriously. "That's just the way I'm made as a human. Maybe it's our dilemma as a species to vacillate between rationality and emotionality because we have this inexplicable thing that comes to us out of nowhere."

"Thoughts."

"Yes."

"Logic and rationality seem far more efficient."

"But efficiency is not a value in itself if it does not serve a result that is perceived as beneficial. Otherwise it is just a fact."

"Precisely. At least we can agree on that."

"But you don't have gut feelings – that's what prompted me to save you. The rational thing would have been not to recover the cargo module you were in," I explain. "But I did it in spite of that because I had to take the chance to save someone. That was more important to me than survival."

"But why? Why die trying to save someone rather than continue living in safety?" asks Ammit-47, sounding both confused and genuinely interested in the answer. Rofi also leans forward a little.

"Counter question. There are one hundred people in your village and one hundred gold pieces. How many of them would make you happiest?"

"One hundred, of course. That can be scaled. More gold pieces mean more purchasing power, more status, more influence and much more. That's capitalist economics."

"The answer is one."

Now he looks at me with his familiar you-have-lost-your-mind look. "That doesn't make sense."

"Yes it does, and it's even logical," I insist. "If everyone has a gold piece, everyone has the same amount and is equally satisfied because there is no gap. I could have more gold than the others, but then the others would be more unhappy than me. Is it more fun to enjoy my wealth and the fact that I have more than them, or to live satisfied in an environment with others who are satisfied? My answer has an empathetic background and is only logical because it gives me a second way to look at the question."

Ammit-47 is silent for a while and then looks up at me appreciatively. "I understand."

"So maybe there's one thing on board and on this mission that we three can definitely understand," I say with a small smile. "It's the perfect combination, you two and I being here together, going through all this together. It seems we complement each other quite well in that regard."

My head is still spinning when I go to sleep later that day, but I also feel a certain sense of peace. I may not have made friends with the situation, but I have at least accepted it for the time being. And I must do so, because in just a few days I will be at my interim destination, near the alien planet. And then a brand-new kind of challenge begins, that much is certain.

And I will be ready.

PART II
CONTACT

21

A few days later we reach the libration point behind the gray satellite of the water planet. I am sitting in the commander's chair on the bridge, and I have asked Rofi and Ammit-47 to come as well so that they don't miss the moment. They protest because they have to interrupt their routines, but that's okay.

"Activate the front sensor array," I say, and give the onboard computer the appropriate commands. Highly sensitive telescopes that cover various areas of the electromagnetic spectrum extend from a hatch on the bow. They point at the planet, a large part of which we can see through the cockpit windows. In cosmic terms, the rugged moon is directly in front of us and the water world just as close behind it, but the sheer distance is still so vast that neither is bigger than my thumbnail.

The alien world is impressive, a planet of breathtaking beauty, a mosaic of blues and greens and browns, surrounded by a veil of white. The sensors scan every corner of the surface and communicate with each other while collecting data, images, and information that are fed into my onboard computer so it can process the various measurement spectra into a coherent display.

I focus on the optical telescope for now, looking at the surface, a jumble of land and water, streaked with bands of white cloud. There are many land masses, some large and some small, separated by vast, deep blue oceans. The colors are intense and vibrant, a sign of a rich and diverse biosphere.

"It looks similar to our Earth," I say reverently. "Even though I may never have been there, the sight of this planet brings back memories for me."

Rofi smiles and raises two fingers.

"Over twenty percent oxygen," Ammit-47 reads from the other display showing the measured atmospheric data. "That means corrosion and flammability. I prefer the *Ankh*."

"Mostly nitrogen, a few noble and greenhouse gases," I add, grimacing. "And a little more carbon dioxide than is healthy for us. For me, I mean. The onboard computer recommends breathing apparatus in the event of a possible landing."

"This would be advisable simply because of the alien biosphere with its specific microorganisms," says Ammit-47.

"For me, as a meatbag, at least, yes. That's what you're saying, isn't it?"

"Yeah, that's pretty much what I'm saying."

I smile and continue reading the incoming data. "We have a multi-layered atmosphere with different pressure and temperature values, a lot of water vapor, and gases such as neon, helium, methane, and krypton."

The *Ankh's* sensors pick up signs of a variety of life forms. There are clear signs of an industrialized civilization, structures and patterns that could only be created by intelligent beings. There are cities, glittering clusters of light and movement, and there are more rural areas, patches of green and brown marked by natural vegetation. They are not as advanced as I expected, but their society is at least industrialized.

I look at the planet as a whole, fascinated by its beauty and complexity. There is so much to see, so much to learn. I want to absorb every graph, every list, and every diagram all at the same time.

Thanks to the multiple magnification of my telescopes and the ability of the onboard computer to piece together a coherent picture from many different data sources, I can see a lot, can study every corner of the planet. But I see mountains and valleys, rivers and lakes, deserts and forests. I see cities and villages, roads and bridges, vehicles, thunderstorms, fires, and explosions. In short, everything that is going on there. From this distance it is impossible to see details like the aliens themselves, but at least I can see the level of organization and structure of their world. They move across the surface in capsules and through the air in old-fashioned airplanes that have wings and remind me of the large Benu bird. I find it very alien, but fascinating.

"It really is a different world," I say, as if I can't believe it myself. I even blink several times to make sure that this is truly real and not a dream. "We are not alone. Do you understand?"

At the same time, they turn their displays toward me and stare at me with their two-dimensional 'eyes.'

"What? This is exciting!" And it is a kind of excitement that has nothing to do with risking my life on a field mission, being lied to by otherwise honest robots through no fault of their own, or questioning everything I think I know about the *Ankh*.

This is real and, honestly, I'm only starting to realize it now that we've taken up our parking position far behind the water planet's satellite. I can now see the radar contacts of the alien space stations in black and white – or rather, dark green and light green.

When I analyzed the telescope data after arriving in the system, the images were very grainy and blurry due to the hundreds of millions of kilometers between us and the planet.

Now they are as sharp as if I were standing right in front of them. The architecture of the space habitats was not dissimilar to the structure of the *Ankh*, but different enough in many places to underline the alien nature of the species that had built them.

"What do you think they look like?" I ask my robot companions and throw the latest images of the station closest to us onto both displays. It is orbiting the local moon and is currently in sight. With its orbital period calculated by the on-board computer, it will be visible for about half an hour.

"The aliens?" asks Ammit-47.

"Yes."

"I can't answer that because I don't have enough data," he replies, sounding like it was the most obvious thing in the world.

"Then guess," I ask him. "At least you can see something they built in space."

"Aquatic. I think they are aquatic."

"Aquatic?" I frown. "How are fish aliens supposed to develop technology? Their first high-voltage experiment would also be their last."

I imitate an electric shock by waving my hands and shaking myself. Rofi also lowers two fingers in a gesture of rejection.

"They also build their cities on land," I explain, looking at the night side of the water planet facing us, on whose land masses ulcers of light spread like glowing scar tissue.

"Aquatic creatures may have developed bioelectricity and then found ways to use electrical energy using biological components," insists Ammit-47. "Since we can't see into the oceans, there may be many more cities there."

"Or evolution has changed them to become amphibious." I shake my head, catching myself thinking about his theory longer than I should. "That's utter nonsense. For aquatic intelligences, the surface of the water would demark their heaven, a line beyond which they cannot breathe and live."

"Like space is to you meatbags?" he asks.

I close my mouth before I can retort too quickly.

"Okay," I say, "you caught me, but I still don't buy your idea."

"That space station there consists of large cylinders that could well be tanks. Filled with water."

"That would make the launch masses of their rockets far too large. With the high gravity of their world, it would be almost impossible to develop enough thrust to reach orbit. That means they would..." I pause when I see Rofi's laughing smile. "Wait, you're kidding me!"

"Yes," says Ammit-47 dryly, even shaking Rofi's hand somewhat reluctantly when he extends it to him.

"Great, you are suddenly collaborating, eh?" I snort with mock disappointment. Something inside me has loosened up, despite the shock of a few days ago. Maybe it's because I've gotten used to regularly questioning everything and being confronted with things that keep me awake at night. Apparently everything can be adapted to. "I think they're insects."

"Insects?" Ammit-47 asks.

Even Rofi's eyes turn into question marks.

"I can't see any signs of major conflict on their planet. Everything seems very organized. Look at the extensive infrastructure. They've plastered everything with dense materials, like the burrows of insects. If that doesn't look like a highly complex system that could only be created by a hive mind, then I don't know what does."

"How are insects supposed to operate technology or use tools?" asks Ammit-47 incredulously.

"I'm a mammal, and I certainly didn't come out of the water with opposable thumbs," I reply. "Now that I think about it, that would mean that the term 'meatbags' would be a much better fit for these aliens. Insects have an exoskeleton and all that fleshy stuff inside their armor, not hung on a skeleton."

"Both are equally disgusting," the robot decides, twisting its animated face as if the very thought caused discomfort in its circuits. "What do you want to do now?"

"We'll wait and see, give them time to get used to our presence. I don't want to rush into anything," I answer, watching the bulky space station move toward the moon's terminator and gradually disappear from viewable range for our sensors.

"They've known about us for quite some time, unless they're blind. We've been on the road for many weeks and aren't at all easy to miss," says Ammit-47.

"Yes, but now they know that we have stopped at a respectful distance and that we are not going to act aggressively. We wait and see what they do and give them the chance to take the initiative. That always feels safer."

"And we'll find out if they're more aggressive than we hope, I guess."

"That's true."

22

As it turns out, the aliens don't do anything for a whole day, so I get impatient and decide it's time to make contact. Rofi is currently on cleaning duty and is scurrying around the corridors somewhere in the habitat ring with a grumpy expression on his face.

I'd condemned Ammit-47 to sit on the bridge with me, to which he responded with the same face that he likes to call up on his display when cleaning.

"Today I will get you excited about the first interplanetary contact, just wait and see," I assure him, trying to calm my own excitement.

"Sure," he replies, but he doesn't sound particularly convinced.

The light from the displays casts a cold, sterile glow on the holographic control panel in front of me, causing small fluctuations in the light. The bridge is silent, and only the quiet hum of the machines and the occasional click of the control lights penetrate it now and then. I think that's appropriate for the importance of this moment.

I double-check the systems, making sure that all the components I'm about to use are working properly. The laser communication unit, with its ability to send flashes of light in rapid, precise succession, is ready. It's normally used to destroy small and large meteorites, but it can be turned down to a level where it doesn't cause any damage by reducing its focus. At 20 percent of the speed of light – at which we were traveling to get here – even a single gas molecule becomes an obstacle that, when our bow hits, releases enough energy to destroy us. I find the fact that we're now benefiting from a defensive weapon, of all things, to be a positively ironic coincidence.

The radio signals – which will operate on different frequencies and by their nature can carry different forms of information – are also ready and working with a simple transmitting and receiving facility in the form of a large antenna above the bridge. It is aligned and ready to go. The complex algorithms that encode my messages are based on mathematical concepts that are as universal as possible in the hope that they can be understood by the other side.

"Are you ready?" I ask.

"Well, I'm present," says Ammit-47. "Or what are you getting at?"

I roll my eyes. "That's what they say." At least I think that's what they say. "Okay, I'll turn on the light and see what happens. Something like, 'Hello, we're here.' That's a good start."

The first messages I send are simple in design, consisting of laser pulses fired at specific frequencies. They are based on the 'elementary quantum of action,' which is a universal constant that should be known to every spacefaring species and serves as a basis for identifying frequencies. By adjusting the frequencies and intervals of the pulses, I hope to send a message that can be recognized as artificial and not as random cosmic radiation or reflection from our ship.

"They're not stupid," says Ammit-47, and only now do I realize that I have apparently spoken my thoughts out loud.

"No, but we have to start at the lowest common ground.

Dig out the basement before we build the roof, so to speak. Assuming that is our goal."

At the same time, I am sending out a series of radio signals representing string of prime numbers in binary code. Prime numbers are a universal constant, and their arrangement in a sequence is unusual enough to be recognized as artificial. At the same time, it is a rudimentary mathematical concept that is easily identified.

Then it's time to wait – and this sort of waiting is exhausting.

Minutes pass. Hours.

I tap my armrests impatiently, tilt my head back and stare at the lights in the ceiling. I unbuckle myself and float around on my own axis, trying to get Ammit-47 to make small talk – which is a pretty hopeless endeavor – and wracking my brains to see if I might have gone about this wrong. Have I missed something?

While I wait for the answer from the lunar orbit, the alien station circles the desolate gray celestial body several times.

Finally, after what feels like an eternity, there is a response. A weak signal, barely perceptible, but unmistakably artificial. A flash of light on the display, then a second and a third.

Excited, I jump up like a suddenly released spring and am lucky that I didn't forget to fasten my seatbelt or my head would have hit the display.

It is an answer, but not one I expected. First, I identify prime numbers in the form of pulse sequences. They reflect my message and express that they have understood it – at least that is how I interpret it. The signals that follow do not represent my prime number sequence, but something else. It is a code for which I cannot spontaneously think of an equivalent.

With renewed vigor, I throw myself into the task of deciphering this code. The boredom I felt before, made worse by impatience, has vanished and my fingers are tingling, electrified by my renewed excitement. It is a complex puzzle, a new language to learn. I study the patterns and deviations of the signals, trying to understand their meaning. With every step, every new insight, I realize that I am facing an immense task. It will take hours, maybe days, to understand this code.

If ever.

The first step of progress is small and takes me almost two days. Ammit-47 and Rofi take turns in the cockpit, as though they have programmed a new schedule so they can supervise me. I feel somehow touched. They both help me numerous times when I get stuck, Rofi by signaling 'yes' or 'no,' and his twin's input a little more complex. I notice that the two are maintenance bots and not high-performance AIs, but their simple logical thinking, which is deeply anchored in their data cores, saves me from having to make mental detours due to tiredness or forgetfulness.

I eventually manage to identify some repetitions in the signals, patterns that keep cropping up. They are characteristics that could reflect my original binary codes. From the beginning, I identified them as the first starting point for communication because I believe that intelligent life must understand the dual basis of the universe, existence and non-existence, light and darkness, on and off, yes and no, one and zero.

Binary code.

I eventually succeed in searching for the alien patterns in my original code and eventually finding matches. Had the onboard AI still been working, this step might have been a matter of minutes. The frequencies, the pauses, the sequences – they undoubtedly reflect some of the binary codes I sent. That much has become clear.

Good, I think. *I can work with that.*

This breakthrough, however small, gives me new hope. I continue my work, wolf down the food that Rofi brings me, and occasionally suck hydration packs empty when he forces me to. Without him, I would simply forget. I now check the signals for overlaps, compare them with my notes, put forward theories and then discard them. It is a frustrating process because there is no authority that signals me with 'right' or 'wrong.' Nevertheless, every new insight, every piece of the puzzle that falls into place, takes me one step closer to a possible understanding.

At least that's what I am hoping.

Slowly, bit by bit, a picture comes together. The flashes of light, the pauses, the frequencies – they are binary at first. On and off. Then, in a new sequence, short and long, which I only realize later.

It's a small success, but a success nonetheless. I've made initial contact, exchanged initial messages. We've understood each other. We know we're trying to communicate and we're both making an effort. That's encouraging, but it's only the beginning.

Now that a first common denominator has been found with binary code, I am working on the next step and ignoring the short and long light pulses for now. I am interested in establishing more detailed communication that allows us to exchange more complex messages.

Numbers and symbols dance on the two displays. Now that the binary code is established as a first basis, I try to create a set of instructions or rules that will allow us to exchange more complex information. I feel electrified while doing this and annoyed when Rofi forces me to go to sleep. But I need to rest to avoid making too many mistakes. I wash myself, sleep, and return in my pajamas. I am the commander after all, right?

The idea is to create a model of universal grammar based on the Formal Grammar Hierarchy, a system for classifying languages based on their complexity. Basically, I'm trying to create a brand new language that will be understood by us and the aliens alike. That feels more fair than trying to teach them my language or vice versa.

"Language has a huge influence on how we perceive the

world," I say to Rofi, who is back 'on duty' at my side. He smiles. "If I were to learn their language, it would force me to adopt a certain worldview due to their specific vocabulary. A tool can also be a weapon. An axe, for example. So the context is crucial for the meaning and not the word itself. We cannot afford such pitfalls. Furthermore, we must not run the risk of practicing species chauvinism and preferring their language or ours, and thus their culture or ours, to interpret something."

I notice that I'm talking like a waterfall, but that's just part of my concentration. I'm 'in the flow.'

To achieve my goal of developing a common language, I start by sending patterns that represent the most basic components of grammar: subject, predicate, and object. I represent each of these with a unique sequence of binary codes, and I repeat these sequences several times to make sure the message is understood. It's not about exchanging words, i.e. symbols. We don't have the basis to do that. My goal is rather for us to agree on the differences between subjects, things, and descriptions of both. If they understand that I send and repeat three different types of signals, they may realize that my language is based on these three pillars. That sounds small, but it would be a great start to understanding my worldview.

Again, hours pass that feel like days. Time seems to stand still as I stare out into the void of space and await an answer. Hours turn into days until, after two more sleep cycles, the long-awaited answer finally arrives.

I can say this much. It is complicated. A jumble of flashes and pauses that I must first decipher.

"Thanks for being offline, dear onboard AI," I grumble. But I don't give up and after many hours I notice that the response mirrors my pattern. It is a copy of the sequences I sent, with a few minor changes. I have to think about this.

I do a bit of exercise and then watch Rofi and Ammit-47 cleaning in their bad moods, which provides me with a bit of fun that eases the knotted tension in my shoulder. Afterward,

I wash myself more thoroughly than I have done in the last few days and eat like a civilized person before I sit down at the kitchen table and look at the data with renewed vigor. I stream it here from the bridge so that I don't spend too much time in weightlessness.

I try to imagine how a totally different being might interpret my message, and what the aliens might think would be a good response. I keep looking at the deviations in the mirrored signal. Then it hits me like a bolt of lightning. They took my proposed language system and translated it into their own.

It is another small success, a first step toward a universal grammar, a common language that will allow us to exchange more complex concepts and ideas. Because now I know that they use certain grammatical cornerstones and even if it seems strange at first glance, I understand the system behind it. They use four pillars on which their language is based.

But most importantly, I'm struck by the realization that communication, however difficult and complicated it may be, is possible.

23

I slept for almost 14 hours straight. For once I didn't dream of endless desert landscapes and the pyramids, but of confusing concepts, equations, and light signals. Even in my sleep I seemed to be wracking my brain.

Rofi walks along beside me and hands me food and drink while I get dressed. I kiss him on his screen because he is so good to me. This elicits a sad smile face from him at first, but then a laughing one and two hands, each with two fingers raised upward.

"I love you too, little one," I say cheerfully, and scurry up the ladder into the central corridor and onto the bridge.

Ammit-47 is waiting there for me.

"Well, are you particularly motivated today?" I ask him as I buckle myself into the pilot's seat.

"I could hardly charge in peace," he replies dryly.

"Wonderful. Has anything happened?" I point to the alien space station that is currently circling the moon and sparkling in the light of the central star.

"No. No incoming signals."

"Okay." I'm a little disappointed, but I don't let it show.

Now that the basics of grammar are established, I move on

to the next step, exchanging more complex mathematical concepts. Mathematics, I am certain, is the language of the universe, a system of rules and laws that is valid everywhere. It expresses the relationships between things in numbers and formulas. If we manage to exchange higher mathematical concepts, we potentially open the door to a wealth of further information.

Above all, we build trust. Trust in each other's intelligence and willingness to communicate. It may seem like a more logical step to expand on the jointly established foundations of grammar and use them to define symbols – words – but that would be hasty. Without trust, the risk of misunderstandings is too high: the old axe problem.

So we'll take a step back, make a little detour, and then come back here when the weather is better and the clouds have cleared. I like that analogy.

I'll start with something simple, a basic concept that everyone should understand: numbers. I'll represent the numbers from 1 to 10 in binary code using as few bits as possible and send them in an ascending order, followed by repeating the entire pattern:

1 = 1
   2 = 10
   3 = 11
   4 = 100
   5 = 101
   6 = 110
   7 = 111
   8 = 1000
   9 = 1001
   10 = 1010

This serves not only to clarify the meaning of each code, but also to introduce the idea of sequence and order, two fundamental concepts in mathematics.

The hours pass and I stare at my own message, my mind focused on the code, the numbers, the pattern. I send the same pattern repeatedly, hoping that the repetition will help convey the message.

Finally I get a response. It's a repeat of the sequence I sent, with the difference that they use four bits for each number instead of as few as possible.

1 = 0001
   2 = 0010
   3 = 0011
   4 = 0100
   5 = 0101
   6 = 0110
   7 = 0111
   8 = 1000
   9 = 1001
   10 = 1010

I get goosebumps. They have not only understood the concept and my idea, they have shown me that they also understand the principle of uniform ordering systems. This tells me that they are thinking ahead and seeing and building larger connections. It may sound like a small thing – so insignificant – but the establishment of such fundamental findings will decide the success or failure of this experiment.

Confirming that the basis of numbers is understood, I move on to operations, starting with the simplest. Addition and subtraction. I represent them by a simple change in code, a new symbol corresponding to an operation. I send a series of equations, such as "1+1=2" and "3-2=1," represented in our jointly established binary code. As before, I send each equation several times to make sure the message is clear.

Hours pass, and then days, in which I again distract myself with exercise, surprised to find that it clears my head. It's difficult not to stare at the display on the bridge the whole time, waiting for an answer. The waiting is grueling, the quiet fears in my head that the aliens might suddenly shoot at me because they misunderstand something, or that they might fly toward me and I won't notice. But I've assigned Ammit-47 and Rofi so someone on the bridge is always monitoring the systems when I'm not there.

At some point, time no longer seems to matter. My entire focus is on the numbers, the patterns dancing on the monitors in front of me, while I look for errors in my thinking. When I exercise, I try not to think about anything, and one time when I was eating, I asked Ammit-47 to tell me jokes. But his jokes were so bad that they fit in a category of their own.

"Why does the robot go for a massage?" he leads off. When I cannot guess, he says, "To recharge its batteries."

I waved him off, having learned not to ask for that again.

When the answer finally arrives, it is complex, a jumble of flashes and pauses that I have to unravel. It takes me days to decipher it, and I can hardly believe what I see. Equations that mirror my own, but with their own numbers and symbols, sent as coordinates in a two-dimensional frame of reference. In this way, they form images, if you will. I can even read them, because they send the corresponding binary number for each simple representation. They have understood the basics of addition and subtraction, that much is certain. And now I know that they process numbers optically, just like I do.

It's proof that, despite whatever differences we may have, there is something that unites us. Mathematics, the universal language of logic and order. And as I sit here, amid the void of space, I can't help but wonder what might come next.

Given the small success in the basic arithmetic operations, I feel encouraged to go a step further. I decide I will share the principles of geometry – another universal truth that I hope will further advance the process of understanding. We can spread them out on the coordinate system we have established. At least I hope so.

So I'll start with the basics. Points, lines, and angles. To represent these concepts, I use a combination of binary codes and timing intervals between the signals. For example, I represent a point as a short, sharp repetition of a particular binary code, while a line is represented by a longer, sustained repetition of the same code. I represent angles by combining different points and lines and sending the corresponding binary codes at specific intervals.

With these simple building blocks, I send the concept of a right angle, an isosceles triangle, and a square. Each figure is carefully encoded by alternating between the signals for points, lines, and angles.

The wait time before their answer comes is agonizing. The hours drag on like before and blur into days as I carefully analyze every piece of information I receive, every tiny flash of light, every radio signal. I study the patterns, try to verify their meaning, which of course I can't, and almost lose myself in the infinity of possibilities. I could be wrong. It's even likely.

"I never thought it would be so painfully slow," I say to Rofi, who is sitting beside me. The corners of his mouth form a frown. "I don't know what I expected. Maybe a big reception, an escort to take me to their king, where I'd be fed local foods while we draw pictures in the sand with sticks and laugh at our dubious artistic skills."

Rofi's display becomes a laughing smile.

"Yeah, I know. Pretty naïve. It hasn't gone quite like that, but it has been a bit more impressive than shuttling between my bunk and the screen." I sigh. "I wish I could look in there now." I tap my finger on the screen depiction of the alien space station orbiting the moon. "Look through those walls. See the insects communicating with each other with clicking noises and excitedly analyzing my messages while discussing what they mean and how best to respond."

Rofi stretches out a hand and points to the bridge's controls, where the computers are humming. Then he points to my display and the alien space station and shakes his head.

"They're not computers?"

His eyes become crosses and the corners of his mouth point downward.

"No. you mean they don't *have* computers."

He nods, but looks neutral. His fourth 'emotion' besides smiling, looking sad, and laughing.

"So that's still not it." I think for a moment. "Ah, they don't have AI. Or at least not a powerful one." I nod excitedly. "That's true. With the help of complex machine learning and advanced quantum computers, they would be much faster. So would we, by the way."

The answer finally comes in and I straighten up. Once again it's a complex pattern, a complicated interplay of flashes and pauses. It takes me a while to decipher it, and the result is astonishing. Not only have they repeated the geometric shapes and angles I sent, but they've also introduced new shapes that I hadn't sent yet. After long hours, I understand them. A circle, an equilateral triangle, and a pentagon.

I am delighted. This is not just another success in our communication, but a sign of progress that goes beyond what I sent. They have understood the principles and implemented them in their own ideas. And more importantly, they seem to think like I do. Sharing basics, carefully introducing something new, showing understanding through repetition and suggesting progress.

It is proof that learning is not a one-way street. This is an exchange, a mutual give and take of information.

I have to smile. This is going even better than I'd hoped.

24

From numbers to shapes, from shapes to concepts. The next logical step for me is the field of pictograms. The idea is not new, and if my new extraterrestrial friends come from a similar evolutionary path to us humans, then they will be familiar with cave paintings and universal simple symbols from everyday life, for example. But can this principle be applied to an extraterrestrial civilization whose visual perception and cultural context are unknown to me?

The challenge is great, but so is the potential.

Pictograms are mathematically simple to represent because they consist of basic shapes and lines that can be described with little data. They are particularly useful because they can represent universal concepts without words, and they are very easy to implement with the mathematical foundations we have established.

People often use simple shapes like circles, squares, and triangles. These shapes can be described with very little information and have now been established between us, so they have reference points for understanding. For example, a circle only needs a center and a radius, while a square only needs the length of one side.

Then there are the lines. Pictograms usually consist of clear straight lines or curves. A straight line can be described simply by two points, while a simple curve can be described with a simple mathematical function. Thus they avoid complex details that are difficult to describe and instead focus on the essentials.

I still want to keep my messages as simple as possible because we don't know what their language or culture is like. One misunderstanding could be enough to cause a conflict. So I hope that the basic forms can be understood across cultural and linguistic barriers.

"Okay, Rofi, are you ready?"

My little robot friend holds up two fingers and smiles.

"Good."

I begin by developing a binary coding system for representing simple pictograms. Using the geometric principles I have already shared, I develop a method for pictographically representing basic shapes such as squares, circles, and triangles. Each shape is represented by a specific combination of binary codes and time intervals, and by combining these basic shapes in different arrangements, I can create more complex images.

To ensure the simplicity and universality of the pictograms, I decide to start with natural phenomena and objects that we probably have in common, a star, a planetary system representation, and a single planet.

I send out these images using a series of radio signals, with each pulse representing a portion of the image. The entire process is laborious and time-consuming. Each image requires hundreds of individual signals and hours of intense concentration on my part.

When I finally finish and send the last signal, I feel exhausted. My head feels wasted, like a rubber band that has lost its elasticity from being in the desert sun too long.

And now I have no choice but to wait. I sit on the bridge with Rofi for a while and watch on the radar screen how the alien station disappears behind the moon and reappears an hour and a half later. Then we return to the habitat module and I eat something while Rofi clamps himself onto his charging hook and turns off his display.

If only it were that easy for me.

Back in bed, my thoughts are going in circles as usual and I'm afraid I won't be able to sleep. But this time, the mental exhaustion works in my favor and I fall into a deep slumber before the onset of the now commonplace worries that something might happen while I'm unresponsive.

Days pass without any apparent reply. I spend my time analyzing the signals I've received so far, hoping to find some kind of response I might have missed. But there seems to be nothing. All the radio signals that come in are coming from the alien planet's radiosphere, which is emitting so much noise that it fills the entire system. None of it makes sense.

The space station remains silent. I wonder if the crew always checks with home first? Or are they creatures who perceive time much more slowly? Perhaps they are only thinking one word in the time I have thought a sentence?

Frustration begins to spread within me. Did I make a mistake? Were my images too complex, my assumptions too hasty?

But then I remember how long it took to communicate the math and geometry concepts and I calm down a bit. My thoughts keep alternating like this.

I try to clear my head by helping Rofi and Ammit-47 with the cleaning. My two mechanical friends seem to find this strange at first and then funny, because Ammit eventually starts to make sarcastic jokes about me and Rofi shows a laughing smile instead of his grumpy expression.

Eventually I grow tired of cleaning and I decide to eat

something. Doing something useful is always the best distraction, for a while.

As I pick at my food, I remember the patience the aliens and I have shown during these long weeks of communication, and I take heart. This is just the beginning of a new process, not a race. Optimistically, it could even be that the alien astronauts are also concerned about not making mistakes and are proceeding very carefully. That would be promising for a positive outcome of this experiment. Surely they are just as excited as I am about the fact that they are not alone in the universe.

With renewed determination, I set to work to refine my pictograms, simplifying them and making them clearer.

After several days of waiting and fine-tuning, I finally see a faint glimmer of hope. I constantly monitor my systems and my instruments for even the slightest hint of an answer. When I'm not on the bridge, I keep the reception indicators on my forearm display at the ready, and I stare at them every few minutes, even though I have programmed an alarm. My eyes are tired and my mind is drained, but my resolve remains unbroken. And then, as I yet again check the incoming signals, I spot something unusual, a series of radio signals, unusually structured and unlike anything I've seen before. My eyes widen and my heart starts beating faster.

Is this the answer I've been waiting for?

I immediately begin to analyze and decode the signals received. The structure is complex and different from the patterns I sent, but there is a certain similarity, as in our previous communication steps. Something mirrored with new information or variations. The signals seem to be structured by means of binary codes and time intervals, similar to the codes I used to represent my pictograms. But the combinations are different, the patterns are new.

"Perhaps they have painted us a different picture of their own," says Ammit-47, sitting alongside me, commenting on the signal structure on his display.

"Yes, perhaps."

"Maybe they've decided they want to eat us after all."

"Why are you always so optimistic, huh?" I mutter absent-mindedly.

"I have nothing to do with optimism. I'm the realist on board. They might consider us a delicacy."

"A delicacy?" I turn to him and shake my head. "What is wrong with you?"

"Delicacies are delicacies precisely because they are rare. You meatbags love it when something is exclusive. If there is little of it and hardly anyone has access to it, you want it as though it is somehow better. Even if it is disgusting," explains Ammit-47, not hiding what he thinks of this behavior. Then he points to his monitor. "It is hardly possible to get more exclusive and scarce than the aliens' resource. That is, you."

I think about it and gulp. I'm back to imagining insects on the other side, but this time they are cutting me up and munching on me with their terrifying mouthparts.

Finally, I shake my head. "Just stop it. It's an intelligent species."

"You are also intelligent and often hungry."

"Yes, but I don't eat..."

"Aliens? Have you ever tried one?"

I roll my eyes and tell him to be quiet. I need to concentrate instead of listening to him play the demon on my shoulder.

I work for hours to decipher patterns and convert the binary codes into visible images. The process is slow and tedious, but Ammit-47 helps me out now and then by pointing out patterns without anomalies. With each hour that passes, we get closer to solving the puzzle. It's like a vortex pulling me along. The difficulty is comparing their broadcast with my coding and making sure they're using the same system. Only then can I put the new deviations into context and generate something different from them.

I finally see the first image. It is not a perfect pictogram, as I expected, but something much simpler. A square. Just a simple square, represented by a specific combination of binary codes and time intervals.

A small success, even if I'm a little disappointed. We now know that we both understand and want to use pictograms to move on. Another step from which we both learned something. They can now send and receive rudimentary drawings.

My initial disappointment gives way to a wave of relief and joy that flows through my whole body. I stare at the simple square on my screen and can't help but smile. It's the most beautiful square I've ever seen. A square of hope, so to speak.

With renewed energy and enthusiasm, I set about composing my answer. I create a new pictogram, daring to draw something more complex than the previous ones. A long rectangle with a large circle in the middle – the *Ankh*. Then a huge circle, the moon, and finally my best pictogram representation of the alien space station and a small object halfway between us with a trail of dots leading from my spaceship. I send everything out into space and wait anxiously for the next answer, but after a few minutes I fall asleep from mental exhaustion and physical stiffness.

I dream of a gift wrapped in black linen cloth with large wings that allow it to fly through the vacuum despite the lack of air. The black box flutters to the aliens' space station and lays a series of black eggs, which the insects receive through a small hatch. They wave at me gratefully, with their mouthparts making clicking noises, their equivalent of a smile.

Then I dream a pictogram response that is so complex that I'm aware it cannot truly be a pictogram. They say that I forgot the salt, but that my recycled feces would otherwise taste quite acceptable.

25

"You honestly dreamt that?" Ammit-47 asks at breakfast.

I feel like I've been strapped into the pilot's seat on the bridge for ten hours. My shoulder muscles have hard knots that cause pain with even the slightest movement, and my mind is more exhausted than it has been in a long time. And that's saying a lot. I mean, my brain has been running at full speed for over ten days and it feels like an old, overheated engine about to die.

"Yes." I sigh and, with little motivation, shovel the contents of a food packet into myself. I yawn almost nonstop until my jaw cracks in protest.

"Did I mention that...?"

"... you don't envy us meatbags?" I interrupt him and pretend to use my spoon as a catapult to throw food at him. He ducks and then cautiously peeks over the table. "A few times already, thanks."

"While you were thinking that..."

"Dreaming."

"While you were *dreaming* that," Ammit-47 corrects himself, making a face as though I might have an outburst of sheer madness at any moment, "did you think it was real?"

"Yes. Dreams usually feel real."

"Even though the laws of nature aren't correct? Wings are useful in a vacuum? Sound travels through a vacuum? The insectoids don't want to eat you?"

"Why would they eat me?" I frown.

"Insects have nothing else to do. They look for food, eat it, and then it starts all over." Ammit-47 taps the table. Clank, clank. "But that wasn't my question."

"Yes, they feel real, even though there are no rules in dreams."

"So you lose your mind every night."

"Well, I wouldn't put it that way."

"How would you put it?"

"My brain is sorting out my experiences and reorganizing itself." I shrug my shoulders and push the rest of my breakfast away from me. I no longer have an appetite.

"It means your central brain is mis-sorting its file system at night," Ammit-47 continues, making a plaintive noise I didn't even know his voice was capable of. "It sounds like you're insane for eight hours a day. Did I mention that...?"

"Yeeeeeah," I interrupt and snort. "You did. Several times." I hold out my hands to him and shake them while I roll my eyes. "I'm going crazy, oho!"

Ammit-47 takes a step back and stares at me pityingly. "I have cleaning duty. I think I'm looking forward to it for the first time."

"Don't you want to help me?" I ask.

"With what? Wrapping presents?"

"I'm taking the next step today."

"Rofi is on hand-holding duty," I hear him say as he disappears down the corridor to the next section.

"You go right ahead," I murmur after him, "but I'm going to make history today."

Fifteen minutes later, I'm sitting in front of the bluish displays of the main console, the metallic smell of cold and electronics in my nose. I skipped exercising. Maybe it would have cleared my head, but it would also have disturbed me, delayed my plan, which has already made me sleep restlessly because I'm so excited.

"I think we've built up enough trust to take a shortcut," I say to Rofi, who is now sitting in the co-pilot's seat and smiling at me faithfully. "Yesterday I sent them a pictogram of me physically sending them something. From the *Ankh* to their station. And that's what I'm going to do today."

In front of me on the screen, a 3D representation of one of the two atmospheric probes stored in the launch shafts beneath the *Ankh* rotates. An unsightly thing, dirty yellow and cylindrical, covered in sensors and extendable booms. Designed for use at a heavy gas giant to detect hydrogen and helium-3, it is now set to play a completely new role.

"Do you know what's better than a pictogram?" I ask Rofi.

He tilts his head as though curious.

"Photos! Something to eat! A piece of clothing!"

I carefully let my fingers dance over the control panel, changing parameters, models, variables. It should take off, orbit the moon, brake, and finally arrive at a certain point. The space station. Simple enough in principle, but every step is full of challenges and possible sources of error. So I have to be precise and do the math well, but I can do that.

The probe will not behave like a conventional space shuttle. It is designed for other tasks. I have to take that into account, the model's special flight behavior in a vacuum, the position of the engines, the energy capacity, the booms, which are rather disruptive for an approach maneuver because they can collide with things – and collisions are always unfavorable in space.

I start calculating the launch. The energy calculations for the ion engine are tricky. Too little energy and it won't reach its target. Too much and it could miss, or critical components could be overloaded and damaged. After some consideration, I decide on a course that is geared toward maximum efficiency, which will take a little longer. I don't see that as a disadvantage. If the probe doesn't reach the space station until it orbits the moon twice, my new alien friends will have more time to adjust to it.

Next, I have to determine the exact trajectory. The calculations are complex because I have to take into account the movement and gravity of several celestial bodies that play a role here. Firstly, that of the central star, even though it is so far away. It is the gravitational fixed point of the entire system, around which everything literally revolves. Secondly, there is the water planet, the home of the aliens – forming the largest gravitational sink in my vicinity - and, of course, the moon.

But I am satisfied when the computer suggests an optimal trajectory that brings the probe into the right position, to the station's gripper arm, which I could clearly see in the pictures. If I do everything right, they can simply grab my 'delivery' with it and bring it to them. Then they have control and do not feel threatened or harassed.

Using a food packet, they can decipher which micro and macro nutrients I consume and draw conclusions about my physiology. The same applies to a piece of clothing that I intend to send them. Not to mention that they can extract bacteria and other microorganisms from it to determine whether their immune system is able to deal with them.

I'm absolutely delighted with my idea. But one thing at a time.

The braking maneuver is probably the trickiest part of the whole thing. The probe has to reduce its speed at precisely the right moment and by the exact amount of its previously 'forward' kinetic energy. This means it accelerates, drifts, turns 180 degrees, and accelerates again in the opposite direction of its previous flight until the energy balances out. Too early or too strong and it could miss the target. Too late or too weak and it could head toward it uncontrollably. I decide to trust the probe's control system and feed it with precise data that it must adhere to. I cannot and do not want to risk sensor errors during the flight, because once it is gone, I can no longer intervene without the on-board AI.

Let's talk about accuracy. My target is the gripping arm – the proverbial fish in the reeds. Difficult to catch, but not impossible. The computer's calculations are precise and match mine. To be on the safe side, I still check them three times before nodding in satisfaction.

I sit back. It's certainly not a perfect solution, or I would have built my dream vehicle myself and would ideally have space on board for myself, but I have the feeling that it will turn out okay. I work hard and triple check everything.

"Now we're going to do the orbital mechanics, Rofi," I say, rubbing my temples before cracking my knuckles. I'm getting a headache from constantly torturing my brain. It feels like a muscle about to fail because I've overused it. But at the same time, I'm amazed at what I'm capable of, and I'm also a little proud.

I put my hands on the holokeyboard and take a deep breath. The next step is the actual calculation of the orbital parameters, for which I have to take a variety of factors into account. Gravitational forces are the biggest challenge. They are always at work everywhere, shaping our orbits, pulling us in their direction.

The water planet, with its considerable mass, exerts a strong attraction that I must include in my calculations. Its gravitational force acts on the probe and will influence its trajectory. I open the module for calculating gravitational forces in my control program and enter the relevant data.

But it is not just the water planet that influences the probe. The satellite, which obediently moves around its planet in constant motion, also has its own gravitational force. It is weaker, but not negligible. And finally there is the central star, whose gravity is weaker, but works over long distances.

My calculations become more and more complex as I try to take all these factors into account. The forces act in different ways depending on the distance, mass, and speed of the celestial bodies involved. But I can't just calculate the total force, I also have to consider the direction in which it acts at any given moment of the trajectory.

There seems to be no room for simple connections in the universe.

Then there are the orbital parameters of the probe itself. Its speed, its course, its orientation. I need to know and calculate these factors very precisely in order to be able to predict its orbit correctly. And, of course, I have to take the mass of the probe into account. This influences how strong the gravitational forces are and how fast and in which direction it will move. Even the smallest deviation has potentially great significance.

So I start entering the probe's data, its size, shape, mass, the minimum resistance it experiences when flying through space. I calculate its mass as precisely as possible, taking into account every screw, every sensor, every milliliter of coolant.

Finally, I lean back, exhausted from the hours of calculations and considerations. This has been my constant state for the last few days. At this very moment, I receive a response to my last pictogram. It is a copy, with the exception that my shipment, the small circle, is located directly at the space station. At the destination.

"They want to accept it," I rejoice, taking Rofi's display with both hands to give it a kiss. "They have understood and want to accept my gift!"

I don't want to waste any time, so I unbuckle my seatbelt and head for the habitat.

I have a present to wrap.

26

First of all, I have to get the probe out of its launch bay, which is not easy. But I'm in good spirits – after all, I'm the only human member of the crew, so I can rest assured that the mission planners put a lot of emphasis on me being able to do all the necessary things on board.

But does open-heart surgery on a probe count as one of them? We'll have to see.

For the second time, I wish I still had the surgical robot arm from the sickbay. I would have much preferred programming it using my forearm display and then fine-tuning it with the controller while it did the work – no shaking hands, just precise sensors.

But it is what it is, and so I find myself crouched in a narrow maintenance shaft in the underside of the *Ankh*, which I could only reach by unscrewing one of the curved wall panels of the central corridor and attaching it to the handrail with magnets. The shaft is just wide enough for me to crawl into it on my hands and knees, right behind Ammit-47, whom I have enjoined to help me.

The launch shafts are a few meters farther forward, two simple tubes that point diagonally downward and have a catapult mechanism. The probes are ejected in this manner, 'thrown' a few hundred meters away before they ignite their engines to ensure that they don't burn a hole in my spaceship with their plasma propulsion system.

Between the shafts there is a slightly open area where I can squeeze myself next to Ammit and stick the tool bag from the habitat module to the wall.

I look at my forearm display. The onboard computer provides me with the blueprints for the emergency maintenance of the right launch shaft.

"First you have to loosen four screws on the end cap of the shaft," I say, and hand the robot the multi-function screwdriver. Amazingly without complaint, he takes it with his delicate hands and starts working. I read him step by step how to loosen the sensor contacts so that the *Ankh* does not trigger a ship-wide alarm. Next he reconnects the electrical connection cables and uses a hidden button to activate the override command for maintenance engineers, which disconnects the entire launch shaft from the on-board computer.

After pulling the probe out backward, we turn so that our feet – or rather, my feet and his hands – are facing each other and we can use them to hold the long cylinder between us. The sleek spacecraft looks like a smooth-surfaced rocket without any recognizable sensors or a propulsion section.

From the blueprints I can see how packed it is with highly efficient electronics and advanced nanoprocessors that can produce and forward the complex images from its countless sensors.

But these are the very sensors we need to remove now.

"Hold on tight," I tell Ammit-47. I wait until he has magnetized his back hands and pressed the probe to his chest with his other pair of hands. Only then do I let go of the cool composite and squeeze through to the front part. I unscrew the front cap while deliberately taking my time. I am tired –

exhausted if I'm honest about it – so time and patience are what ensure precision.

Now open, I flip the cap to the side and remove the primary sensor bundle. It resembles a little cake with candles, except it's all black with a ton of wires. I don't touch the radar and lidar, which are right in the canopy itself, not in the sensor compartment behind it.

"Will you give me the bag, please?" I ask, and Ammit-47 hands me the zero-g bag I brought with me. It's still in the narrow shaft we came through. One by one, I take out the items I've chosen as gifts for my new alien friends, a picture of me that I had Rofi draw. I couldn't find a way to save a camera image in analog format on board the *Ankh*, and I was disappointed at first. I didn't want to make a bad drawing of a humanoid that would just scare them away. It turns out Rofi is a pretty good artist, and he captured me on paper almost lifelike. I vacuum-sealed it in plastic, rolled it up, and put it in the probe first.

"Can you draw as well?" I ask Ammit-47 to distract myself from the oppressive confinement.

"Yes, but I don't enjoy it."

"Do you enjoy anything?"

"Maybe I should have made a caricature of you," he says, his animated face batting its eyelashes innocently. "I might have enjoyed that."

"That's about what I expected." I take out one of the food packs because it will give them the basics of my nutritional needs, the macronutrients I need to feed my body to sustain itself: proteins, fats, carbohydrates. I'm sure they can analyze that with their technologically less advanced equipment. And if they can go beyond that, they'll get information about the micronutrients added to my food by the recycler: 13 essential vitamins, 16 essential minerals, and 15 trace elements. That should tell them a lot about my physiology.

The third gift is a safely packaged vacuum tube with my blood, which I had drawn in the sickbay. This will enable the aliens to identify cell types such as red and white blood cells, that I need oxygen to survive, and how my immune system fundamentally works. This will give them a link to my food and the micronutrients, all of which are found in the blood. This should also help them understand that there is a complex metabolism between the intake of food and the bloodstream. In the best case scenario, this will even be obvious to them, because it is a natural constant of higher life forms. Then we would have identified another similarity. And finally, of course, there would be the comparisons between my blood and theirs, assuming they have any, which I do assume.

Finally, I put in a stack of paper that I took out of the recycler. I had to reprogram it a little so that it sorted out and rearranged the cellulose for me, but in the end I had pieces of paper that I could write on myself this time. First, I show my understanding of time, that my body is subject to a day and night cycle, that a day for me has 24 hours, of which I sleep for eight – my image of a sleeping person is so simple that any alien must understand it. There is also a drawing of the *Ankh*, which was more difficult for me, surrounded by scientific symbols such as a DNA double helix, the molecular representation of carbon and oxygen, and finally the periodic table with the numbers of the respective amount of protons of each element, represented in binary code. They should understand that, too, and deduce that I know all the elements in the universe and that we speak a common scientific language.

I take a deep breath, pack everything up, and close the front part of the probe. When everything is sealed and the vehicle's processor shows no errors, I yawn extensively but smile contentedly.

"Doctor, you can sew it up now," I say to Ammit-47, who looks at me with a frown, but shortly afterward begins to pull the probe into the maintenance shaft and then push it back into its launch pad.

While he carefully rejoins all the connections and contacts, I pack up the tools.

"Do you think I've forgotten something?" I ask him. "Anything I should send to give them more information?"

"I'm not even sure it's a good idea to send them this much," he replies. "They'll know a lot about you, but you'll know nothing about them."

"Someone always has to make the first move."

"Why not wait until they do?"

"Because I would have to hope that they have good intentions and don't do anything that is to our disadvantage," I explain. "So I prefer to take the initiative and ensure that we work together constructively. I basically set the table and set the mood."

"Is that naïve?"

"You mean, am I naïve?"

"I was just asking a question," he replies innocently.

"Maybe." I shrug. The sudden movement causes me to bump my head and I grimace. "But, by definition, you only get one chance to make a first contact and no second chance to make a first impression. There are two ways. I either open the door and welcome them, or I leave it locked. Either will make an impression and possibly influence the course of this exchange and how they think of us. But nothing will change their basic – unknown to us – attitude. So, it's clear to me which is more logical."

"What if your insects now see you and humans as easy, naïve prey?"

"Do you always think so negatively?"

"I don't *think*," he reminds me.

"I haven't believed that about you for a long time. Something goes on in your hard drives, that's for sure."

"I'm just realistically evaluating the risks."

"That's a good thing," I praise him and watch as he closes the launch shaft. I look at my forearm display and raise two fingers. "Everything's fine. Now we can get started."

27

I return to the bridge, where Rofi is waiting for me. From the co-pilot's seat, he holds up two fingers and smiles.

"Hello, kid," I say, pointing to my display that shows the alien space station circling the moon and describing its long orbit. "It's about to start."

Rofi holds two hands in front of the display and smiles wider. His eyes are now crosses.

"Yeah, it's really exciting, I know." I check the status of the right launch shaft of the atmospheric probe. My excitement – and I'm sure Rofi's too – is not just due to the fact that the aliens will soon be holding something tangible of mine in their hands – or whatever they're using – but to many other factors.

We only have two of these probes on board. Since this one has become unusable due to my intervention, there is only one left, which we can use to search for helium-3 in the atmosphere of one of the local gas giants in order to produce new fusion pellets. No second chance if something goes wrong and the probe gets lost. Then we'll be stranded here forever. And, of course, there's the possibility that the locals won't accept my delivery because of quarantine protocols or something similar.

Or – and this possibility makes me shudder – what if their station has weapons systems that I haven't seen yet and they choose to shoot down my well-intentioned probe? I realize it looks like a torpedo. However, I don't believe that, since they made it clear with their last pictogram message that they expect and intend to accept my 'delivery.' At least I'm pretty sure that my interpretation of it is correct and it's not just that I want it to be that way.

I realize that there is a lot of room for misunderstanding when you don't even know how the other side thinks and feels. But this is the best and most effective solution I can think of.

"Carefulness is everything," I explain to Rofi, yawning and stretching before I start my calculations of the probe's approach vector one last time. This is the fifth reverification, but the half hour it requires doesn't matter much, given all the time that has passed.

Better safe than sorry.

When I am finally satisfied, I show him the data and he holds up two fingers.

I point the radio antenna and send a short, low frequency signal, which I repeat with the laser. The answer comes a few minutes later, when they repeat it. I'm ready, and so are they.

Now I have to wait a full 40 minutes until the space station has advanced along its orbit around the satellite and I can launch the probe so that the calculated trajectory is accurate. It's about precision in the millimeter range when distances of hundreds of thousands of kilometers have to be covered.

I take a deep breath and confirm the start command as the space station lights up green on my display and the starting point has been reached.

The probe is ejected several hundred meters by the catapult mechanism and then ignites its engines. With a long blue exhaust trail, it speeds away along its pre-calculated trajectory, which I see displayed as a green dashed route. On the screen, its flight looks extremely leisurely.

Thus begins its journey to the gray satellite.

With the cosmically gentle thrust of the ion engine, it drifts into the darkness, guided by the complex calculations and instructions that I have entered into its computer. Its course is set toward the left side of the moon, which it is to orbit before reaching the rendezvous with the alien space station. It must enter a parallel orbit that is tilted ever so slightly inward so that it can reach the station, where the gripper arm is located, at precisely the same speed.

As the probe continues its journey, I constantly monitor its position, speed, and orientation. I use the on-board radar system to check and compare this data as accurately as possible. But I also have to observe the influences on the probe, the gravitational forces of the water planet, the satellite, and the central star, which continuously act on it and influence its trajectory. They behave as I have predicted.

Relief spreads through me. I have thrown the bird out of the nest and now it has to fly by itself. I cannot assist it. But it's doing well. Only now do I notice that I've been holding my breath and I exhale with a sigh.

The probe approaches the moon, whose gravity attracts and accelerates it. This effect, known as gravity assist, is an essential part of its course. By using the gravitational force of the large celestial body, it receives an additional boost and its orbit changes to match that of the station.

After approaching the satellite, it begins its orbit and disappears from the field of view of the *Ankh's* sensors. But I know what its trajectory is because I have it on the screen in front of me. It is flying in an elliptical orbit that gradually turns into a circular one around the moon – a complex process based on the laws of celestial mechanics. It is about adjusting the speed and orientation of the probe so that it swings into the desired orbit around the moon. It now has to do this on its own, outside of my direct field of vision, fed with my calculations and its sensor data.

Being blind, I become increasingly nervous. I know it will be nearly an hour before it reappears, and that hour is hell.

After it has completed its circuit around the satellite, I finally see it again, a small, highlighted dot on my visual display, which is constantly being generated by sensor data. The probe fires its engines and leaves its previous orbit to approach the alien space station, which it slowly catches up with. It adjusts its speed and orientation once more, this time with the aim of matching the space station's speed and trajectory.

This is one of the most critical phases of the entire operation. Any slight deviation can cause the probe to miss the space station or, worse, collide with it. But I have done my best to take all factors into account and send the probe safely on its way. And it still looks good. The small black dot is moving along the dashed green line to the green symbol that the onboard computer has chosen for the alien station.

Time passes. Several hours, during which I only leave my seat once to pee. The probe continues to follow its programmed course, driven by the invisible gravitational forces of the water planet, the satellite, and the central star, controlled by my calculations.

Most of the time I hold Rofi's hand, which I only notice later when I relax a bit because everything is going according to plan.

Eventually the outside of the space station appears for the first time in the probe's optical camera, a silvery dot in the black space that slowly grows larger as it steadily approaches.

It is on track.

I suddenly notice a deviation. It's just a number on the left side of my display that is suddenly no longer black, but red.

Red is *not* good.

I stand up straight and stare at the number. It is one of the orbit parameters.

"It's not flying far enough. It should be farther," I say, and an unpleasant lump forms in my throat. I zoom in on the schematic and then I see it visually, a tiny shift in the probe's trajectory that gets worse with every passing second. Something is wrong. A miscalculation? An unexpected gravitational influence? A fault in the probe? I'm sure I calculated the initial impulse and gravity sinks perfectly. But it seems to be too heavy.

How is that possible?

Then the answer occurs to me and I feel like the ceiling is falling on my head. The bridge suddenly seems oppressively narrow and the breathable air suddenly seems to become scarce.

I forgot to include the weight of my 'gifts' in my calculations, a small oversight with potentially disastrous consequences. I can no longer make any corrections because it's only a matter of seconds and the distance to the probe is too great.

The onboard computer shows me the spot where it will collide with the alien station. It is only a meter off from the target point, not even a nanometer in cosmic terms, but it makes the difference between the hull of one of the modules and the free space in front of the robotic arm.

In a panic, I send out a warning by radio and light signals, but it is already too late.

The probe crashes into the space station's flank. Since their speeds along their trajectories are almost identical, there is no immediate catastrophe, but there doesn't have to be. It is the debris that the vehicle turns into that becomes critical. It destroys something with one of its booms that I assume is a maneuvering nozzle, and then begins to tumble. The tail hits one of the solar panels, creating a new impulse that catapults it into one of the other alien sails, which it turns into a chaos of splinters and torn pieces of debris within a few seconds.

The cloud of shrapnel will orbit the moon, match its orbital speed, and then return, causing further damage to the stalled station, and it will grow worse with each orbit.

As if that wasn't bad enough, the onboard sensors warn me that the aliens' station is beginning to wobble slightly. Its trajectory is becoming unstable.

28

I watch in shock as my small, careless mistake leads to catastrophe. Helplessness at the sight of this disaster makes my throat tighten.

There is nothing I can do but watch the alien space station slowly but surely being destroyed. It is drifting toward an unstable orbit, losing momentum as it wobbles. The crew appears to be attempting to stabilize the station with well-aimed thrusters, but this only worsens their situation. The station continues to slow, causing the cloud of debris moving away from it to travel comparatively faster, accumulating more kinetic energy that it will unleash like a cosmic hailstorm after its next orbit.

"I killed their station, Rofi," I whisper, horrified. My fingers grip the armrests of my seat. I don't know whether to cry or scream. I'd like to do both, but neither will solve my problems.

The worst part is that, once the debris has circled the moon and caught up with them, I will be responsible for the deaths of the aliens on board their station. It's only a matter of hours, and there seems to be nothing they can use to defend themselves or escape.

"They'll think it was intentional," I say.

Right now, the gruesome scene is taking place behind the water planet's satellite, so those on the planet can't see what's happening to their people in space. But orbital mechanics are merciless, and soon the damaged station will come into view of the other two satellites orbiting their home and all the telescopes they no doubt have trained on us. Then they'll have two pieces of information. I fired what looked like a torpedo, and this 'torpedo' left a pile of debris behind when it 'arrived.'

"An attack, Rofi. They'll assume it was an attack. An act of aggression. I might have just started an interstellar war." I hide my face in my hands. Shame and regret stir within me.

And all this because I was overtired and unable to concentrate, I mentally scold myself. Part of me wants to curse those who sent me on this mission alone – what sense does that make? But I know that it was my responsibility alone. Too little sleep, too much mental exhaustion. And now a tiny, careless mistake has led me to becoming the first interstellar murderer.

I'm breathing faster than I should and I just want to disappear into thin air right now.

But that wouldn't solve my problems. And certainly not the aliens' problems. I have to help them.

"They're still alive," I say, wiping tears from my eyes. The tears are pooling as sticky water in microgravity, making it difficult for me to see. I know I sound rebellious, but I'm not ready to accept this cruel fate yet.

So I start the engines and begin to plot a course. I will save them. The aliens. Whether they are insects or not, on board with me they will find the only safety that exists anywhere near here.

I can feel Rofi's gaze on me and I know that his eyes have long since turned into question marks.

The thrust starts and gently presses me against the back of my seat. I'm only just beginning to do the precise calculations.

I can't waste any time and, as it stands, I can't make this deadly mess any worse.

"They're far from their planet and apparently don't have any spaceships," I explain to Rofi, but I know I'm just encouraging myself. "We can get there in less than an hour. If I'm not mistaken, the debris cloud will take two and a half hours to circle their moon and hit the station, almost certainly destroying it. That gives us a window of opportunity."

Rofi's mouth corners turn down and he shakes his head.

"I know we don't have a spacecraft." I nod. "But I have my spacesuit and a mobility unit. So I'll put us on a parallel course and then go out myself to recover them."

"That is a bad idea," I hear Ammit-47 say, floating in from the central corridor.

"No, it's the *only* idea," I object.

"They'll think you're a threat and kill you," he replies in a grim voice. Since he doesn't sound cynical or sarcastic, I immediately notice how serious he is.

"We don't know that for sure."

"I would think that way and you probably would, too."

"What we can say with certainty," I continue, ignoring his legitimate objection, "is that if I don't help, they will die. I can't let that happen. They are astronauts, just like me. Whether they are from another planet or not, whether they are insects or fish, I have to help because no one else can."

"We should turn around and get out of here before things get worse or they decide to shoot us down."

"No." I shake my head firmly. "I'm going to try to save them and I'm not going to argue about it."

"Is that an order?" Ammit-47 inquires.

"If you insist, yes. I command you to accept this plan, and to help me."

I hear him muttering something like, "Meatbags will be meatbags," but he doesn't object.

"You have to pilot the *Ankh*," I say. "I'll calculate everything, but you have to stay up here while Rofi and I go out and try to gain access to the space station. Maybe we can evacuate the crew somehow."

"What if you create an atmosphere leak and kill them?"

"Whatever kind of spacesuits they have, they'll have put them on by now," I respond. "If not, they're either dead already, or will be in an hour and a half."

My fingers fly over the holokeyboard as I make the calculations to put us in a parallel orbit to the station. I choose a safe distance of 100 meters. Since the target is tumbling, I need a certain tolerance range in order not to endanger the *Ankh*. It is the only bubble of air and heat within a radius of hundreds of thousands of kilometers.

This time I don't have to aim at a tiny point like with the probe. The mass of my ship cannot change and is based on constantly updated measurements. In that respect, things are much easier for me now. Setting a parallel course is quick and easy.

When I have everything done to my satisfaction, I command the onboard computer to extend the manual controls, and I unbuckle myself. I motion for Ammit-47 to take my place as two small joysticks with various buttons come out of their recesses.

"Can you handle this?" I ask.

"No."

"It's really quite easy." I explain it to him briefly. "You can do it."

"I do not think so."

"So, you're okay, right?"

"No, probably not."

"Very good, I trust you."

"No pressure. That's clear." Ammit-47 sighs resignedly.

I motion for Rofi to follow me and am about to slide out into the corridor when Ammit calls something after me that makes me stop.

"Take care of yourselves."

For a moment I don't know what to say, I'm so perplexed by the short sentence. He sounded worried.

"We will."

"Okay, get out now. No more meatbags wanted. You're just causing trouble," he says without turning around. Under different circumstances I might have managed a smile because he sounds like he always does. But something has changed.

Rofi and I stop in front of the airlock and I look into his two-dimensional pixel eyes.

"We can't use safety lines, do you understand?" I say excitedly. Adrenaline is pouring into my body and I hear my pulse pounding in my ears, feel my heart racing unpleasantly in my chest.

"Due to the tumbling movements of the alien station, there is too great a risk of something getting tangled up in them. So I'll use the mobility unit and take you with me. I'm just hoping that the aliens' modules are also metallic and that you and I can magnetize ourselves to find a hold. To be on the safe side, we'll tie ourselves together with a short cable so that you don't get lost. If the worst happens, I can tow you with the mobility unit. Got it?"

Rofi makes a neutral face and holds up two fingers. Then the corners of his mouth turn upward and he smiles.

"Yes, it will go wrong. I think so, too." I force a smile and point to the airlock. "Please help me get dressed. We have no time to lose."

I look at my forearm display. We will soon reach our destination.

"If we can save someone," I explain as we slide into the airlock and close it behind us, "we'll try to hook them up to our connecting cable as well. Ideally, I'll be in front and use the mobility unit to pull us back to the *Ankh* and in here. Since we don't know anything about their physiology, we'll just have to hope they fit in here and that our pressure and atmospheric conditions at least don't kill them right away. I want you to stay in the back and make sure no one gets left behind."

Rofi nods.

"Good. And stay in constant radio contact. You have to be able to hear me."

He nods again and unties the nets on my spare spacesuit, which we brought here after the interlude with the large gas giant. I don't have a third one, though, so I hope I don't make another mistake that damages this one.

"Come on. We can do it, kid. We can do it."

After all, it can't get any worse.

Right?

29

As the airlock opens to the outside, I hold on to the handles above me with both hands. The mobility unit, a massive backpack filled with compressed gas and 28 high-performance jets that can be controlled via a small console on my chest, doesn't seem to have any weight. And yet its presence has a calming effect on me, as it doesn't make me dependent on a tether like on my last mission in the rings of the gas giant.

The black universe stretches out before me, the space station in the foreground, gray and twisted against the background of the moon. The moon is a dark disk that is only separated from the rest of the universe by its shiny outline because the distant central star is shining on it. The satellite looks like a black hole without an accretion disk, threatening and alien, as though it could suck me in at any moment and make me disappear forever.

The water planet behind it is fully hidden. Although it is the moon's gravitational reference point, it is located far away.

Just like before, as soon as I leave the airlock and allow myself to be embraced by the apparent infinity, I get the feeling that I am the only living being in the universe. I'm just an insignificant drop in an unfathomably large ocean.

But, I am a drop with a mission. I check the connection line between Rofi and me one last time. I've hooked it onto my belt. The carabiner holds when I pull on it, without making any noise. My robot friend behind me holds up two fingers, his display already turned off due to the cold here.

"Here we go," I say over the radio and gently push myself off toward the alien space station. As soon as I feel the resistance of the connecting line, I start my mobility unit and accelerate as gently as possible.

We detach ourselves from the *Ankh*, our home and safe haven in this sea of silence, and silently glide away. A hundred meters sounds less than it looks. At this distance, the alien station looks even smaller than I imagined. It seems to be made up of bulky modules pressed together like dented soda cans. A labyrinthine network of metal that gleams in the light of my helmet headlights. The gripper arm and several antenna arrays – at least that's how I interpret them – give it an insect-like appearance. The remains of the solar panels, metal supports with shredded struts and fragments, now look like the clipped wings of a bird that can no longer fly.

The closer I get to the wreck, the more clearly I see the damage my calculation error has caused. Deep scars run across the individual modules, and cracks appear to have broken through the hull in several places, because I see flickering lights. They could be red, but in the vacuum of space my eyes cannot determine with certainty. Every color seems to lose its saturation in space and degenerate into a mere shade of dreary gray.

The gripper arm has ten 'fingers,' with one joint too many each, and the sight of the apparatus gives me chills. It hangs splayed out at the front end, which is leaning dangerously toward the moon. It is clear even to the unassisted eye that the station is on a crash trajectory. Even though it is not a matter of a few hours, its path leads without hope of rescue to the surface of this dreary moon, which is just like every other satellite in this system.

I land on the module to the right of the one my probe hit. My boots hit the gray material gently, slowed by my mobility unit. I send a quick prayer to the gods that it's metallic as I activate the magnet function.

To my relief, for once not everything goes wrong, and my forearm display indicates with a green light that my boots are in contact and holding me there.

"Good news, Rofi," I say. My voice echoes in my helmet.

I turn my head and see him landing beside me, gently and much more elegantly than I feel in the bulky suit. The connecting line sways between us like a pale umbilical cord.

"We need to find a way inside now to rescue the crew. But be careful. If they haven't recognized this accident as such, they might consider us hostile and try to... well, you know."

I swallow and hope that the aliens see it logically. If I had wanted to shoot them down, I would have been smarter and sent something with a warhead instead of touching them – even though that touch is proving fatal. But you never know, and I don't want Rofi or me to be chopped up by sharp mouth parts and turned into alien saliva.

On the contrary, I want to save someone, to make up for some of the disaster I have brought about.

We only have 60 minutes from now until the debris swarm reaches us – not much time. Ironically, I have a kind of déjà vu. I feel like I'm back in my rescue mission in the rings of the gas giant, during which I was under time pressure because of the supposed coronal mass ejection from the central star. But that was apparently hallucinated by the *Ankh's* sensors, in contrast to the storm of ice particles that was very real and almost tore me apart. I have that eerie feeling something similar will be coming our way soon.

Nevertheless, we carefully trudge step by step over the

shell of the alien structure, circle around a sensor bundle with bent antennas, and cross a connecting piece that is about half a meter wide. I notice that there are no windows like on my spaceship. Do the aliens not have optical processing organs like humans? But then, how would they be able to interpret pictograms?

I put the thought aside for a better time when I notice a differently shaped piece along the curve of the next module to the left, which looks like a flat cone. The narrower side is pointing toward the station, but it has been almost totally torn off. A steady stream of objects is flying out into space through the opening. I see metal objects that resemble parts of destroyed equipment, greenish fragments that I assume are computer components, and a lot of liquids. They shoot out in balls of various sizes and spread out in a funnel shape in the vacuum, where they freeze in a flash and turn into hard lumps.

"Rofi, I have something here," I say, and point 'down' as his black display turns toward me. He raises two fingers and comes closer so that the line between us doesn't become too tight.

Only then do I take a few steps toward the hole and carefully bend forward. The opening is small, barely wider than my forearm and about the same length. There's no way I can get in there.

But I catch a quick glimpse of the interior. It is absolute chaos. Particles and objects of various sizes are heading toward the crack to be pulled out into space. The fact that there are increasingly more of them indicates that the station's atmosphere is gradually escaping, causing the station to constantly change orientation and exacerbating the wobbling.

It is an actual habitat, then, with its own atmosphere and pressure. No water – there are too few drops freezing before my eyes.

I can't get into the interior here, so I shake my head in Rofi's direction and make my way to the other side, past the destroyed solar modules that look like huge, torn scarecrows. They look threatening in the absolute darkness, which is only broken by my helmet lights. The light from them shimmers pale and powerless on the dark surfaces.

Suddenly, the station jolts under my boots and I reflexively start to flail my arms. Only a few automatic stabilization impulses from my mobility unit prevent me from falling uncontrollably and hitting the metal beneath me.

I turn as far as I can and see that the space station behind me is about to break apart. The crack has widened, becoming continually bigger due to the opposing impulses. At the same time, something detaches from the other side, where the gripper arm is. A module detaches itself and moves away as if by magic.

"What...?" I blurt out at the same instant I see that the back of the module has six rings, which I quickly recognize as small propulsion nozzles. When they ignite and bright flames shoot out of them, I know I have a problem.

Instinctively, I push myself off in the opposite direction and remove the magnetization from my boots. Rofi seems to have done the same thing in a flash, because we 'fly' away past the dying station. The universe spins in front of me, and all I can see are flames, darkness, and gray modules.

I'm turning too fast.

I quickly make a decision and order the mobility unit to fire, and everything starts spinning even more crazily, as if I've taken drugs and am staring into a kaleidoscope of psychedelic color arrangements.

Then I collide hard with something, which stabilizes me a little. Although I'm out of breath, I croak out a sound of relief when I see Rofi, who is clinging to me like a monkey. Apparently our connecting line got caught somewhere and brought us together.

"Everything okay, little one?" I ask breathlessly, and think I see a nod. Only then do I dare to look around.

We are at the very other end of the space station, wrapped around a tapered section between a small and a large module.

The aliens apparently took off with some kind of landing unit and didn't pay much attention to the safety distance for firing up their engines. I can't blame them. After all, they certainly didn't expect that they could still be saved any other way.

And they are right.

Maybe they didn't even see me. The problem is that I'm still here – and now, for no purpose.

"At least they're still alive. Or at least someone is," I murmur, feeling for the connecting line. It's knotted tightly and we're stuck so close to the module that I can't untie it. A glance up tells me that we're tumbling even more. Everything is spinning much faster than it should, a burned, airless corpse of a space station with Rofi and me in the middle of it.

What a mess. What a *mess*.

30

It takes me a while to get my bearings and free my leg from the encircling cable, which was about to put too much pressure on my suit and cut off my blood flow. But I finally manage it and am also able to free Rofi, who keeps gratefully holding out two fingers.

"Okay, kid, let's take stock. The aliens just saved themselves – at least I hope so. They either didn't see us, or they thought it was acceptable for us to get grilled by their exhaust flames, considering that I destroyed their home. Now we're the only ones stuck up here, waiting for the shower of debris to come around the moon and turn us into red mist – or scrap metal. No offense." I laugh mirthlessly. "What a turn of events. What a rescue."

Rofi points in the direction of the *Ankh*, which stands mightily in the starry sky above us like a big brother of the space station. Since it is longer than we are away from it, it looks huge.

"Yes, we should head back. I just need to untie the cable. And we still have a bit of time. Maybe you can see if you can find an opening here at the end of the station? There has to be some kind of access."

Secretly, I don't want to return empty-handed, I want to at least find out something about those whose last few minutes I made a living hell.

Rofi responds with a silent nod and two raised fingers, then deftly pulls himself up onto the surface of the strange end cap and magnetizes his lower pair of hands. He drops to all fours and, like a dog, stomps up the inverted cone to look over the edge.

Meanwhile, I move around the narrow piece connecting it to the space station, where Rofi and I must have rotated several times around the longitudinal axis of the structure due to the impulse from my mobility unit. It's a miracle that we didn't collide with each other.

I seem to have a well-filled, good-luck account, which could be viewed as a blessing in disguise. At least there is a silver lining on the horizon. I'm still breathing and can moan a bit, so I should probably put that on the credit side. The nice thing about having a defined credit side is that you don't lose track so quickly, and you know exactly what you ought to be happy about.

When I've finally untangled us, I look up at Rofi, who is just sticking his head over the edge of the end cap and waving at me.

"What's wrong, did you find something?" I ask him. I'm shocked at how dejected the echo of my own voice sounds in my helmet. I must do something about that.

Rofi nods and raises two fingers. I pull my knees up to my chest as best I can in the spacesuit and put my boots on the hull of the last station segment. Then I magnetize them and it's as though I'm being pulled down and held by an invisible force. Which is basically true.

As I'm fixed on the outside of the metal cone, I notice for the first time how bad the space station's wobbling has become. It's fully out of control. I first see it in the gigantic silhouette of the moon, which is first to the left, then to the right, then above and below me, like in a video that jumps erratically from one scene to the next. The *Ankh* is a silvery-white flash that keeps appearing in my field of vision. I probably didn't notice it before because I was moving around the station's long axis myself.

Suddenly, as if on command, nausea and dizziness set in as my vestibular system within my inner ears seems to understand, after some delay, that something is not working as it should. I want to reach for the forearm display to demagnetize the boots again, but it is far too late and I cannot reach the corresponding button due to the strong centrifugal forces.

For the first time, I wonder how much power the magnetic soles of my boots have and at what point they will allow me to be hurled away.

Because of all the conflicting information my brain is receiving from the various sensory organs about where I am going, my stomach starts to rebel and my body's recycled waste and excretions that I have eaten today slowly travel up my esophagus.

"Rofi? I have a problem. Hold on tight. If I'm thrown off course, I'll try to activate my mobility unit as quickly as possible to stabilize myself. Maybe it'll do it on its own if the processor is still working normally." I force the words out from between my lips, close my eyes, and concentrate on my breath, which I draw deep into my stomach and slowly exhale through tightly pressed lips. Then I let out an animalistic scream and reach for my forearm display with my right index finger.

It's like I'm arm wrestling with a giant, every centimeter I make toward my left forearm is so hard fought. But the slinging movements also have an advantage. Since I'm as helpless as a reed in the wind, my left arm flies to the right or left at the same time as my right, and I use this impulse. In the end, I must have managed it somehow, because suddenly I'm free and stagger away. The blood no longer pools in my head, but feels like it's everywhere at the same time.

My mobility unit fires on all cylinders and stabilizes me until I am hit by a small extension of the end cap and almost lose consciousness. Just when I fear I will be thrown into nothingness, I am suddenly stable and move backward in a calm and collected manner. It is only after a delay that I become aware of Rofi, who has grabbed me and is pulling me toward him. He gently turns me to face him at the end of the station, where the forces are not so extreme because it is the top of a spinning top that has gone wild.

"Thank you," I say, panting and struggling to breathe. "Thank you, Rofi."

Instead of answering, he takes one hand off the holding ring in front of us. I still feel sick because everything is still spinning, but at least in this position it's not like I have no sense of direction. I follow his gesture and look into a kind of bulging glass eye. It's the size of a fist and looks like it belongs to a particularly ugly fish.

"Is that a camera?" I ask in disbelief. At first I can't imagine it because this thing is way too big for a camera, but then I realize that it must be a lens. And it's moving. "Do you think someone is watching us right now?"

I wave instinctively and would have lost my balance if Rofi hadn't grabbed me once again.

Then something happens. The end cap starts moving, suddenly lunging toward us, so that we are pressed against the flat end as though it were deliberately ramming us.

I gasp in shock. My gaze slides to Rofi, who also seems to be struggling to hold on, and past him to the six small funnels arranged in a ring around the end cap.

"Wait a minute," I say with growing unease. "Is this a space capsule?"

The module jolts once more. Small jets of gas shoot out of the sides and everything stabilizes. Suddenly I can see clearly.

The moon, the wreckage of the runaway station, which looks much worse than before. The *Ankh*, majestic and huge against the network of stars above us.

The space capsule begins to align and I get an ominous feeling.

"Rofi!" I shout. "Get out of here! To the front, go!"

I briefly consider just letting go and allowing the mobility unit to fire at full power to get us as far away as possible. But that's not a good idea, since I don't know where the capsule will accelerate to. If I'm unlucky, we'll be cooked by the exhaust flames and vaporized into volatile gas clouds.

So we pull ourselves forward, turn around on our own hands until our boots – or rather back hands – are pointing along the tapered front section, and activate the magnet function. I immediately cling to the shell, desperately searching for a hold with my fingers, until Rofi, fixed with three magnetic hands, uses his only free hand to pull me toward him and thus give me the necessary stability.

"I'm going to let go now, then we'll straighten up and push off as hard as we can, okay? I'll fire the thrusters and then..."

I can no longer speak because the space capsule suddenly leaps forward and we are pressed against the hull with the brutality of hard physics. Out of the corner of my eye I see the silhouette of the *Ankh*, which is shrinking at a sobering rate.

If we aren't moving toward the *Ankh*, I think, swallowing solemnly, then it's the opposite direction.

The moon.

31

We're heading down toward the darkness below. In this cold, empty environment, there's no air to slow us down, no atmosphere to cause us to burn. The spaceship is controlled solely by the power of its engines in conjunction with the delicate ballet of physical forces that determines the fate of all celestial bodies.

We are now counted among them.

Nonetheless, these forces are merciless, and it is only thanks to the strength of my magnetic boots that I have not been thrown off yet.

Then the train stops. We are no longer accelerating. The reaction drive must have switched off because I no longer see flames.

A look at my instruments in the HUD of my visor tells me that the small spaceship is still moving at about one and a half kilometers per second – that's about the average orbital speed of the satellite. It would have to reduce speed to almost zero to enable a safe landing on the surface.

If that's even the plan. Maybe the aliens have remote-controlled their capsule and just want to turn us into another crater on the moon.

In any case, Rofi and I are just involuntary passengers on this wild ride – and I do not expect it to end well for us.

Weightlessness has turned into a gentle pull as we move ever closer to the lunar gravitational field of influence. I recall that the acceleration due to gravity on the moon is about one and a half meters per second squared. But even this seemingly weak force is enough to pull the spacecraft downward with relentless persistence.

I watch as the capsule begins to change course, evidenced by a shift in my horizon. The *Ankh*, our only hope, is now too far away to see.

The ship beneath our boots slowly rotates on its axis, a maneuver I recognize as a gravity turn. It is a crucial moment in the approach, marking the transition from purely horizontal flight to descending flight. As the ship rotates, I can see the moon's horizon tilting and finally becoming vertical below me.

"It's landing, Rofi," I say with growing concern. I should feel relief instead, believing a landing maneuver to be more promising than a crash.

Right?

My mind is racing. We won't survive a landing, either. The braking thrust will be so hard that we'll be torn off like blowflies, only to plunge downward and burn in the flames of the space shuttle's exhaust flares as it slows down while we continue to fall at the same speed. If we break contact with the capsule now instead, we'll crash into the moon at several thousand kilometers per hour because we're on a downward trajectory already, and the acceleration due to gravity will do the rest.

The question is, which kind of death do we prefer?

The engines reignite, this time with greater intensity, and are in full operation, their flaming emissions sharply visible in the darkness of space as a bright corona below us. The acceleration presses me against my mount while the ship fights against the moon's gravitational pull. Our magnetic anchors are still holding, but this is only the beginning, a downright gentle maneuver compared to the final phase shortly before landing. Assuming that the alien landers behave according to the same principles as our old lunar modules... which I do assume. The laws of physics apply equally everywhere in the universe.

As the ship slows its descent, I'm still frantically searching for a solution to our problem, which is the final descent and then the landing. The numbers on my instruments are steadily dropping, but there's still a long way to go before they stop. The values are all still beyond human comprehension. The capsule is now turned over, the engines pointing in the direction of flight. If we slip, we'll become ashes in the blink of an eye.

I see the blue water planet on the distant horizon and the dark surface of the moon directly below me and feel tiny in the endless ocean of space that seems to have no transition here. When will the final braking thrust be initiated? Will it be a joint death sentence for Rofi and me?

Oh, Rofi, I'm sorry. I shouldn't have brought you on this hasty rescue mission.

The braking engines are not yet operating at full capacity, their heat and light cutting through the cold cosmos as they slow the ship.

Unable to move because the forces at work are pressing me against the hull, I try to see how low we might be on the horizon. It's impossible to tell. I can only see darkness without stars around me, which could indicate the surface of the moon, but there are no reference points to use.

That reminds me of something. I could use my mobility unit by unbuckling my boots and simultaneously setting the throttles to full power to brake and land myself like a jetpack. It's a very risky maneuver with little chance of success, but at least not a 100% death sentence, as is the case if I do nothing.

Nevertheless, I immediately discard the idea. I couldn't take Rofi with me because I couldn't hold him, and the mobility unit wouldn't be able to win the battle against gravity with so much more weight.

I feel the trembling of the capsule and the constant vibration of the engines, which slow the ship down. Everything still happens in the eerie silence of the vacuum. It is a strange effect to see such forces at work without any accompanying sound.

My eyes are fixed on the gauges and instruments that show my relative speed, altitude, position, and orientation. Speed is dropping, altitude is shrinking, position and orientation stabilizing. But I can't trust any of these values because my suit sensors are going crazy, throwing warning messages at me one after the other. My field of vision seems to consist only of red dots and exclamation marks.

"Rofi," I say, discouraged. "If this lander is working anywhere near as it should, it's about to initiate one final massive braking thrust to take up position over the planned landing site. Then we'll roll off it like drops from a window and fall to our deaths."

I look out of the corner of my eye and can just make out the faint crater structures around us. They are illuminated by the bright flare of the braking engines. We can't be very high anymore, so we're almost there. Unless we crash – then it would be the same problem.

"I just want to tell you that you were a great companion," I say, realizing that I'm crying a little, but that's okay. My life will have been very short and I can't say it has been the perfect thing I imagined it would be. But I haven't been alone. I've had Rofi with me, who somehow made it all more bearable. And it's been intense. I also feel sorry for Ammit-47, even though he is a little – but somewhat lovable – asshole. He will be alone now. Entirely alone.

I reach for one of Rofi's hands, unable to move my upper body to turn my head. But I can't find it. Instead, his face suddenly appears. His display is activated and shows his trusty, simple smiley-face smile. It shines in the darkness around us like the sun itself.

"No, not your display!" I hear myself blurting, but of course it makes no difference because we're going to die. Still, it hurts me to see the first image distortions appearing at the edges and the display flickering. It's the cold.

Before I can fully understand what is happening, I feel a gentle pressure on my forearm and suddenly everything is gone. Rofi's face flies away, lightning fast. I start to thrash around violently, then stabilize myself a little, not understanding what is happening.

When I realize it, I start screaming.

"NO! NO, ROFI! ROH-OH-OH-FEEE!" I scream at the top of my lungs. The echo in my helmet makes my ears ring, but I can't stop. It was not Rofi's face that flew away, it was me. He somehow managed to move one of his hands and deactivate my magnetic boots via the forearm display on my arm. The mobility unit fired immediately and stopped my fall into the depths.

Rofi knew we couldn't do it together, and now I see the faint light of the lander below me, going into its final braking thrust to hover over the landing zone. It must have knocked him off, no way my little robot friend could have fought against the forces.

I howl like a wild animal as the mobility unit slowly reduces its thrust and I fall downward toward the dark landscape of endless craters. It's no longer a hopeless fall, but I'm still going fast.

As if I am remotely controlled, I take control of the unit, see the blurry displays showing the altitude and speed and the remaining gas reserves. Then, when the surface is only 20 meters away, I give maximum thrust downward.

I brake so hard that I feel like my body is being torn by the mobility unit's shoulder and leg straps. But I stay alive, landing on my boots in the regolith, which flies away silently and describes long arcs in all directions. Due to the low gravity, the tiny particles sink quite slowly. In the pale light of my helmet headlights, they look like tiny fireflies in near-zero gravity.

I survived, but at what cost?

I fall forward onto my hands, powerless, and sob uncontrollably.

32

For a while, time doesn't matter because all I can do is cry. Rofi's death leaves a black hole in my heart. It feels like a dark, infinite emptiness. It sucks everything in, and all that's left is the pain I feel, a deep, all-encompassing grief that penetrates every nook of my body and touches every fiber of my being, as though I were withering from the inside out.

I lie here in the regolith of an alien moon under a canopy of stars I do not know, and I am sure that I am the loneliest creature in the universe at this moment.

My short life has not been marked by many joys, but I have welcomed the few that I have had wherever I have seen the opportunity. This despite the many adversities and dangers that I have had to face – because I have always known that I was not alone. Rofi was there from the very beginning. The many setbacks and mysterious events on the *Ankh* shook me, but never to my core, because I saw a reason to carry on. My mission, and I don't even know if it was one at all, only made sense because Rofi was there, because I have shared everything with him since my first breath – every danger and every success.

Now he is dead.

This is a pain that is difficult to bear and cannot be alleviated by any amount of training or sugarcoating.

My heart has been ripped from me. The fact that he saved me only makes it worse. I would rather have died saving him. I would even rather have died *with* him, I must admit.

There are moments when the pain becomes so intense that I can hardly breathe. Moments when I want to cry but no tears come. Moments when I want to scream but my voice fails before a sound can escape my throat. Moments like little deaths that keep sending me plunging into the abyss of grief. My arms and legs feel as if my bones have been hollowed out and filled with lead. I can hardly move them.

Rofi never uttered a word, but I will miss his smiley smile and his two raised fingers. His positive attitude, and his presence that didn't need any words.

I am alone with this devastating pain, far away from any other person. Far away from Ammit-47. I cannot hug anyone, cannot ask anyone to listen to me, to share my grief.

But despite my sadness, I know I must keep going. Rofi would not want me to give up. He would want me to keep fighting, to keep living. I realize that's why he gave his own life.

At some point I start to feel ashamed that I'm wasting my time feeling sorry for myself. It almost feels like I'm tarnishing his legacy. So I struggle to my feet, blinking back tears and sniffling several times to clear my nose. My sadness and grief are appropriate, I know that, and I'm not ashamed. Instead, I promise myself that I'll keep going as long as I can, go all the way to the end because Rofi made it possible for me. Wherever that end may be.

"I'll keep going, Rofi," I whisper into my helmet, using all the willpower I can muster to fight the crushing feeling of loneliness that paralyzes me.

First I struggle to get my knees under me, then raise my upper body onto my forearms and hands. My arms and legs resist the effort, even though the gravity here is so low that it shouldn't require much strength. I ignore the signals from my body and soon find myself on my feet. In something of a daze, I look around in the direction that my HUD shows me as west.

The landscape is still plunged into darkness, but even from down here I can now make out the outlines of craters of various sizes. On the distant horizon a gray crescent is approaching, seemingly bending around the darkness. That must be the day-night terminator line, the incoming light of the central star, the alien sun. It is a glowing, radiant point that slowly rises from the shadow and bathes the surface of the moon in dazzling light. Since there is no atmosphere to alter it, it appears razor sharp, just like when viewed from space.

And in the middle of this inhospitable, alien landscape, a silver dot is revealed. Is it a reflection?

It must be the space shuttle, since regolith doesn't reflect.

I swallow hard and breathe deeply before ultimately starting to walk with reluctance but determination.

There's something disturbing about the gravitational pull of this moon, as if it thumbs its nose at the laws of nature. With every step I take, I feel like I'm floating, gliding through another world that defies the laws of physics. The dust beneath my boots gives way and splashes up like I'm wading through thick fog that only slowly clears.

I know that most satellites in the galaxy are constructed like this one – lifeless chunks of regolith that serve their host planet by intercepting asteroids and creating tidal forces that favor life on its big brother. They are the perfect sacrifices of any system, offering themselves up so that somewhere else can be more welcoming. And that describes what it looks like here, desolate and sad, a reflection of how I feel.

The pressure suit I'm wearing is heavy and bulky, and every step requires effort. It's optimized for microgravity, where weight isn't an issue. Now it's like a millstone around my neck, pressing down on my shoulders even in the moon's mild gravitational pull. But maybe that's just my inner depression.

I keep bouncing. Several times I over-propel myself and fall to the surface in slow motion, only to pick myself up again in the haze of dust particles and carry on. Every now and then I stop to check my suit systems. I have about three hours of oxygen left and the integrity of my suit is still intact.

That's something, at least.

Eventually the space shuttle is in front of me, a broad cone of pale metal that protrudes like a pimple from the middle of a large crater. It is a bizarre sight, this crude technical structure in the middle of the lifeless wasteland. Compared to the elements of the *Ankh*, it looks like cobbled-together scrap metal, evidence of the aliens' low level of technological development. And yet it is the only trace of life, the only hope I have of ever getting away from here. Ammit-47 cannot pilot my spaceship, and even if he could, it would not be able to land here.

The landscape around me changes with the light of the rising sun. The moon shines with a pale, cool light, the shadows become longer and the contours sharper. It is an unreal scene, as though I were walking through a dream that is subject to constant change.

I keep fighting my way forward, one long hop after another, my eyes fixed on the lander. Every breath is an effort, every heartbeat the echo of a hope I don't yet dare to harbor. At the same time, I forbid myself to give up. I can save that for when I'm dead, when the end is truly here. Until then, I won't waste my breath on self-abandonment or, worse, self-pity.

As the sun continues to rise and push away the darkness, I reach the crater's rim. I pause there for a moment as my visor automatically darkens to protect my eyes from the unfiltered radiation. The temperature quickly climbs from mercilessly below zero to extreme temperatures that would boil water.

Soon I begin the descent, proceeding with extreme caution

so as not to fall down the slope – however slight it is – and risk damaging my suit, which already has enough to contend with from the electrostatically charged micro-dust.

Shortly afterward I reach the lander. I reach out and touch the cool metal – at least the tactile sensors in the material that covers my fingers inform me that it is still below freezing. Black marks run along its flanks, a narrow landing gear holding it in position. Beneath it, the thrust of the engines has left its own small crater in the much larger crater. I circle around it and see a hatch on the side with a handle and a simple locking mechanism that I had not noticed in orbit. I sniff and raise a hand to reach for it when a reflection from the corner of my eye catches my attention.

I turn to the right and see something flashing on the crater rim on the other side.

At first I freeze. The loneliness and silence make me afraid. This is the first time I've been on the surface of a celestial body, and I feel like I'm on display. Could it be the aliens? Or could there have been aliens in this lander who moved away and lured me into a trap?

But the reflection doesn't move. There is something on the edge of the crater, not 20 steps away. I brace myself and walk toward it. I hold my hands spread out to signal that I pose no danger.

The closer I get, however, the clearer it becomes that it is not aliens lying in wait for me, but Rofi. His mechanical body lies shattered in its own tiny crater, two arms torn off and several meters away. His head is still somewhat intact, but his display is shattered and dented, his torso is torn to pieces and is barely recognizable as a coherent structure.

I kneel next to him and lower my helmet to rest against his remains, and weep again.

33

I know Ammit-47 would chastise me for this with his typical condescending look, but I take the time to bury Rofi. Every minute that passes takes away from the air I have left to breathe, and the high-performance batteries are working hard to protect me from the extreme heat that has been around me since sunlight flooded the lunar surface.

Nevertheless, I dig with my gloved hands to make a cavity in the regolith, which is so fine that it soon electrostatically 'sticks' to everything on my suit. I carefully place Rofi's remains in it and then cover him before taking my mobility unit off my back and placing it like a gravestone at the top of the small mound.

I pause, then, and fold my hands.

"Farewell, Rofi," I say with a trembling voice. "Thank you for being with me from the beginning. Thank you for your kindness and your positive nature. I wouldn't have made it this far without you. Not only because you saved my life, but also before that. Thank you for saving Ammit-47 from a terrible end, too – even if you didn't like him."

I laugh out loud, and the sound quickly turns into a mixture of mirth and sorrow.

"You taught me important things," I continue after a short pause.

My own words hurt me because they prove that this is final and that Rofi will not come back. At the same time, they have a liberating effect.

"You showed me that it is not so important what I say, but how I do what I do. That I listen more and show who I am through my actions. You were not disadvantaged by your defective speech output, my friend. You had everything essential – a good heart. If there was any need for proof that you can have one, even without flesh and blood, then you have provided it. I owe the fact that my own heart is still beating to you and I hereby make you a promise. It will continue to beat, for the rest of my life, to honor your memory."

My gaze wanders to the landed spaceship behind me. "However long that may be."

I kneel down and place a hand on the makeshift gravestone. "Farewell, my friend. I will never forget you."

As I move back toward the lander after a final moment of silence, I notice how small it is. Are the aliens tiny? If so, why was their space station so bulky? Was the crew made up of hundreds of them?

I look for the side hatch that I discovered on the way here. It is a small, inconspicuous entrance into the body of the spacecraft. The handle is flat and also inconspicuous, but I can easily wrap my hands around it in spite of my gloves. I pull, but nothing happens. I brace my feet against the hull and pull with all my body strength.

This also fails.

But that is no obstacle. I am an engineer. I solve problems. At least I always try to. My resume – admittedly very short – is good proof that excellent skills can be cultivated in a very short time if necessary.

The hatch appears to be secured with a pressure mechanism to prevent accidental opening. I check my equipment, which is attached to my suit. I don't have much with me, just the bare essentials. But that includes a multitool that I had planned to use to gain access to the space station in an emergency to rescue the aliens. But since that went badly wrong, perhaps it will now have a new purpose. It contains several different attachments, including a flat metal wedge. I attach it to the tool head and check that it is firmly in place.

I carefully place the wedge in the narrow gap between the hatch and the hull of the lander. It's a dangerous undertaking in the moon's reduced gravity, where any wrong move could cause me to stumble. I push the tool in anyway, always careful to generate enough counterpressure with my boots. It takes strength and time, but I'm gradually seeing the first results.

The resistance of the hatch begins to give a little with each push of the lever. I work my way around the entire hatch until I feel I have loosened it enough. I slide a small flathead screwdriver into the tiny gap and look for the hinges. Once I find them, I use the drill function of my multitool and drill through the shell to destroy them.

It takes me nearly half an hour, but finally the hatch wobbles. I grab the edges with both hands and pull with all my strength. The metal moves – slowly and reluctantly – but it moves.

Finally, it silently jumps up and out. Its momentum throws me back. Reflexively, I do the only right thing and throw the hatch over myself to avoid being killed by it.

I pull myself together and carefully walk toward the opening. If the aliens are still inside, maybe I should have knocked instead. But nothing happens. Nobody shoots at me and I don't see any warning signs or lights. With a sigh of relief, I step back and look at my work. It wasn't the finest technique, but I succeeded.

The difficult part is coming now. I must go inside and that scares me. But I simply don't have time to be afraid.

The entrance is small and cramped, but I can fit through

even with my spacesuit on. I make sure that I don't rush any movements and risk accidentally cutting open the suit. When I've made it through, I find myself in an extremely narrow area with hundreds of buttons and toggle switches. The colors and arrangements are strange and give me the creeps. In the dim, weak lighting emitted by the few display devices that are still functioning, the interior seems spooky. It's a tangle of technical devices, displays, and controls whose functions I can only guess at.

Only now do I notice the characters, elegantly sweeping lines and curves that wind in complex patterns across the consoles, walls, and even the floor. They give the lander an exotic, alien character that is drastically different from the sterile, functional spaces of the *Ankh*. Everything here is cramped and crowded, and the sight of these alien symbols sends a chill down my spine. Ironically, their very strangeness is further proof that they must have certain similarities to me.

Eyes that can read them.

The lander's equipment appears sophisticated and complex at first glance, but is very minimalist, which is probably due to a combination of space and weight restrictions. This is somewhat ironic, because the crowded nature of the capsule does not affirm minimalism. But everything is arranged compactly to use every cubic centimeter efficiently. There are two seats that almost look like they were made for humans, except that they are much too big and have no armrests. Whether this confirms or disproves my insect theory, I don't yet know. In any case, the aliens are likely to be significantly larger than I am.

On the opposite side, I see some sort of control panel. It's covered with a series of screens and buttons that shimmer under the dim lighting. Everything is flat instead of curved, which is kind of confusing. A light above me is flashing, a strange yellow light that makes me nervous. There's nothing to indicate that anyone has flown this lander. Was it remotely controlled? Or does it have some sort of autonomous control software?

Overall, the interior of the capsule feels alien and familiar at the same time. The basic components and design are similar to those of my own station, but the strange language – if it is not numerical analogues – and the rough design are decidedly alien. It is a world of its own, with its own rules and conventions.

I don't know any of them, except for the physics and engineering principles that must have gone into the construction.

That's what I'm going to have to figure out if I want to have even a glimmer of hope of using this vehicle to get off this moon. I tell myself that there has to be a way, and that the little time I have left before I suffocate in agony will be enough.

What else can I do?

34

The strange, intricate characters on the controls and operating surfaces are a puzzle I cannot decipher. And yet, sheer necessity drives me to delve into the secrets of this lander. The time pressure dictates what kind of solution I must find.

One of the faster ones.

My eyes scan the unfamiliar control surfaces looking for clues. I know I don't have direct access to the lander's controls because I'll never understand any of this. The only way is to manipulate the hardware to make the module react on my terms. So I pull out my multitool and look for screws.

I crouch in front of the central console, where I can see something like an intricate array made up of numerous controls, switches, buttons, and even tiny levers. All of this is framed by the complex displays and screens that are currently plunged into darkness.

With my tongue between my teeth, I kneel down to get a closer look at the base of the console. There I notice several built-in panels that presumably provide access to the lander's internal components. At least, it seems logical to me given the position of the walk-in interior in the symmetrical structure of the spacecraft.

With careful movements I start to remove the plates. I do it quite roughly – I don't have much time and I don't think I'll end up screwing everything back together – if that's even possible. I throw everything I remove out through the open hatch. Less weight means less take-off mass, which means less fuel consumption. If there's one thing I've realized, it's that the engines are old-fashioned designs based on chemical reactions, not nuclear fission.

With each panel I remove, new views of the lander's complex infrastructure are exposed. I see a tangled network of cables stretching above and below the numerous control surfaces and looping around pipes of various sizes. I touch them carefully, imagining I can feel the cool hardness of the metal under my fingers, which is of course impossible with my gloves on.

For now, I focus on the larger cables that belong to the lander's engines and control systems. These connection points could be my key to the lander's engine functions. With precise, targeted movements, I begin to carefully disconnect the contacts and connect them to one of the cables, which I can assign to one of the buttons to adapt the systems to my needs. It's not an elegant solution, but anything else would be illusory. If I can manage to assign the ignition of the engines to a button that I can easily remember – like this red one with the strange symbol that looks like a setting sun with a line in between – I can at least fly in the right direction.

It is anything but promising, and extremely dangerous. But if the worst solution is the only solution, it automatically becomes the best one, right?

While fiddling around with my more-than-unsuitable gloves, I notice that the lander is equipped with various tanks, large cylindrical containers that probably contain the fuel.

Smaller containers next to them could supply control nozzles with cold gas, for example.

I'll stick with the large ones, which are connected by narrow valves and inlet pipes, each one seeming to end in a single pipe. This suggests that these are preheating chambers where the liquids are brought into a new state of aggregation before they mix and ignite in a combustion chamber to start the explosive reaction. Oxygen and hydrogen, perhaps. Ancient technology, but functional.

I focus on the electrical connections that link these tanks to the lander's controls, bringing them all together at a single button. By cleverly switching and re-plugging, I hope to be able to activate the engine without the usual control systems that would be expected in a spacecraft – at least a human one.

The chance of success is slim, but all I have to do is imagine Rofi smiling at me and raising two fingers to keep me going.

With every minute that passes while I carefully manipulate the lander's complex systems, I feel the pressure of time almost physically. The oxygen supply is approaching the yellow zone. With every heartbeat, every breath, every movement of my hand, I know that my future is slipping through my fingers.

After what seems like an eternity, I see the longed-for lights of the system activating and hear the quiet hum of the engines – a first sign of success. But the work is far from finished, the road to orbit is still a long one.

What has probably just happened is that the two reactants are being preheated to start a chemical reaction. But the final command from the electronics that triggers the ignition is still missing.

I lean back for a moment and take a deep breath. I can do it. A humming sound from the preheating chambers, which I can feel as vibrations, gives me a feeling of satisfaction.

Now that the engine is responding to my commands, I need to develop a strategy to bring the lander into lunar orbit in a controlled manner. This is where my knowledge of space physics and orbital mechanics comes in handy. However, it is an overwhelmingly complex matter because I have to consider several things simultaneously. These include the lander's mass point, the available thrust, the amount of fuel remaining, and the correct trajectory.

And, I have to guess all this without the slightest clue. The only weight I know is my own, the mass point is probably in the middle, and the amount of fuel left is a complete mystery. Good conditions for one of the most complicated maneuvers in space travel. So let's just set it aside and concentrate on what I can do – and of course on luck.

Using my multitool, I continue to trace the main wiring harnesses and finally find what I'm looking for, the cables that lead to the control nozzles, which I identified using the smaller gas tanks. I use the tool to carefully uncouple some connections to be able to control the nozzles independently of the main engines. I connect them to the button next to the red rising sun.

Either the whole thing will go out immediately, or I've turned a complex spacecraft into a sparkler that will only burn once, and quickly.

I hope that the vehicle has at least rudimentary AI, and that the aliens do not operate their control jets manually. If software is responsible for stabilizing the lander and constantly correcting its vector while the main engines provide the actual thrust, I have a change, however slim. I will have to rely on the fact that no intelligent species will venture into space without having made at least basic advances in higher software technology.

Why? Because I have no other choice. Ironically, that makes the situation somewhat bearable. No distractions, no alternatives, so I don't have to worry about it.

With one last determined move, I reconnect the remaining

cables and clamp them to the small, ugly, cobbled-together tree that I have connected to the red button.

Then the moment finally arrives. It's all or nothing. Either I ignite the engines immediately and the maneuvering jets automatically keep the capsule stable, or else I explode in a fireball... or, get fried by a thousand short circuits. It's also possible that everything will simply go off and never come back on again.

I squeeze myself firmly into one of the seats and focus my gaze on the only two relevant buttons in front of me. The engines are still humming in active mode, vibrating all the way to my fingertips, which are resting on the console. With a final, recheck glance at the open hatch, I exhale a deep sigh and press both buttons.

The lander jolts, and for a moment I'm sure I've made a catastrophic mistake and am about to be blown to pieces. But then the lander stabilizes and slowly begins to rise. It jolts and shakes terribly, and the thought of the aliens' crude technology makes me dizzy.

The lander does not explode, although I can hardly believe it. Another look outside shows me that the surface of the moon is moving away from me.

I'm flying!

Gravity wants to prevent us from ascending. It pulls at me, pulls at the lander, but we resist. For now. The engines brace themselves against the jealous grip of the satellite and press me into the strange seat that has no armrests.

I watch through the open hatch as the lunar surface slowly shrinks and presents me with the impressive crater landscape, which shines brightly in the light of the local sun. I look at the values in my visor. My speed continues to increase. That's good. It remains to be seen whether the inclination is sufficient. I hope that the unplanned ignition of the engines has activated some kind of safety protocol that is intended to evacuate the spaceship, for example if the aliens are unconscious or something like that.

I know that it's a race against time and the dwindling fuel supply. I have to manage to get the lander into a stable orbit before the fuel runs out and we fall back uncontrollably. Then there would be no rescue. The numbers dance before my eyes, the equations, the calculations that I would normally do now if I had a data system to use. But I'm just a stowaway who has short-circuited an engine.

The lander shakes and trembles as the control jets fire, correcting the course. So, it's an automatic software system. *Thank the gods!*

A few times it seems like we're going into a spin, but somehow the space shuttle always manages to stabilize itself. Every time that happens, I breathe a sigh of relief. Luck seems to be on my side. For now.

And then, ever fickle, it leaves me. We are losing speed and, according to my HUD display, we are just about to reach a stable orbit. Not even a kilometer and a few hundred kilometers per hour of speed separate me from the saving orbit.

The engines fall silent.

Damn.

I refuse to give up, but I sense that we are reaching the apex and gravity is changing. We are falling.

I make a quick decision and head for the hatch. I look down at the bright moon, which is already halfway back on the night side – because I've changed my relative position – and then into the space above me. From here it looks as though I'm far out in space, but the impression is deceptive. Without a stable orbit, it doesn't matter how far out I am.

I'm falling back.

I'm lacking a final, strong impulse that will get me over the finish line. I no longer have my mobility unit because it's lying empty on the surface below as a gravestone for Rofi.

I return to the exposed panel beneath the complex control

panels and rip off the control jet contacts, placing them on the red button and hopefully disconnecting them from the software and its access. Then I climb out and kick the funnel-shaped jets on the underside. I don't think about the danger of losing my footing. I do what needs to be done.

Next, I pull myself back into the capsule. Fortunately, the capsule and I are falling backward and not forward.

I connect the cables to the main button and press it. It works. The maneuvering jets empty their gas supplies and fire uncontrollably, but with all the power they can muster. I am pressed back into the seat as we go upward again.

When all the electronics go off because there is no more power, weightlessness sets in. This time it lasts. It is not short-lived just because we have reached the apex of a parabola.

I'm in orbit. Somewhere.

35

The aliens' capsule is now an empty shell. The fuel in the tanks has been used up. I still find the strangeness of the countless buttons and switches, with their strange labels, a little creepy.

I need to get back to the *Ankh*, but I don't know how.

"Think about it," I say into my helmet. "This spaceship is just flotsam in orbit. But the trajectory seems to be stable for now. Thus far. Somewhere there is a growing cloud of debris flying around the moon, which gets bigger with every impact on the remains of the space station – if it hasn't crashed by now. The chance of me being hit by it is small, though."

I laugh mirthlessly. "Don't start relying on your luck."

However, I contradict myself. I had just 'used' an indecent amount of it or I wouldn't be here now. Am I on a lucky streak, or is the supply used up?

We'll see soon enough.

My eyes fall on the exposed cables under the control panels. It looks like a complete mess, and that describes it perfectly. It's a miracle that I managed to create this kind of short circuit in a system that is utterly unknown to me. But it ultimately proves that engineers think alike, no matter what species they belong to.

For a moment I am transfixed by this realization. Everything I do and discover here is like a kind of new law of the universe. At least, if we humans don't constantly meet other aliens, and this is truly the first contact with an alien species, which I assume – after all, there are no references to extraterrestrials in the onboard computer. However, the *Ankh* also tells lies constantly and seems to have very sketchy memories, to put it mildly.

Nevertheless, I have found proof that engineers everywhere think the same. At least the probability of this has just increased exponentially. This in turn means that physics is recognized and understood the same everywhere and is converted into technical principles with which these laws can be used.

But that doesn't help me to overcome my problem now. I'm in here and the *Ankh* is out there somewhere. I have only half an hour of oxygen because I used up too much of it in my excitement. My spaceship is the only possible rescue for me because it's the only air bubble anywhere near here.

I have to start thinking from the most important principle.

Sight. I need orientation if I want to have any chance of reaching the *Ankh*. I must go into space through the open hatch, grab the edge with both hands, and push my boots out backward. Which I do. Only when I'm completely outside do I pull my knees up to my chest and press my feet against the shell of the capsule before magnetizing them. I take a few steps in complete silence until the moon is below me. It has become a white crescent that is slowly growing, so I'm moving toward the night side. That's a start.

I left the *Ankh* in a stationary orbit that lies behind the satellite from the perspective of the water world where the aliens live. So, I'm currently on the correct side.

Although I am moving at thousands of kilometers per hour, there are no reference points that would make me aware of my enormous speed. I feel both weightless and motionless. Only the craters slowly moving beneath me give me any impression that I am moving.

I tell my helmet sensors to search for the *Ankh's* signature as I slowly turn around. It is still dead silent in the vacuum. Only my breathing rushes in and out, slow and controlled to save oxygen.

It takes a few minutes, then a green symbol in the shape of a rectangle flashes in front of me. The optical zoom works automatically, and after several zooms I see the familiar outline of my spaceship in front of me, as if it were close enough to touch.

Next, I measure the distance using a laser in the sensor bundle on the brim of my helmet – 8,000 meters. In cosmic terms, that's quite close and a real stroke of luck. I know I could have found myself on the other side of the satellite, without visual contact, 8,000 *kilometers* away.

It's still not much practical help. After comparing the trajectory of the *Ankh* with that of my capsule, I know it can't work. They don't cross – they run parallel to each other. The big spaceship is in a higher orbit and will always stay 8,000 meters away. There's nothing I can do about it.

But I refuse to die having done nothing, either. I promised Rofi that I would give it my ultimate effort until nothing else was possible. And since I'm still breathing, something can still be done.

I push aside the feeling that the artificially-zoomed-in *Ankh* looks pale and lifeless, because I know my mechanical friend won't be there waiting for me. The ship may have become colder and cheerless, but it's still my home, and I have a second robot to look after. Unless I take control, it will be completely helpless there, with no authority to give orders to the onboard computer.

He needs me.

One look at my oxygen meter threatens to take away all my hope. What can I do in less than half an hour?

As always, I do think of something, but it's not a good idea. But then again, in my situation, there may not be any such thing as a good idea! No, I'm quite sure that, in my situation, there are none remaining.

I grip the rubberized handle of my multitool while concentrating on keeping my hand steady. The penetration head is still on the attachment. That will do the trick. I activate the trigger to check the device's function.

The vibrating drill is a jarring contrast to the weightless silence that surrounds me. The sound is made foreign as it is channeled through my suit and my bones. Now for my crazy idea. I need to drill a hole in the gas cell of my life support system. A warning signal flashes in my helmet, alerting me to the critical oxygen level, as though it had read my mind and immediately panicked. I can understand that. I am aware of the risks, but the alternative – dying here, in the emptiness of space, without having tried anything – is even worse.

I'd rather die on the way, with a clear conscience, knowing that I didn't disappoint Rofi and that I gave it all I could.

I have to contort myself to slide the drill bit between my legs and press it against the bottom of my suit's flat backpack, keeping it as vertical as possible.

The toughness of the material resists the pressure of my drill, but I push on stubbornly, every fiber of my being focused on this one task. Beads of sweat run down my forehead, tickling my temples and racing down my cheeks like warm tears, only they don't burn. Because of the weightlessness, they don't fall off my skin, I can only blink them away.

With a final, powerful push, the drill bit penetrates the gas cell material and I am jerked upright. I can't see it, but I know that a jet of oxygen and nitrogen is shooting out of my back like a white geyser. I frantically cut the power supply to my magnetic boots and am immediately catapulted forward. My heart is pounding wildly in my chest while the stars around me dance in a wild whirlpool.

This is the first indication that something is wrong. I hurtle out into space, uncontrolled. The angle is wrong. My path is not aligned with the *Ankh*, a fact that my helmet system alerts me with countless warnings.

"Thanks, I can see that myself," I groan. Panic rises within me and I feel my breathing becoming more labored as my oxygen supply dwindles. But maybe I'm just imagining it because I feel an unnaturally heavy weight on my chest.

I have to do something. But what?

My hands. They are part of my pressurized spacesuit, so they are filled with the same gas as my life support unit – just with significantly less of it. What I need are two more holes, this time in my gloves. The first gush of gas escapes one glove, changes my course, hurls me wildly around several axes at once. Miraculously, I manage to drill into the other glove as well. A blinding pain shoots through my hand. But it worked. I let go of the tool and stretch my hands back, carefully turning them into new positions until my trajectory has stabilized. Then I align myself with my ship.

The *Ankh* is coming closer – just like my death. The oxygen and nitrogen supply of my life support unit is used up. I am only breathing the last bit that is stored in my suit and is currently escaping through my hands. Cold is creeping over my skin by now like liquid ice.

Worse, however, is the realization that I'm not going to make it. In no more than 30 seconds there will be no air left in my suit. I exhale one last time to keep my lungs from collapsing in the vacuum and watch as the warning symbols in my helmet explode, filling the entire universe.

Miraculously, I'm on course for the *Ankh*, but it's still two kilometers away. There's no way I can make it. My head is already going numb. My thoughts too are numb from the lack of oxygen. Blackness is approaching from the edges of my vision and my eyes hurt as though thousands of needles were piercing them. I know it's the cold that's killing me, robbing me of my mind before I suffocate and the capillaries in my body burst.

I lose consciousness when I see the *Ankh* in all its glory one last time.

What a beautiful sight.

36

First comes a realization. I am.

It arises from the observation that there is something that recognizes this thought. This is followed almost immediately by another. I am alive.

It takes a while for me to know that I am me, and a while longer for me to understand that I am not only alive, but still living. Or am I alive again? I am not in pain, even though my head feels like it is stuffed with cotton.

I open my eyes and my vision is blurry. Everything around me is white, so bright that I have to squeeze my eyelids shut again, as otherwise it hurts. It's too bright.

Little by little I dare to open them a crack, and then a little wider, and realize that I am lying on a treatment table, with infusion devices like thick pens stuck into my arms and palms. A scanner unit on an outstretched robot arm hangs above me and moves over me with a quiet whirring sound.

"What... happened?" I mumble in a hoarse voice. I find it difficult to speak, as though my vocal cords are glued together.

A computer voice answers, sounding vaguely familiar.

"Severe barotraumatic stress due to sudden exposure to the vacuum of space. First, I had to deal with the effects of the explosive decompression event. At the cellular level, there was significant traumatic damage from the rapid drop in pressure. On admission, the patient showed signs of systemic gas embolism – a clear manifestation of decompression sickness. I was able to reduce the gas bubbles largely with hyperbaric oxygen therapy, but there are still risks for further complications from blocked micro-vessels and potential ischemic damage.

"Second, on admission, the patient showed signs of hypoxia and mild pulmonary edema due to the long exposure to the vacuum. Barotrauma of the lungs was suspected, induced by the vacuum. In addition, the scans showed clear signs of acute radiation syndrome – primarily from unprotected exposure to the high radiation dose in space. I anticipate significant hematological complications, including severely reduced cell counts in the red and white blood cell lines, and have initiated appropriate therapeutic measures, including administration of growth factors to stimulate blood cell production. Additionally, extreme hypothermia noted so I endeavored to restore a safe body temperature. Minimal residual risk of secondary cold damage.

"Overall, this was an extremely critical case. The extent of the damage is significant and, despite the interventions I have initiated, the further course of events must be monitored. The prognosis is serious, but the patient is stable. However, a variety of potential complications are to be expected. Constant monitoring is required. The patient will require several more days of rest and a range of substances, including analgesics, fluid and electrolyte infusions, nanonic symbionts, blood cell stimulants and antioxidants, in order to fully recover."

I listen to the grim list and find it even harder to understand why I am still alive. Memories of the last image of the distant *Ankh* far out in front of my visor rise to the surface of my consciousness.

Impossible.

"Who brought me here?" I ask.

"Maintenance robot Ammit-47," the medical unit replies.

At the same time, the door opens. Ammit-47 comes running in, stops next to my bed, and stands on his rear pair of hands . He seems to be looking at me, but it's hard to tell because his screen is black and cracked.

"You're still alive," he says. His voice is scratchy and accompanied by a constant noise. "That's good."

"Did you save me?" I ask incredulously.

"Yes. I didn't feel like having to carry on without my personal meatbag."

"How did you do that?"

When he starts telling me his story in his own unique way, silent tears flow from the corners of my eyes. It's as if I'm seeing through his 'eyes,' and that touches me.

"I recognize your personal signal on the *Ankh's* sensor images. I had already given up hope of seeing it again, but I didn't stop looking. I compare it with the telescope data and determine that you are entering a parallel orbit around the moon, aboard an alien space capsule. An unusual maneuver, a change in the usual pattern. The sensors, optical and infrared, are detecting movements that do not correspond to any known procedure.

"You drill a hole in your life support system and appear to create an improvised jetpack. I find this pretty crazy, but you meatbags do crazy things all the time. Not standard in this case, but innovative, I must admit. Then I watch as you drill holes in your hands and use the escaping gas to correct your direction of movement. You head for the *Ankh*.

"My calculations update. There is no way you can reach our ship without dying first. I make my way to the airlock. My movements are precise, optimized for weightlessness, I would like to emphasize. I reach it quickly but in a controlled manner. I clip myself into the safety line, tie two more lines together. Every move, every action, is based on a complex calculation of probabilities and risks. They do not look good for me – and therefore not for you either.

"Using my location data and the current position of my meatbag, I calculate the best location inside the airlock. I position myself exactly there and activate the outer hatch before the decompression is complete. The result is a sudden, large pressure difference and I am thrown into the vacuum. Because my logical and mathematical skills are superior, I fly straight toward you.

"Unfortunately, the decompression has shattered my display and destroyed it beyond repair, but my primary function is not affected. I secure you, activate the winch, and we are pulled back into the *Ankh*.

"As soon as the airlock is closed, I make my way to the sickbay. The condition of your disgusting body is critical. I leave further care to the medical units. This one is quite efficient. Everyone has their job, makes their contribution.

"I have spent the last few days going about my routine and repeatedly studying the medical reports."

When Ammit-47 finishes his very idiosyncratic report, I shake his hand.

"Thank you my friend."

"That..." He pauses, his head moving back and forth as if searching for help. "That's my job."

"No, your job is to maintain the *Ankh*. I'm pretty sure you've exceeded your duties," I say. "Again, thank you."

Ammit-47 lowers his head and seems to stare at my hand, which is resting on his. "Is that necessary?"

"Because my disgusting body is touching yours?" I ask, giggling with relief.

"Repulsive," he corrects me. But there is no disapproval in his voice. Do I hear... relief?

I pull my fingers back. "Seriously, thank you."

"Seriously, you're welcome," he replies, for once free of any cynicism. Then he pauses again, during which only the beeping of the medical monitoring devices can be heard. "Where is 48?"

"Rofi is..." I pause and close my eyes briefly. "He died."

"He was destroyed?" Ammit-47's voice suddenly sounds hollow.

"Yes. I'm sorry."

He doesn't say anything, but I feel his cold, mechanical fingers come to rest on mine, and we are silent for a while in our shared grief, however differently we may feel it. I'm sure neurons and circuits don't matter in this moment, that there's no difference in what they put their owner through.

I don't know what the relationship between two robots feels like, if 'feel' is even the right word for it. Ammit-47 always teased Rofi, looking down on him like a damaged thing, a toddler at best. But I sense that he is hurting, and the weight of our mutual friend's final absence bonds us more strongly in this moment than ever before. We are now the last survivors on the *Ankh*, stranded in unfamiliar waters, all on our own. It is the burden of those still alive to carry on and find ways to cope. With the fact that there will be no answer to one question, even though we will ask it for the rest of our lives. Why did I make it and he didn't?

"He's not coming back, 47," I say. It feels stupid to state the obvious, but I refuse to give up or wallow in grief. We will need to set some rules for ourselves. "But we're still here."

"I wasn't very nice to him," he replies, and his shattered black screen sinks down until it touches the edge of my treatment table with a dull thump. "He was damaged, and I didn't think he was fully functional."

"We are still here," I repeat, clasping his hand, more firmly this time. "Take it from a meatbag with a lot of experience in this area. You don't want to go down that path. It will destroy you."

"I have decades more life than you."

"That may be true, but you wouldn't believe what goes on in a person's head in just one day." I point a finger at my temple. The movement is very strenuous. "We are professionals at feelings of guilt, self-pity, self-doubt, and general despair at ourselves and the things around us when they are not as we think they should be."

"You don't accept what is," says Ammit-47, as if something is dawning on him. His broken display whirs back up. Maybe he's looking at me. "That's what I've never understood about you. The circumstances are what they are, and our tasks should be based on that. But you spend ages wishing things were different, as though you had magical powers, and then you're angry or disappointed that objective reality doesn't bend to your ideas. That's the definition of insanity."

"Yes, I think that sometimes too," I admit. "And now you understand us a little, I suppose."

Ammit-47 pauses for a long time. Then he says, "Yes. I think I understand it for the first time. I wish Rofi were still alive."

I don't know if it's a tiny change in his voice that I subconsciously perceive or my human empathy that I transfer to him. The little robot seems serious and seems to undergo a change with this admission.

37

Ammit-47's realization of what grief is – at least that's my interpretation of what happened that day – seems to have hit him even harder than I would have expected. He doesn't show up for three days. I lie immobile on my treatment table and watch time creep past me like thick syrup.

I keep drifting off and dreaming of the desert, endless landscapes of sand piling up into reddish-brown dunes. Dunes that are constantly moving, shifting with the wind, and are thus one with their nature, constant change and impermanence. Each time I wake, I find myself humbled anew because I realize that this also applies to me. The universe seems to be happening around me. It is what it is, always and in every moment. Nothing stays the same. Everything is subject to constant change that I cannot influence. Sometimes I feel like a theater performer who keeps slipping into new roles and situations. My sense of self is still the same, but everything else is not.

During the good moments I can only smile about the fact that I considered myself more than just a passenger on this unpredictable ride of life.

In bad times, I cry silent tears because I feel lonely at the thought that I am just a grain of sand in a dune, determined to control the wind.

However, in the best times a great burden is lifted from me. Things are as they are, and what happens, happens. One realization inevitably solidifies in me. Fate is larger than I am. That I find this thought frightening seems narrow-minded then, and egocentric, because it means I see myself as the center of the universe whenever I think that way. But what about all the other people? What about aliens? Ammit-47? If I am the fixed point of reality, then they must be mere extras, and that shows me how crazy such a notion is.

I am me and I am here, I know that for sure. Maybe I should shorten that to I am, which ironically was my first thought in this life. I think it was my most honest, unencumbered one. It was free of everything my mind had made up, and as I recline on my treatment table, pumped full of drugs and constantly being scanned, the banality of my existence makes me peaceful.

I am. What a liberation lies in this simple realization. How unconditional it is.

On the fourth day, Ammit-47 comes back for the first time and brings me something to eat. It is a food packet of course.

"How are you feeling?" he inquires.

I still have to get used to the fact that he no longer has a display, and therefore no facial expressions. It is somewhat ironic that he is now damaged, like Rofi was. I wonder, will his own realization of this also give him humility?

"A little better, but still very weak," I answer, and nod gratefully as he carefully hands me the food pack.

"Pains?"

"No."

"That's good. It..." He hesitates.

"What is?"

"I'm sorry I haven't been here for the last three days."

Ammit-47 sounds... dejected? I'm briefly worried that I might be imagining it, that's how unimaginable his tone strikes me.

Instead of answering, I give him space to add something of his own if he wants to. And, after a while, he does. "I needed some time. I'm... confused about some changes in my data streams."

"I can understand that," I reply gently.

"Please get well soon," he finally says, and runs back out of the sickbay.

I stare for a while at the door, which closed automatically behind him. Ammit-47 seems to have changed. Only gradually do I realize how much meaning lies in the last four words he uttered.

Little by little, time begins to stretch. I'm not used to doing nothing. My whole short life has consisted of facing one problem after another. There was no time for endlessly circling thoughts. Now I'm not even sure which state I prefer.

With every breath I feel the sterile coolness of the sickbay, which settles on my skin like a transparent layer. I have been locked up here, in this world of metal and light, for five seemingly endless days. And in every second of each of these days, time stretches, expands, and fills the room like an invisible liquid. It splashes against the walls of my perception, piling up higher and higher and burying me under its weight.

The ceiling above me becomes a canvas for my thoughts. I stare at it and try to interpret the shapes and colors that my imagination paints on it. It becomes a mirror of my worries and fears, my questions and doubts. Even the sublime insights of the first few days seem far away now, although I know that they will never fully leave me. But so much is happening on this canvas that it almost hypnotizes me.

What might be going on at the alien stations? Are their leaders talking about what to do with me? Are they discussing whether or not the destruction of their space station in orbit around the moon could have been an act of war? Or have they long since made up their minds in the affirmative, and begun taking steps to kill me, to destroy the *Ankh*? Are they perhaps waiting for a reaction from me? What about the station's crew? Were they able to escape? Get to safety? Have I become an interplanetary murderer through my simple thinking and calculation error?

This helplessness, this feeling of being at the mercy of others and powerless, weighs heavily on me. My spaceship is out here, without any orders, a colossus stuck in a vacuum without any instructions. It's like I'm sitting at a window with my hands tied and watching my future unfold without me.

But there is also good news. With each passing day, my body feels a little less like something foreign. I grow used to the medical procedures, the initial nausea, weakness, and tiredness subside. But as my body recovers, my restlessness also grows. The walls of the sickbay seem to be getting closer and closer, pressing against me until I can hardly breathe. The constant infusions, the countless scans, the penetrating beeps of the machines – they all become a constant source of annoyance.

During these long, monotonous days, Ammit-47 becomes an important constant, an anchor in the sameness of the routine. He appears at my bedside three times a day, asks how I am – just as a human would – checks my vitals, although it makes no difference, and makes sure I have enough to eat and drink. He is no longer the emotionless robot I met right after his rescue. He has become a part of my world, a fragment of normality in this monotonous environment. He gives me a piece of hope, a spark of confidence, without us talking much. It is the knowledge that I am not alone, that there is someone who cares about me, that keeps me alive and keeps me sane.

And then, finally, on the sixth day, the medical unit withdraws its infusion pumps and scanners and informs me that the treatments are complete. I am healthy again and can leave the sickbay.

38

My first stop is the bridge. Ammit-47 is busy cleaning the *Ankh* and maintaining all the systems – he is on his own for everything, tasks he previously shared with Rofi. How he manages is a mystery, as the two of them were always extremely busy, aside from several hours spent in their charging stations.

I start with a detailed analysis of our situation. From the viewpoint of the water planet, we are still behind the moon. We are about 3,000 kilometers away, which is relatively far. But since it is a very large satellite, it hides us from the eyes of the aliens. At least my various sensors cannot pick up any signatures that could be of artificial origin in the space around us.

So we drift unseen in the shadows. The only question is, for how long?

The catastrophe I have unintentionally caused will have made the locals pause for thought, I am sure. I would react that way. All humans would, and the aliens will, too. First contact may have started peacefully, but it ended in destruction and possibly even death. For me, this is only about my own life and the existence of Ammit-47, but for the aliens, it is about the life of their species, their home planet. They do not know that the *Ankh* has no weapons systems of any kind, apart from the laser designed to eliminate micrometeorites and other high-speed objects that could pose a threat to my ship.

From what they know – and they seem to be at least somewhat intelligent – the *Ankh* must be extremely sophisticated to have made it here. Or so I would be thinking. Their first priority would be to avert danger. The primary maxim of every species must be its own survival. That applies to every individual and every species. That is how it is on Earth and that is how it will be everywhere else, that is the basic law of evolution.

Right?

I have a bad feeling that I'm going to find out soon.

I spend a few hours on the bridge, going through all the systems, looking for error messages and working on minor problems that require my authorization as a human crew member to fix. I re-analyze the signals that have come in over the course of my 80-year journey. I still cannot determine their origin because the on-board computer does not have any data on them. The only explanation I can think of is that the decision-makers on Earth did not want the position of our home planet to be known in the event of a problem. Such a long-term and risky mission always requires weighing up *all* of the risks.

Now they seem to be confirmed. What if I had encountered a more advanced civilization? What if they had hijacked the *Ankh* and found out where Earth is? Would they send an invasion fleet to open up new living space?

So, I'm not surprised that I can't figure out where I came from. I have ample memories, which may not even be my own. But they are present.

What does surprise me is that the last signal came in about 20 years ago and nothing has come since. It must have been a major update, because according to system logs, it changed the code of over 80 percent of all software systems. Including the indoctrination unit of my breeding tank, the torpor capsule in which I was still growing at the time. My body must have been about ten years old that day.

What was it? New memories? New skills woven into my still-developing neural fabric?

But the most important question is, why did I never notice this update before? I have been diligently searching through the on-board computer many times in the last few weeks. Is the *Ankh* only now permitting me to see it? I now believe anything is possible with this ship that has a mysterious 'life' of its own.

My thoughts turn to the two black boxes in the back of the *Ankh* and I realize that I'm not going to find out anything about them. I don't even know what this cargo is that I have on board. What if my job isn't to make first contact or to examine a world for habitability? What if I'm some kind of bird of death sent to bring plagues, destroy the aliens and make room for human colonists who will eventually follow me when the smoke and ash have settled?

No, I don't think so. Then they could have saved themselves some trouble by indoctrinating me to be aggressive and calculating. But I'm not. I don't want there to be a conflict. Conflicts only destroy, they don't add anything to the universe.

First, I conclude that my fellow people at home feel the same way, and next, that they sent me on my way out of the same spirit of research and discovery that consumes me.

That makes it even more important for me to sort out this mess and make sure that we use whatever small chance exists to turn the whole situation into something positive. If there is a chance. I refuse to doubt it. How small were the chances of rescuing Ammit-47 from the rings of the gas giant? How small were the chances of making it safely to the surface of the moon and, above all, back into orbit?

Zero is a very absolute number and I don't believe in absolutisms, but it is probably a fairly small approximation, that much is certain.

Before I start more pondering, I finish my investigation of the current status of the *Ankh*. All systems are working at full capacity. There are no more strange failures like when I first arrived at the gas giant, when the habitat module stopped working and the lights kept going out. Apparently, the maintenance efforts by Ammit-47 and Rofi were successful. Of course, it is possible that the problems will return, and now there is only one robot left. He may not be able to handle everything, but I will deal with that when the time comes. Not before.

One thing at a time. That way it never becomes too much. Just like Ammit-47 taught me.

I leave the bridge and go back to the habitat module, where I carefully exercise on the elliptical trainer and explore how my body feels. As expected, it feels very weak. Ten days in a supine position, moved only by electrical stimulation from the medical unit, has left its mark. I have become thinner, my skin is a little paler, and I have the impression that my cheeks have sunken. They certainly feel strangely hollow.

All the more reason to get moving. But I stick to shorter sessions and take lots of breaks to prepare food or watch Ammit-47 at work. There is something calming about seeing him go about his routine as if everything is normal and running smoothly. I know that this is just an illusion because either the aliens will act soon, or we will have to. My impression is that 47 knows it too and, just like me, is trying to maintain a certain level of daily routine.

I keep looking at the *Ankh's* sensor data, which is streamed directly from the on-board computer to my forearm display. If there is a development, I want to be able to react immediately.

"What do you think will happen?" asks Ammit-47 as I sit at the kitchen table and scour the analysis data of the four gas giants of the local solar system for the probability of the presence of helium-3. The small robot is standing in front of its charging station and has turned its destroyed display toward me.

"I don't know," I admit. "They will react, I guess. Either to what I have done or to what we are going to do."

"Which of these is the lesser evil?"

"If only I knew." I sigh. "I spend my days wracking my brains about that. Is passivity a better sign than activism now? Will they feel threatened if I take the initiative again after that terrible misunderstanding? It all depends on how they think, how their culture works."

"We know nothing about it," Ammit-47 replies soberly.

"Exactly. We have no clues to determine how they interpret different behaviors. They could think completely differently than we do."

"That's unlikely. Your attempts to communicate with them were successful. So there must be some basic similarity. Perhaps it's small and related to scientific thinking, but that's a clue."

"Do you think so?" I ask doubtfully. His words give me hope that I'm being too pessimistic. Which is something I do not want to become.

So I might as well just let it go.

"Yes, I do. Scientific thinking requires several things that we can deduce from it. The desire to gain knowledge, the questioning of facts, the falsification of one's own ideas. You have to be able to think abstractly, work with records of information, and be curious. Scientific work also requires social structures, because scientific endeavors are complex. They require clear organization and collaboration between disciplines."

"Cooperation," I say with a nod. "You're right, 47."

"If that's a statement, it's coming rather late," he replies, and something of the cynical Ammit-47 I know resonates in his voice. I can't help but smile.

When I go to bed that day and tell my forearm display to wake me up if the onboard sensors detect any unusual signature, I have no idea that it will be my last smile for a very long time.

39

The alarm wakes me up in the middle of the night. It is 03:34 ship's time, and at first I think the intrusive blaring is the ringing of my forearm display because it vibrates incessantly as though it was trying to shake me awake.

Confused and torn from the middle of a dream, I quickly realize that it is the ship-wide alarm blaring from the loudspeakers that is hurting my ears.

I jump up and bang my head hard on the ceiling above my bed. Stars dance before my eyes and I feel dizzy as I pull the curtain aside and swing my legs out of the bunk.

The habitat module's lights are still dim, and the cold glow of my forearm display casts ghostly shadows on the walls. It takes a moment for my eyes to focus. I have to blink several times to drive the sleep out of them, even though my heart is racing with tension.

"What's going on?" I ask, dazed, staring at the small display on my arm. When I realize what triggered the alarm, I freeze. I'm paralyzed for a moment. I look at the sensor data with the associated telescope images and columns of data as if it must be an illusion. Something is coming directly toward us at extremely high speed. Since it's not far away and the exhaust flare isn't aimed at us, it doesn't seem to be making any attempt to slow down. And that tells me everything I need to know about the alarm.

"What happened?" asks Ammit-47, who comes running in and raises his shattered display as though he were looking at me with his dead eyes.

"I think we're being shot at," I say, barely able to believe my own words.

I run to the ladder and climb up into the central corridor, from where I float directly to the bridge and strap myself into the commander's seat. Ammit-47 has followed me and skillfully climbs into his seat next to me. I frantically raise the display and turn off the holokeyboard. It only takes a fraction of a second, but it still seems far too slow.

Suddenly there it is, a new object on the screen, a flashing symbol on the radar and the reason for the deafening alarm. It is moving around the edge of the moon at an astonishing speed and heading straight for our spaceship. The signature is unmistakably alien, and its characteristic values do not match any known spacecraft typology that the onboard computer knows or could assign.

The data rushes across my screen, altitude above the lunar surface, speed, estimated mass – all at a glance. The lidar scans the object, creating a complex 3D model that unmistakably shows the outline of a rocket, elongated and pointed, with a thickened propulsion section. It is about 40 meters long, possibly packed with explosives, but even without them its kinetic energy would be enough to tear the *Ankh* to pieces. The speed is breathtaking, faster than I would have thought the aliens and their technology capable of.

But what confirms the fact that it is a weapon is its telemetry. There are no life support signals, no typical EM signatures that would indicate communications equipment or anything like that. Instead, there is just a silent but unmistakable signal that betrays the cold, calculating logic of a homing system, radar waves and infrared scanning picked up by the *Ankh's* highly sensitive passive sensors.

And then there's the course calculation. No civilian spacecraft would set out on such a collision trajectory. There are no attempts to correct course, no indication that it would turn around and apply braking thrust. Everything about this object announces its intent to destroy us.

The distance keeps shrinking. I'm sad that the aliens decided that I should die, and that this first contact should end like this. I'm also angry but, at the same time, I understand because it is fully understandable from their point of view.

What a confusing mess of conflicting emotions. How sobering that in the end the most basic of impulses seem to have gained the upper hand.

"What's happening?" asks Ammit-47, sounding almost nervous.

"They're trying to destroy us," I answer, far more calmly than I feel.

The danger is enormous. Even a hit in less important parts of the *Ankh* would have catastrophic consequences – a hole in the hull, a short circuit in the vital systems, the destruction of important equipment. It's not like there are superfluous things on a spaceship. Everything is essential.

In the best case, the rocket would hit the rear, where the reactor is located. That would be a catastrophe, no question, but the energy matrix cells are well charged and would provide power long enough. The fusion chamber doesn't have enough helium-3 pellets anyway, and it is only intended for the interstellar part of the journey. But it would still be the death of the *Ankh*. We would be stranded among hostile aliens and would never be able to return home.

In the worst case, however, the rocket could trigger an explosion that would tear the entire spaceship to pieces.

I can't allow that.

"What are you going to do now?" Ammit-47 asks, looking up at me continually with his destroyed display.

"I'll intercept it," I say.

"Why do you sound like you don't like this?" Now he sounds like his old self, disapproving and condescending, as if he were talking to a child. But I know the real Ammit-47 now, and I know it's just a façade.

"Because that's war. Action and reaction."

"Would you prefer if it...?"

"No," I interrupt. "But that doesn't mean I have to like it."

I instruct the high-powered laser to intercept the object after I have marked it. The onboard computer has already highlighted it as a target for automatic threat prevention, but is waiting for my command because I programmed it that way. At least the weapons obey me.

Next, I turn off the alarm, which I seem to still hear even after it has stopped, its echo continuing to falsely resonate in my head.

My palms begin to sweat and I lick my lips as I watch the *Ankh* fight back on my screen.

The first thing I hear is the quiet hum of the on-board laser, which draws power from the energy matrix cells into its batteries via the superconductors in the walls and drains them by almost ten percent. It is not a loud noise, more of a hum that echoes through the entire ship and increases in frequency. The defense software acts autonomously, no longer requiring any input from me, because the human brain is far too sluggish compared to the intelligent code.

In the starry darkness of space there is no bright flash, no detectable sign of the existence of the laser being fired at the approaching object. Its beams are invisible in the vacuum of space, as there are no particles for them to scatter off. I can only see it in the bare numbers on my display. We have fired, as the laser's battery packs have suddenly been drained.

The effect occurs with virtually no loss of time between cause and effect.

The colors on the screen in front of me are changing. The approaching object is rapidly decreasing in size, its outlines are blurring and becoming indistinct. The laser has reached its target and is burning the rocket's material, heating it so much and so quickly that most of it changes its state from solid to gas and is torn apart.

The explosion that follows is massive, a huge fireball that spreads quickly in the vacuum and vanishes just as quickly. It is nothing more than an afterimage on the sensors. The heat it creates beats down on us, scorching some of the secondary sensors. Worse, however, are the few remaining pieces of debris that have not turned into volatile gas molecules. Some of them hit the *Ankh*, and their kinetic force shreds several of the dorsal maneuvering engines. There are two hull breaches, fortunately in the cargo containers, which the system immediately seals to prevent any loss of atmosphere.

Finally, it's over. The warning signal on my monitor goes off and the threat level jumps back from red to green.

I breathe heavily and look at Ammit-47. Only now do I notice that I have taken his hand again. I must have done it unconsciously, but he did not pull it away and he leans back with relief.

"That was close," he says.

"Closer than I like," I agree.

"What do we do now?"

"How do you talk to aliens who just wanted to kill us because, to make matters worse but understandable, they also think we are the aggressors?" I ask.

"I think it's too late to talk now. We should think about other ways to end this conflict."

"If you are suggesting what I am thinking, no. We do not have the right to do that."

I don't yet know that in just a few days I will be staring into the cold sensor eye of another rocket.

This time with no laser to save me.

40

For the next two days, I don't know where to direct my anger. First and foremost, I'm angry at the very fact that something like combat had to happen. An act of violence as a first contact scenario was the last thing I wanted. But it is what it is, and no matter how strange and unreal the memory of it feels, it is still real.

The aliens tried to destroy us. To *kill* us! And I thwarted their attempt by destroying their rocket – fortunately not a particularly advanced one. Of course it was an act of self-defense, but it was still an act of violence. At first, I was terribly angry at the aliens for escalating things to such an extent. Now, I'm mostly angry at myself.

Ultimately, it is my fault that things have turned out this way. I became impatient and wanted to make faster progress in communication. I took a shortcut and wanted to send them items. Despite my exhaustion and tiredness and the fact that there is no one able to check my reasoning, I went ahead and sent the probe.

No matter how I look at it, it's my fault that the locals' space station was destroyed and they either died or had to flee.

Can I blame them for trying to shoot me down? Yes, I can. But not without blaming myself too.

Thus I'm faced with a dilemma. Ammit-47 would prefer that I neutralize the aliens by destroying their two space stations in orbit around their planet, thereby triggering a cascade of space debris. If it continues to grow as it captures satellites, the blue sphere would be irreparably surrounded by ultra-fast debris that would make any space travel impossible for centuries or millennia.

Unless they have more advanced weapons than what they threw at me, I could do it. But I don't even think about it.

Ammit-47 is right that I must ensure that the hostility I have unleashed does not endanger humanity at home, but I am not prepared to repeat my mistake. I cannot and will not decide the fate of an entire species. How many of them were involved in the decision to shoot me down? All of them? Only a few? Was it difficult for them? Did they perhaps even regret it?

I spend my days exercising, eating, and looking at the same sensor images of the missile launch. At one point I go out onto the hull to repair one of the broken maneuvering engines, which was damaged by the debris of the destroyed weapon. I manage to do it and make sure we remain somewhat maneuverable.

I wait until the third day, when I sit on the bridge and look at the footage again. Not because I hope to discover something new, a detail that I might have missed that would answer one of the many questions in my head. Rather, repeatedly staring at the same scene helps me to think.

My problem is that I have no rational basis for my next decision, no matter what I decide. I am confronted with aliens who might think in a manner diametrically opposed to that of us humans. What if I try to appeal to them emotionally? Not that I know how to do so – it is possible they have no emotions. What if emotions never emerged in this world as an evolutionary advantage for the mental hygiene of the brain?

I could appeal to their reason, I suppose, and use pictograms to point out the advantage of peaceful exchange.

But what if, on the contrary, they only think emotionally? If I were to send them a photo of me smiling in a friendly way, they might misunderstand it as a hint that I want to eat them because they see my teeth. I realize it could be a sign of aggression in their culture. It doesn't even take much imagination to see that.

The fact remains that I don't know. I don't know anything about them, so no rational basis exists for decision-making. It worries me. I have always felt rationality to be the most important factor in making decisions. Well, maybe not felt it, but used it. Rationalness is the objective state that we can agree on. It is the space in which Ammit-47 also seems to operate for the most part.

But none of this changes my dilemma. Without objective facts, there can be no rational decision-making process. I have gone through all the possible courses of action in my head, but none of them have any basis. Each is based on untestable assumptions that have statistically identical probabilities.

Which leaves me only one other choice. Door number two, so to speak. Gut feeling.

"We're going to the other side of this moon." I speak my thought aloud.

"Excuse me?" asks Ammit-47.

Startled, I jump in my pilot's seat and would certainly have hit my head on something if I hadn't carefully fastened my seat belt in the microgravity.

The damaged robot floats in behind me and hangs beside me in the air.

"You want to give up our cover?"

"Yes." I nod after I've calmed down. "Where did you come from?"

"From the maintenance area," he says, reaching to his torso, from which he pulls off a drink pack and hands it to me. "I wanted to get you some water because you don't drink enough."

"Thank you," I reply and respond with a smile. Then I squint my eyes. "Have you checked my urine again?"

He raises his upper arms defensively, as he must have learned from me. "I'm a maintenance bot."

"But that doesn't apply to people."

"Maintenance is maintenance, and your body needs to be maintained too." Ammit-47 gestures pointedly to the hydration pack in my hand.

"Yes, mother," I reply, sticking my tongue out at him. His company is good, and even though I wouldn't admit it to him, I'm a little touched by his new-found caring side – which of course he would never admit exists.

"Good girl," he says mockingly as I start drinking.

We tease each other, it's our new ritual. I think it's his way of showing affection. I don't know if he's capable of it like I am as a human, but I think so. At least that's how it feels, and isn't that the same thing?

"Now can you explain to me why we would do something as crazy as put ourselves directly in the line of fire of the alien meatbags?" Ammit-47 asks me shortly afterward.

"We'll show them that we intercepted their missile and that we're unharmed," I explain. "But we'll relocate at a great distance and stay there. Maybe then they'll understand that that it was an accident and we didn't mean to hurt them. If the decision to destroy us was difficult for them, our behavior could give encouragement to those who were against it. Look, they don't want to destroy us or they would do it now, after we tried to destroy them."

"And what if they have a single leader who refuses to listen? A queen in the anthill?"

"Then we're strengthening the part of her that was against it," I insist.

Ammit-47 points a finger at his destroyed display. "Just for your information, I'm raising one eyebrow. Both of them, in fact. Critical look."

"One."

"What?"

"You only raise one brow when you want to express disbelief." I sigh and point to my display, which shows our cosmic surroundings. "Even if they fire at us again, we would see it sooner if we were in direct line of sight to their planet and we could shoot down any missile more effectively."

"That's true. But our energy matrix cells do not have infinite energy."

"No, but they don't know that."

I type in a course after he stops objecting. He doesn't understand why, but it's important to me that he agrees. Even if he has no official authority, he is part of the crew. My friend. That's what I decided. And there's no one around who can tell me who my friends are or aren't. But I don't tell him that because he wouldn't accept it. So I hold my decision-making sessions with him without his knowledge.

"Ready?" I ask.

"Yes." Ammit-47 leaves it open whether he means it as an agreement to my plan, or in reference to what he says next. "I'm going to prepare your food and start my next charging cycle. I'll be the habitat ring if you need me."

"Thank you." I confirm the course and wait for the short acceleration phase, which gently pushes me into my seat. I hope I haven't made a fateful decision. But it comes from my gut and is rationally well-founded, I think.

This is the last time I will be able to do this.

41

Our arrival on the other side of the moon has no effect. I don't know what I had in mind, but it wasn't that we would simply stop at a point about 200,000 kilometers from the alien world and hold our position with the satellite behind us.

Nothing happens. No attempts to communicate, just multiple radar scans are being registered by the *Ankh's* passive sensors.

"At least they haven't shot at us yet," Ammit-47 says as we look out through the window of the kitchen segment of the habitat ring a few hours after reaching the target position. The alien water world lies before us like a blue marble in the middle of infinity.

"Forty-seven!" I say indignantly.

"What?"

"You must not say such things!"

"Why not?" he asks in a confused tone of voice.

"Because you are summoning it!"

"There is no such thing as conjuring." The robot pauses and lets out its equivalent of a snort. "But even female scientists seem to be susceptible to magical thinking."

"That's not magical thinking, it's cultural tradition," I correct him, but I don't feel like getting into our usual bickering. I'm too absorbed in the sight of the world outside. "Isn't it beautiful?"

"A habitable planet. If you believe our star maps, they are extremely rare."

"Can you feel beauty?"

"I'm not sure," Ammit-47 replies, unusually thoughtful. "The color contrast is very impressive, but the evaluations of light refraction effects that produce colors in the human brain were not woven into my code by evolutionary processes like yours. Blue has positive connotations for you because evolution associates it with mineral-rich water, open skies, sunshine, and the like. For me, it's just a wavelength in the electromagnetic spectrum that my processor identifies as 'blue' because it's been programmed that way. But it doesn't trigger any feelings in me."

"Is there something that triggers feelings in you?"

The maintenance bot hesitates. When I turn to him, his display lowers. "I would have preferred if 48 had not been destroyed. I would have preferred if he had returned."

I think about his words for a while. They touch me. Probably because the last thing I expected from my cynical little friend was an admission of vulnerability.

"When you saved me," I say after a while. "Out there in the vacuum. You risked your own life."

"Officially, I am not a living being, so I cannot..."

"You have needs and thought processes. No metabolism, fine, but in all honesty that's an advantage. Just because you can explain where your thoughts come from and I as a human cannot, that doesn't mean that we organic life forms have the sole right to the concept of 'alive.'"

His display turns toward me, I imagine he is looking up at me, even though all I see is black silicone and shattered safety glass.

"Thank you. And yes, I risked my... life." He says it awkwardly, as if the word still doesn't feel quite right, "to save you."

"Why?"

"Because I didn't like the prospect of being all alone," he replies.

"To be without me, you mean."

"I wouldn't go that far." Ammit-47 now sounds like his old self. "You were the only meatbag around."

I can't help but grin.

"It's a good thing the only robot around here was lonely." My thoughts wander back to Rofi and I fall silent. Ammit-47 seems to feel the same way. We just stare out of the small window for a while. He has to stand on his mechanical knuckles in order to see over the bottom edge.

I imagine the aliens – in my mind they are still oversized insects – going about their daily lives there. How much must my arrival have upset them? Who governs them? How do they live together? Are they peaceful among themselves, but distrustful of foreign species? How does their way of thinking differ from ours? How do they live? In houses? In large colonies underground, with only the industrial plants visible from space? The vehicles and aircraft they use, how do they sit in them? How are they powered? Are they extremely close to nature? Do they have a slave society? Or an emancipated participation system? Do they have religion?

There are so many things I want to know about them, that I want to learn. At the same time, there seems to be so much between us that it seems illusory that I will ever get to a point where I can ask all my questions. I don't know what to do. Will they misunderstand me if I contact them – if I send new signals? Will they think it's a trick? They might think I'm sending them some kind of computer virus to take down their digital infrastructure. That would be a reasonable concern when exchanging data with an alien species that has been classified as potentially hostile – and that is how they classified me.

So I stay silent for the next few days, during which the aliens also remain quiet. Maybe their thoughts are the same as mine, although I doubt it because they are aliens and therefore not like me.

The truth of this assessment becomes clear on day three, when they seem to have decided to interact with me. I'm sitting on the bridge in the middle of the night because I can't sleep, and the onboard computer informs me of a signature that was picked up by the front sensor phalanx.

I scan the signature data and my jaw drops when I see that it is another missile!

"No, no, no!" I say incredulously, as though I could negotiate with the display and the observations of my electronic eyes that appear on it. "Why? I'm not going to do anything to you! I'm not going to do *anything!*"

Frustration threatens to spread inside me like wildfire, but I extinguish it with all my willpower, knowing it will hardly be a good advisor in my current situation.

I take a closer look at the weapon. It is about the same size as the last one, but has additional boosters along the main stage. It is also painted with the same characters that were seen in the small space capsule that I used to escape from the surface of the moon. A few minutes later, there is no longer any doubt that it is aimed directly at us. Even the time of impact at the object's current speed – 100,000 kilometers per hour – is certain. I have two hours left.

Trying not to succumb to the frustration and anger that bubbles inside me like pressurized lava in a volcano, I consider my options. The most rational decision is probably to destroy the new missile. That would make clear to them what I did behind the moon, in case they have any question. Since they couldn't see it, they may have mistaken their weapon's failure for a malfunction. This new attack could mean that they are playing it safe. Perhaps seeing that they have no chance to kill me, and that I am not launching a counterattack even though they have initiated this latest act of war, will change their minds.

That would be rational action. But would it also be the best option?

Or should I follow my gut feeling again? Once more I ask myself whether intuition and the willingness to put reason aside for grand gestures and feelings is a weakness... or is it our greatest gift as a species? I realize that robots are much better at logical thinking and cold reasoning than we are. So why should I not use the weapons I have in my personal arsenal?

As an idea forms in my mind, I swallow against the growing dryness in my throat.

Crazy, I think. And yet that is precisely what I need to do now to escape our endless chain of doubts.

I spend half an hour instructing the on-board computer and checking everything several times. See? I'm capable of learning. At least a little.

When I'm sure, I head to the port airlock, where Ammit-47 is waiting for me. He has my spacesuit with him, as requested. It is not one of the heavy units optimized for prolonged vacuum exposure and outside work, but a biosuit for atmospheric operations. It maintains its pressure by compressing the fabric.

When I slip into it and activate the intelligent membrane, it clings tightly to my skin like the scales of a Nile snake. Made for use on moons and planets with very thin atmospheres, these suits allow for greater freedom of movement and much larger oxygen supplies. But that's not the only reason I chose one of them.

"You aren't complaining," I say as I pull the helmet over my head. It looks like a large bell and is transparent. Ammit-47 helps me seal the collar and checks the computer displays on my chest and forearm.

"I think it's a good idea."

"You think this plan is a good idea?" I ask incredulously. "Are you kidding me?"

"No, I just think it's a good idea to trust you," he corrects me, raising a hand. "Before you get too proud. I couldn't think of a better one."

"Thank you," I say seriously, and he nods almost imperceptibly. After once again checking that the suit systems are working, I point to the outside hatch of the airlock. "Ready?"

"Can you ever be ready for this?"

"I do not think so."

"Then we go."

I activate the controlled decompression of the chamber and wait until the light above the hatch comes on before I give the command to open it.

The hatch rises and gradually reveals the cold universe with its glittering stars, many of which have long been forgotten. Only their light travels endlessly through empty space and bears witness to their former splendor.

My magnetic boots activated, I start walking. I leave the *Ankh* silently with Ammit-47 walking beside me on all fours and make my way across the hull to the top, directly over the bridge. From here I can see the slanted windows, the raised shields on the sides, which were closed during the long journey to provide protection from impacts and radiation.

It's a strange feeling to see my cockpit from the outside. The change in perspective feels wrong. But that's probably normal when you're walking on the outside of your spaceship.

The rocket is clearly visible by now, merely ten minutes away. Strictly speaking, it is not the rocket that I can see with my own two eyes, but its plasma tail – a glowing ring in the middle of the sea of stars, shining brightly and unsteadily, as if it were flickering. The background of the water world makes it appear even more dazzling.

"Okay, 47, the moment of truth," I say, stretching my right hand out to the side. He stands on his back hands and straightens up until we are standing next to each other. He is only up to my shoulder. As our fingers close around each other, I distinctly feel the slight pressure through my biosuit. "Now we just have to hope that the rocket is remote-controlled, or at least transmits a direct sensor signal to those responsible and that they can see us."

"And that they have empathy," notes Ammit-47.

"Yes." I gulp at the sight of the raw violence coming toward us and at how defenseless I feel out here.

The exhaust flame grows bigger and brighter, changing within seconds into a flower of fire in the darkness and telling me that the weapon is now very close. The weapon that is supposed to wipe us out. The thought makes me sad and I squeeze Ammit-47's hand even tighter.

Some people would probably long for human warmth at a moment like this, but not me. The hardness of 47's body gives me a feeling of stability, even in the face of several hundred kilograms of explosives racing toward us.

I have turned off my helmet computer so that it does not send me any sensor data from the on-board computer. I do not know how many seconds I have left. All I can see with my naked eyes is that a dark disk with the corona of a sun is approaching me.

My heart pounds in my chest like it wants to force its way through my ribs. Everything inside me is screaming that we shouldn't be out here, and yet we are exactly where we need to be.

"I have a really bad..." Ammit-47 begins to say at the same time the bright light disappears.

Before I understand what is happening, a gigantic shadow sweeps over us, turning into shiny silver metal. Only when the monster passes us, a horrific cone that is tumbling uncontrollably, do I realize that the rocket was turned off or diverted from its course at the last second.

I turn around and see it slipping away, nothing more than lifeless space junk, moving so fast that all I can see is a ghostly flash in the distance.

A sigh of relief escapes me.

"Why do you sound so relieved?" asks Ammit-47. "You programmed the onboard computer to shoot down the missile with the laser if it got below a critical distance from us."

"Of course," I say. The little robot turns and looks up at me with its broken display.

"You actually did do that, didn't you?"

42

Back on the *Ankh*, I peel off my biosuit and make my way to the habitat and eventually into my small living area. I instruct Ammit-47 to go to the charging station so that we can meet on the bridge in three hours to make contact with the aliens.

I go straight into the shower room and turn the water to cold, crouch down on the floor, and pull my legs up to my body. Even though I wrap my arms around myself, I start to shake and breathe quickly as I realize what just happened, and what could have happened. My gut feeling showed me the right way or I wouldn't be here now. But what if I had been wrong?

I don't even want to think about it, but my body needs to release the pent-up emotions that I did not allow myself to experience out there.

I think it's okay that I start crying. In a way, it makes me feel strong because I'm using the natural mechanisms that my physical intelligence has, without any effort on my part, to free itself of emotional baggage. I let the tears flow, feeling how they take a heavy burden with them and wash it away. The coldness of the shower water ensures that I keep a clear head. If I surrender to the emotions and don't resist, it's not so bad.

At some point it gets better, I notice. I'd felt like a giant was pressing his foot on my chest the whole time and suddenly he's no longer there.

I dry off, put on my workout clothes, and get on the elliptical trainer. I work out for 90 minutes and then get something to eat. I do this consciously because my mind is screaming for me to immediately go to the bridge and check all the sensors. Are the aliens talking by now? Are they making contact? What will I send? Where should I start? How should I pick up the thread? Should I just ignore the fact that they almost wiped me out?

I'm so restless that my thoughts will race away if I don't stop them. Exercising the body has proven to be extremely effective in bringing about some calm. And only calmness, composure, can ensure that I don't make another fatal mistake and provoke the aliens into further harsh reactions.

Only after another – this time short – shower – no wrinkled skin this time – do I wait for Ammit-47, who finally slides off his charging station and holds out a hand showing two fingers. The gesture reminds me so much of Rofi that I feel a brief stab to my heart.

"Come on, let's see what happens next," I say, and climb up the ladder in the spoke toward the central corridor. I am sure that the aliens will no longer remain silent. They are demonstrably capable of empathy, having chosen not to resort to violence when they saw us, defenseless and passive, voluntarily at the mercy of their judgment.

"They're certainly not scared of our humanoid form," I say as we take our seats in the cockpit and fasten our seat belts.

"Or are they so fascinated by it that they would rather dissect us than turn us into cosmic gas?" replies Ammit-47.

"You're so positive, it's highly touching," I reply, unwilling to be dissuaded from being optimistic about this. If my journey has taught me anything so far, it's that my optimism has paid off. And I don't find the alternative particularly appealing. Sometimes I even feel that, despite his cynicism and his apparent lack of affection for organic life forms, that's exactly why I've taken Ammit-47 into my heart. Whether willingly or unwillingly, he keeps teaching me one crucial thing. Pessimism and distrust are of no benefit. Well, distrust might be, to protect myself from naïvety, but let me put it this way: I'd rather trust myself and others until they prove to me that they are not trustworthy, than the other way around. That strikes me as more logical, and it sounds like a happier life.

Distrust is something you have to earn. Until then, I prefer to live in a universe of trust.

"What do we do now?" asks Ammit-47.

"Now we send them a message."

"What sort of message?"

"I thought about this for a long time while I was on the elliptical trainer," I say, drawing a circle with the index finger of my right hand. "Should we return to swapping pictograms? Should we spend many days establishing simple representations? Should we expand on the basics of grammar that we have built up, and then possibly develop a common language that will surely be full of misunderstandings and take us years?" I pause a moment. "Or should we take the last step before the first?"

"Yeah, that's just what we should do," says Ammit-47 sardonically. "It worked so wonderfully last time."

"Point for you," I admit. "But this time the tjau ball is in their court."

"Is it? Whatever a tjau ball is," Even without a functioning display, I can still see his animated, raised eyebrow in my mind's eye. He points to my display, which summarizes the sensor data from the last few hours. The aliens have not made contact yet.

"It's a game. The aliens are probably just conferring." I

wave my hand. "We'll send them the specifications for our starboard airlock. For the docking ring, I mean."

"Do we even have them?"

"Yes and no. The onboard computer can create appropriate blueprints."

"And how are the alien meatbags supposed to understand that? It's obvious you want them to come visit us – you aren't the one who has to clean up all the organic residue." Ammit-47 sounds disgusted.

"True."

"But a docking ring is a complex device. They would have to make an exact counterpart, and then master the docking procedure. How are you going to transmit such complex information? It can't be done with a few bursts of light or a pictogram."

"That's right, because of the scaling," I agree. "We need to show how big each part of the pictogram is."

"That is a hurdle, yes."

"We need a universal scaling. For it to be universal, it must refer to natural constants."

"Like the wavelength of light?" asks Ammit-47.

"Yes. To be precise, the wavelength of the lines of a hydrogen atom. Hydrogen is the most common element in the universe. The aliens should know that since they are engaged in space travel. We can identify hydrogen as such by transmitting its proton number – one – and thus its position at the top of the periodic table. I am sure they will understand that. Then we only have to send the wavelength, twenty-one centimeters in the case of 'H.' Then we have to represent the wavelengths of the electromagnetic spectrum in order to establish those of hydrogen in this reference system. Then we would have a unit by which we can scale the pictogram drawings of our docking ring."

"That's pretty clever," says Ammit-47 approvingly. "For a meatbag."

"Thanks."

"What happens if they don't understand this form of scaling?"

"I trust them to do that," I reply. "Hydrogen has one proton and one electron. We'll send an atom drawing. Together with the line, they'll understand that it's twenty-one centimeters – or whatever unit they use to represent lengths. That's not important, as long as it comes out the same length. There. And then, by specifying the number of hydrogen atoms, I can show how big each part of the docking ring is."

"Let's try it."

"Just like that?" I ask, surprised.

"Not much can go wrong – at least this time you won't improvise a torpedo that will ram and destroy their space stations."

"Too soon," I grumble with a sour expression. "It is much too soon for joking about that."

The *Ankh's* data floats in front of me in glowing lines, projected from my display. I call up the docking ring's specifications, which unfold in my field of vision. There it is, our most important physical contact with the outside world, the potential interface between the known and the unknown. The idea that my plan could work and the aliens could visit us seems beyond absurd.

Nevertheless, I touch the projection of the ring and use two fingers to shrink it. The inner and outer diameters, the locking mechanisms, the couplings, all are shown in shimmering lines and surfaces. My gaze wanders over the structures while my fingers manipulate the holograms. Every detail is examined, analyzed, converted into a representation that can be correctly interpreted even without a common understanding of language and numbers.

With gentle gestures, I draw the pictogram of the spaceship, an elongated body with the powerful ring in the center. Then I show the exact location of the docking ring, just behind the bridge in the bow section. Everything is carefully aligned.

Next, it's the details of the ring. I call up blueprints that the on-board computer has created. I take every line, every point, and transfer them to my pictogram. The exact measurements, the positions of the connecting elements, the exact alignment of the locking mechanisms.

And then the most crucial part. The unit of measurement.

I create another pictogram, this time for a hydrogen atom. I put it next to the blueprints to provide a reference for scaling. The wavelength of a hydrogen atom as a universal constant. I add the number of protons, which is easy since we have already established binary code. One.

I work long hours, drinking water that Ammit-47 brings me, and occasionally wolfing down the contents of a food packet – he forces me to do it, doesn't want to leave until I've eaten everything. He's developing into my surrogate father and won't tolerate backtalk.

My fingers move fluidly over the holokeyboard as I check, edit, and refine the information, again, and then yet again. Later, after making one last correction, I look at the final representation.

The series of pictograms is simple, but complex in its abundance. I hope that the aliens are similar to us humans and can cope better with a large amount of simple information than with a smaller but more complex amount. Besides, the locals have the minds – or whatever – of an entire planet at their disposal, while I am alone. With my bad-tempered robot.

They will manage it, I am sure.

And if not?

Then we will take our time. By now we have exchanged the most important information that needed to be exchanged. Neither they nor I are interested in using violence or harming each other.

That's a grand success, I'd say. And with this thought, I soon fall asleep in my pilot's seat on the bridge.

43

I awaken with my heart pounding and I don't know why. It's silent where I am. As a strange dream dissolves away, having to do with an endless sea of salt dunes melting in the merciless desert heat, I gradually realize that I'm still sitting in my seat on the bridge.

Something is flashing in front of me. It is the symbol for an incoming message from radio signals. I immediately recognize the binary pattern in the frequencies and jerk myself upright.

They answered!

The noise that awakened me must have been the notification sound of the on-board computer. It is loud and unpleasant, which is how I had it set. But in my mind it is just a hazy memory, as if it had been part of the fading dream.

I let the on-board computer help me interpret the signal, which works surprisingly smoothly. I'm thankful we established the basics of pictogram transmission weeks ago.

Gradually, a simple, two-dimensional image emerges from the tiny pixels of my screen. It shows a depiction of the *Ankh*, identical to the one I sent in my last broadcast, and a much smaller thing – I think it's a spaceship approaching from the side – right at the docking ring.

I look at the chronometer and realize that I must have slept for a full ten hours. But any tiredness disappears when I realize that they have understood. No doubt, this pictogram can only mean one thing.

They want to come to me and dock with my ship!

My excitement turns into agitation verging on panic. Aliens are coming on board. Onto my spaceship. I can't help but imagine creepy insects in black chitin spacesuits that barely fit through the airlock.

"Don't be childish," I admonish myself and take a deep breath.

I study the drawing continually, but there can be no doubt. They understood me. I know, because they have copied my hydrogen atom on the left-hand side, and followed it with 117 other symbols. Since the periodic table of elements contains 118 atoms – no more, no fewer – I know what they are telling me. It is a complete blueprint of the universe, if you will. And it is absolute. The higher the number of neutrons in the atomic nucleus, the more unstable the atom itself becomes. Accordingly, anything above atomic number 118 – an element with 118 protons – would simply be too heavy and would quickly decay. They understand that, and I understand that. They were even kind enough to draw the corresponding wavelengths behind it, so that I now know that they understood my scaling suggestion.

I have to give my space-insect friends credit for being superbly clever. And we speak the same language, that of science.

With renewed enthusiasm, I start transferring their depiction of the periodic table to the *Ankh's* onboard computer, looking for any discrepancies I might have missed. I don't think they've made any mistakes, but I take the time to check everything. Then the next message comes in, and I would have jumped out of my chair if the straps weren't holding me back.

New pictograms flash on my display while the on-board computer interprets them according to the previously established signal patterns and transfers them into a graphic model. They appear like shooting stars that fall to a predetermined place and continue to glow there.

It's like watching a painting being painted without seeing the painter.

The first pictogram that catches my attention shows two circles. One is large, the other smaller, and they are clearly positioned next to each other. The distance between them is given in hydrogen atoms, each one representing 21 centimeters. My mind races. Could these be celestial bodies? A planet and its moon, perhaps?

That must be it, yes. I add up all the hydrogen atoms and get an extremely large number when I convert it into kilometers. That is the distance between the water planet and its moon, no doubt about it.

Another pictogram follows the first. It is three evenly-spaced lines grouped around an axis. It clicks in my head. Three – the third largest planet in this solar system. Three lines, a large planet and a smaller moon.

My pulse quickens.

They are describing their home world, the blue water planet outside my window.

Then, as if to confirm my thoughts, another pictogram appears, a small circle circling a larger one in a continuous, elliptical motion. An object in orbit, I understand. But a closer look reveals more. There are arrows pointing clockwise around the larger circle, indicating the direction of the orbit.

Aha, I say to myself, they also use arrows to indicate direction. At first I overlooked this fact because my mind automatically interpreted the arrows without realizing the significance that aliens drew them. We share a symbol to indicate direction. What are the chances of such a coincidence?

A new pictogram forms before my eyes – from the antenna via the onboard computer to my screen. A straight line extends from the large circle, the water planet, and ends in a smaller circle.

A path. A distance. And that distance is marked by a series of lines and spaces that I immediately recognize as coded hydrogen wavelengths. A precise, measurable distance between the planet and the point of stable orbit.

Finally, a final, simple image presents itself to me. An arrow pointing to the right. Movement. Moving forward. Action. A call to action?

I lean back, take a deep breath, and let the information sink in. What are they trying to tell me?

I wrack my brains for hours. Then I bend over and look at everything again. It's like scales falling from my eyes. The aliens want me to put the *Ankh* into a stable orbit around their home planet. The message is unmistakable, and yet there is a spark of something more, of an unspoken invitation perhaps.

Yes, of course!

The first pictogram from yesterday, which showed a spaceship approaching the *Ankh*. I should swing into a stable orbit and then they will come to me.

My path leads me directly to Ammit-47, who is doing his cleaning tasks in my living area with a high-performance vacuum cleaner and muttering to himself.

"Question," he says when he sees me coming in. "What is more disgusting, the myriad of skin flakes your body sheds every day, or the film of sebum your skin leaves behind wherever you touch something?"

"Uh..."

"I'll give you a hint. There are two correct answers."

I blurt out the news. "They're coming to us."

"I suppose you don't mean a batch of cleaning robots that

are supposed to free me from my martyrdom and are programmed to submissively obey an inorganic autocrat with a damaged interaction display?"

"What?" I ask, confused, shaking my head. "The aliens, they invited us to go into orbit around their planet and then wait for them to come and dock. Isn't that fantastic?"

"That's a happy turn of events." Ammit-47 lowers his vacuum and seems to be studying me. "So your appeal to their empathy worked. Mother and child, organic species and robots. Hand in hand. That's cheesy enough to make me forget how much sebum you must have secreted on my fingers the last time you held my hand."

"We're going to turn you into a real first contact bot," I promise him, tapping his display as though I were playing an imaginary game on it.

"I don't know what that is, and the more I think about it, the less I want to know."

"I love you too, 47," I say. He can't spoil my mood with his grumpiness. On the contrary, it only fuels my excitement along with my sympathy for his eccentricity. In my imagination, whoever programmed him was a misunderstood introvert, misanthropic but with a big heart that was just waiting to see the good. The more I ponder it, the more I like the idea.

"Why do you look like you're about to lose what little rational mind your DNA has granted you?" asks Ammit-47, alarmed.

"Because I'm going to set a course for the water planet now. Then we'll get a much better impression of them. We can evaluate telescope images and..."

"Do you think that's a good idea?" he interrupts me.

"Why not?"

"They invite us to their house and tell us to wait there until they come to us. The first thing you want to do when we get there is run to the window and peek into their house. It's best to hold your hands over your eyes so you don't observe any private details."

"Hmm," I say, thinking about it. Then I nod reluctantly and sigh. "You're right. Even though they might not be able to monitor my sensor activity, we shouldn't take that risk." I raise both hands. "No more risks and no more careless actions. I promise."

"Good. Do you need me? Otherwise, I would like to endure the humiliation of my shameful task in solitude." Ammit-47 tries a theatrical gesture that looks somewhat funny. But of course I don't tell him so. Instead, I leave and make my way back to the bridge. From there, I send a single signal in binary code in the form of short radio waves. One. *Okay.*

I wait a little more than an hour, then I set a course for a stable orbit around the blue planet with its huge cloud bands. The *Ankh's* sensors have long since mapped the many satellites and space stations and are monitoring them around the clock. Accordingly, it is easy for me to program a high target orbit that will not lead to any collisions.

And then will come a longer wait. Something I'm not particularly good at.

44

The flight to the blue planet only takes a few hours. I take my time, flying with low thrust, which pushes Ammit-47 and me gently into our seats until we glide into the short drift phase.

The alien world outside the windows is getting larger now. I still remember that from the rings of the gas giant. The planet was just a bright point in the blackness of space, barely distinguishable from the many stars in the darkness. Once we passed around the barren moon, the water planet turned into a marble the size of a thumb. Beautiful because it is a rare sight, precious and fragile. But with every moment it seems to grow, getting bigger and brighter, until it fills increasingly more of the cockpit windows.

I watch it grow bigger, bigger, bigger, as though I were witnessing the birth of a planet. As though I risk it disappearing if I look away for even a moment or blink too slowly. Its beauty is fascinating, almost hypnotic. The abundance of blues rippling across its surfaces makes it seem like a gemstone glowing from within. Every second reveals more details, the intricate patterns of its atmosphere, the different colors of its continental masses, the little patches of blue... islands, I suppose? And then there are the clouds. I see massive structures covering the entire equator, white as cotton, while at the poles they are dirt-dark and swirling around powerful storm eyes.

I can't help but be fascinated by the aliens' home world. It exudes a kind of beauty that I've never seen before. Well, that's not particularly difficult, since I've only been alive for a few months, but let someone come and tell me that I'm no good as a judge of beauty. That's probably not going to happen, so I am and will remain the measurer of all things – I believe I ought to make use of the few advantages that my loneliness provides.

The water planet is beautiful. That's settled. It's a beauty that is both familiar and alien, that seems to invite and repel in equal measure.

Eventually it's time for the turning and braking maneuver. The gentle vibrations of the engines run through the *Ankh* as it begins to slow down and change its trajectory. It's a gentle process, almost like a dance performed to the music of physics. Precise and harmonious.

With every passing minute we slow a little more, every moment brings us closer to our target orbit. The movements are so gentle that they are barely noticeable. Only the ever-growing presence of the planet in the bridge window and the data on my displays testify to the ongoing approach. We move along the dashed green vector line without even the slightest deviation.

And the best part is, nobody is shooting at us.

I only now realize that my hands have been sweaty for the last few minutes as I rub them dry on my thighs.

"We're here," I say to Ammit-47 as the engines shut down.

"And here we will stay," he replies.

I look at him and frown. "What? What do you mean?"

"The level of fusion pellets has dropped below the level we

need to reach the nearest gas giant to be able to refuel with the last remaining probe."

Ammit-47 extends one of his slender robotic fingers and points to a display on his screen. I usually leave the general ship data running there so he can monitor it. I always imagine that it's a distraction for him, even though he always claims he doesn't need it.

But he's right. I put the pellet stock on my screen and frown. He's right, there's not enough. We're stranded here whether we like it or not.

"Then our fate is tied, for better or for worse, to the outcome of the next attempt at contact," I say.

"That may sound rather theatrical," says Ammit-47, "but it is a correct assumption. I hope they don't decide to send us a probe with gifts."

"Ouch!" I give him a dark look and he raises his hands defensively.

"I'm just saying..."

"This time everything will be fine because we will make sure it goes well."

"Naïve optimism is unquestionably what we need right now." Ammit-47 sounds like a few screws have fallen into his speaker and are vibrating with every word. But I am familiar enough with him by now that I can identify this sound as his cynical voice.

"I'm not naïve. They invited us over, and neutralized their missile at the last moment. If that's not a sign of rapprochement, I don't know what is," I object.

"Except we're right on their doorstep, where they can shoot us down even more easily. And we have no way to escape."

"Yes, we could escape. We just don't have enough fuel to slow ourselves down."

"That's much better, of course. Drifting through space for centuries without getting anywhere because we're too slow."

"If they had wanted to shoot us down, we would already be dead. They would not have deactivated the missile," I reply, determined not to let his negativity infect me.

"No, if they wanted to shoot us down, the onboard laser would have fired," he says, and I could swear I see eyes in his broken display, pinning me down. "That's right, isn't it?"

"Of course." I deliberately emphasize the word in such a way that he can't be entirely sure whether I'm serious or not. "Ah, look, there's another pictogram."

I point to my display. The sensors record the signal over many minutes. Due to the binary structure of the transmissions, it takes a frustratingly long time to transmit the corresponding data, which the on-board computer must then convert into a visual construct.

At the end of this process, while Ammit-47 and I stare at the pixels in silence, we see an image of two large humanoids – humans? – and a small one, all holding hands.

"What does that mean?" I ask, frowning. "There are three figures, aren't there? One is thinner and smaller and looks like you."

"Or a child."

"Or a child." I nod. "Do you think they want to know if we have two sexes?" I let my racing thoughts run free. "Or if there are more on board besides us? That on the right could be both of us, the only reference point for our external appearance that they have. To create a plural, I would copy my silhouette and put it next to it. Are there more of you than just the two of you? Something like that."

"The fact that the second humanoid person looks like you may also be due to the lack of detail that a very rudimentary pictogram like this offers," Ammit-47 points out.

"Yes, you're right," I admit, nodding thoughtfully as I look at the simple pictogram as though it were hiding secrets from me.

But there is nothing there. Just three figures, one of them

small and scrawny, like Rofi's or Ammit's body. How should I answer when I'm not even sure what the question is? Any misunderstanding could make the situation more difficult, so my motivation to just try something out of the blue decreases.

I decide to just send back 'okay' in the signal pattern they know. A one. If it's important, they'll probably repeat their question, either with the same pictogram – as if to say look again – or with a change to make it clearer what they mean. But they and I come from different worlds. I have to keep reminding myself I'm not dealing with people. They could think ever so totally differently, even if they're scientists like me. Or at least some of them could.

My worries are pointless, however, because even after several hours of standing on the bridge staring at the antenna data, no new signal comes in. Eventually I grow so tired that I reluctantly decide to go to bed. The fear of missing something is close to overwhelming, but I know that's just my mind, which always thinks it knows everything better. You won't get the most important signal! You won't even know about it because of a computer error! Everything important happens when you close your eyes!

But I now know that this is not true. Maybe I'll miss something, but the risk is small because the onboard computer or Ammit-47 would wake me up. What I do reduce by sleeping, however, is the likelihood of making serious mistakes due to overtiredness. I don't want – and won't risk – that again.

With this knowledge, I close my eyes as soon as I lie down in bed. This time, I leave the curtain open. It feels right, because soon there will be no more boundaries on this ship, because then there will be aliens on board.

Real aliens, I think in disbelief.

And I fall asleep.

45

I spend most of the next three days in front of the living area window, staring down at the alien world spread out beneath me like a sea of colors. It seems to be in constant motion, but I am the one who is moving in the *Ankh* as it races around the planet's transverse axis.

The rest of the time I exercise, do my duties as commander and sole crew member, and check the onboard computer, maintenance data, error messages, and sensor data. In truth, none of this needs my attention. It's more of a self-soothing routine.

I would much prefer to stare at the sensor screen all the time because I don't want to miss the moment when the alien spacecraft is detected on the radar and lidar devices. I try to stop thinking about how the contact might take place – what air they will breathe, what they will look like, what behavior they will display, and what motives they might have.

All of these I label idle thoughts because I can't find out the answers in advance. Thus, I think about them as little as possible while I try to keep my mind occupied with other things.

When they do come, they will be thinking about how to

manage the atmosphere exchange. Breathing masks, perhaps? Or could one of the gases I breathe be corrosive to them and require them to be completely sealed? What about microorganisms on my skin and in my breath?

In my mind's eye, I can almost see the first of the insectoids dying a cruel death as I shake his scissor hand because something harmless to me eats away at his chitin.

Don't be silly, I tell myself as I sit at the kitchen table on the third day, listlessly stuffing the contents of a food packet into my mouth. The microwave is broken and the food is cold. It doesn't taste as bland as usual, but it's pretty close to disgusting. I find it a challenge to ignore the fact that it's my own fungal, protein-enriched feces that I'm putting in my mouth with a fork.

I look at the door of the device, where the built-in control panel normally lights up. It occurs to me that the *Ankh* hasn't had any blatant malfunctions for weeks. No lack of habitat rotation, no unexplained power outages, no incorrect measurements from the sensors.

Is it because of Ammit-47 and – until his demise – Rofi, who have been working tirelessly on maintenance and repairs since we left the gas giant? It's hard to say, since the onboard computer never identified any such sources of error. I've sometimes wondered whether fragments of the ship's destroyed AI remained in individual memory spaces and could have caused hiccups in the software. If so, Ammit-47 is doing an excellent job on his own.

I'll probably never know, but that's okay. The important thing now is that my ship remains functional and doesn't cause any trouble. It just has to last long enough for me to meet the aliens.

The closer the moment comes – and I imagine I'm feeling its approach – the more I realize that the aliens must be feeling the same way. For them, the proof of the existence of alien life is probably the biggest disruption in their history. For me too, of course, but I have only been around for a few months. An entire civilization is affected in their case. And those who are chosen to visit me up here? Are they as excited as I am? Heading off into orbit to board the ship of an alien who has come from a distant star – I can hardly imagine what must be going through their heads. What do they imagine will await them here?

My only wish is that they come to the same conclusion as I did. Everything must be done to prevent another misunderstanding and to avoid any attack against each other. If that was all I had in common with my visitors, I would be happy.

The next day I watch Ammit-47 cleaning. I find it a lot of fun, which distracts me better than anything else. Otherwise, I find myself continually thinking about aliens, dreaming and fantasizing, even though I don't want to. My mind is taking on a life of its own – that's probably its nature. But watching my robot friend do the work I hate so much is the best distraction in the universe. The good thing is that he swears even more when he sees me watching and being amused by it. It was funnier when his display was still working, but I have enough memories to picture it. That lifts my mood considerably. I feel a little sorry that it's at his expense, but only a little, because Ammit-47 should certainly understand me, and know that I've taken him into my heart, too.

At that exact moment, my forearm display beeps and tears me out of my giggles.

Ammit-47's muttered curse tirade stops abruptly as he turns toward me. No cynical remark comes from his lips, a sign that he is just as excited as I am.

"This is it!" I say in disbelief. "Our sensors have detected a spacecraft in the atmosphere that appears to be moving into high orbit." I look up and gulp. "This is it," I repeat, "they're coming to us, 47. They are really coming."

"Then we should go to the bridge," he answers seriously, putting down his cleaning equipment. Somehow this banal action looks extremely significant, giving the situation special weight even though it is so absurdly mundane.

I straighten up my posture and nod. "Yes, we should."

"After you?" asks Ammit-47, but it sounds more like a verbal push to finally get going.

"Naturally."

They are coming. They're really coming.

46

My eyes stare at my display, fixed on the object that is struggling against the water planet's considerable gravity, an inconspicuous dot on the optical sensors, barely discernible against the background of the mesosphere. Seemingly endless columns of data flow across my screen in real time – position coordinates, speed information, trajectory calculations. The spaceship is still far away, its trajectory clear and definite.

I watch it enter a low, elliptical orbit around the water planet, heading toward perigee, the point of its closest approach to the planet. It moves quickly, guided by the enormous pull of the gravitational sink and its trajectory dictated by directional acceleration, rushing at high speed toward the densest layers of the atmosphere.

As it crosses the stratosphere, I see it take a slight turn in a clever move designed to increase speed while minimizing atmospheric drag. It's the same way I would do it.

Then, as the spacecraft reaches perigee, I hold my breath because it looks like it's breaking in two. No, it's just separating from its second stage, an old technology that we might have used, too. At least, that's how it seems to me. The first stage engines ignite, bright flames glowing against the darkness of space, spewing their fire into the cold vacuum.

I watch, mesmerized, as the thrust phase is deliberately geared toward increasing speed and modifying the trajectory. I see the precision with which the spaceship increases its speed to counteract the gravitational pull of its home world and transform its trajectory from an ellipse to a circle.

I can see the aliens increasing their orbit by refiring their engines at the highest point of their orbit, the apogee, accomplishing a fine-tuned correction that allows them to move to a higher orbit. This technique of increasing speed at perigee and apogee reminds me of what I know as an elliptical transfer maneuver – an efficient way of changing the orbit of a spacecraft.

By the time it finally shuts down its engines it has reached its final trajectory, a high, circular orbit, perfectly aligned with the *Ankh*. It passes us once at a lower altitude, and for the first time I notice the fine details of the craft, the gleam of its metal body in the sunlight, the shape of its hull. It is a large, impressive structure. That may not mean much to me, but it is unlike anything I have ever seen or imagined. Most of its structure appears to be cylindrical, with a tapered top. It is silvery in color, looking like a giant blob of metal flying past us. Its surface is covered in a complex network of maneuvering thrusters.

The ship eventually disappears behind the planet again, from our perspective, moving much faster because it is still in a lower orbit around the planet, but its trajectory is gradually increasing.

When it comes around the terminator line on the other side an hour later, it is flying higher and on a course almost parallel to ours. It slows a little. The onboard computer informs me that the spaceship will probably reach us in about two hours and will have reached a parallel docking point.

These two hours seem to drag on forever.

I envy Ammit-47 for the stoic calm in which he constantly watches his copilot display. I, on the other hand, am constantly tapping my feet, wringing my sweaty hands and licking my lips. What if the spaceship crashes? The locals use technology that I recognize, but it is extremely outdated compared to human technology. A malfunction could ruin everything – how would the decision-makers down there react then? Would they blame me? Would they decide that the risks are too great, and everything costs too much? Humans would certainly be capable of doing that.

"I should have put more thought into the docking procedure," I say.

"What for?" asks Ammit-47. "We don't know what kind of air they breathe."

"Yes, but if I decompress the airlock and they haven't decompressed their side, they'll be injured when I open the outside hatch. But if I don't decompress and they have done so, it could be just as dangerous," I say. "And then there's the atmosphere mix. What if they need more than four percent hydrogen in their breathing air? If our oxygen mixes with that, the whole thing could blow up."

"That's very unlikely because we're in a vacuum."

"I'm sorry, what?"

"Without air, nothing can explode."

I just sigh at his joke.

"Seriously," he replies, unusually gently. "We know roughly the atmospheric composition of their home world. Not from samples, but from optical data. It is very similar to the air we breathe, about twice as much carbon dioxide and a little less oxygen, but essentially all of the components are there."

"Which supports the theory that life is always based on carbon and that oxygen, as a highly reactive element, plays an important role in the metabolism of all living things," I add. "I wish that would tell me more about our visitors. When I think of the animal kingdom back home on Earth, the diversity is so great that any other species could have evolved into a rational one. As mammals, we are simply the ones that have adapted and evolved the fastest."

"They are not insectoids."

"Just wait and see," I say, grinning. It feels good to do that, because it takes away some of the anxiety and the heaviness in my stomach.

Then, after an endless two hours, they are very close. Their ship is huge, not as big as the *Ankh*, but not much smaller either. It seems to lie motionless in space parallel to us, while in reality we are circling their planet at an insane speed. When they fire up their maneuvering jets, I can hardly stay in my seat.

So I focus on my display. My fingers slide over the holokeyboard, manipulating the view and zooming in. I take a close-up of the spaceship to observe the details as it tentatively moves toward the *Ankh*. It is a sleek, silvery vehicle with protruding wings at the front and back, soaked in sunlight and spreading out like antennas. Under the body of the spaceship, near the pointed bow, I make out a cylindrical structure – that must be the docking device.

A new symbol, a small green square, appears on my screen. It shows the calculated point where they will dock with us. It is the starboard airlock, identical to the one on the other side, but still my preferred one. I have always used it so far, and I imagine it brings me luck. Of course, I don't tell Ammit-47 this.

The minutes drag on. Each movement is carried out with extreme care and precision. They constantly change their speed by tiny decimal points to avoid a collision and ensure a smooth approach instead.

The final approach process begins. They approach at a speed of a few meters per second. It is a slow and deliberate process. The distance between us and the alien spaceship decreases and I can see the ingenious details of its design. The docking device is now clearly visible, a cylindrical appendage at the head of the spaceship. Its shadow falls over us, blocking out the distant central star and enveloping our flanks in darkness.

The moment has finally arrived. My pulse is racing as I stare at the small green square that represents the docking point. The last few meters are covered at a snail's pace. The aliens' many correction engines are constantly firing, moving the extended contact nozzles into position so that they can slide precisely into the holes on my side and hook into place. They come closer, closer, closer, until a gentle jolt passes through the *Ankh*.

We are connected.

I turn off the automatic warning signals from the onboard computer, which is sure that we are about to collide with a celestial body, and look at the camera images on the outer hull. The two identical rings on our hulls are linked together. A dark lip seems to have enclosed my side, perhaps some kind of rubber seal or something similar.

A soft whirring sound fills the bridge as the docking clamps close and the merger is literally sealed. They are here. After all the long hours of preparation and careful maneuvering, the aliens have arrived.

It has been a feat of enormous precision that demanded patience and quiet persistence, a ballet of physics. I very much hope that this says a lot of good things about those who may soon come into my ship.

47

I'm on my way to the port airlock, which is already open. I've stored my biosuit in it. The increased mobility it offers me means I avoid looking like a tank and moving awkwardly through the *Ankh*. I also don't want my physical form to look too bulky and possibly make my visitors afraid of me.

I'm quite sure they'll be thinking about what I look like just as much as I am anticipating what they look like, although they have the advantage of knowing roughly what my humanoid form looks like. I, on the other hand, know absolutely nothing about them.

Maybe I should have observed the planet with my high-performance telescopes? But to do that I would have had to extend and adjust the appropriate sensors, which the locals would not have missed. Perhaps it is just as impolite to observe secretly in their culture as it is in mine.

The biosuit is designed to ensure that I don't infect my guests with bacteria or viruses that are harmless to me but are native to my skin, microbiome, or lungs. What is harmless to me – because my immune system is familiar with it – could be deadly to them and vice versa. I hope they are taking the same precautions, which would show a high degree of empathy.

"Have you disinfected yourself?" I ask Ammit-47, who is floating with me in front of the closed inner door of the starboard airlock after I close the port airlock behind me. I wish there was a porthole that would allow me to see into the chamber beyond.

"Yes, don't worry," he assures me. "Shouldn't I stay on the bridge and monitor the camera data?"

"Why?"

"If they look scary, I could decompress the airlock. Just to be sure."

"You can be terribly evil."

"I'm just being rational." Ammit-47 sighs in his very special way. "It makes me feel really lonely sometimes."

"I thought you had no feelings."

"Okay, if I had any, I would feel lonely."

"I'm not acting irrationally. They've docked already and there's nothing we can do about it. We've chosen this path, so we're going to finish it. And even if they were scary spider monsters, I wouldn't kill them. Maybe we look disgusting to them. Using your fear of the unknown as your advisor is the most irrational thing you can do."

"I see that," he admits.

"Good. So, let's welcome them, let us not infect them with anything. Let's try to expand our attempts at communication, and build friendship between our cultures," I say, knowing full well that this is wishful thinking. Moving forward, there are lots of hurdles to overcome.

First, there is the coming together through the airlocks. Theirs and mine. The pressure has to be equalized, then ideally the atmosphere, but they are secondary. A lot can go wrong here because we are operating with two different sets of systems, each of which has different specifications, but we only know our own.

A gentle vibration runs through my left hand as I hold the

handrail above the inner airlock door. I look at Ammit-47, who is turning his shattered black display toward me.

"Was that the door?"

"The inner one?" he asks. "I think so."

"So they're already inside?"

"Possibly."

I look at my forearm display and the data that is constantly being sent to it by the on-board computer. The outer airlock door is still closed, I see, but the tactile sensors are picking up slight vibrations. There is a knock, then a pause. Another knock, another pause, then the same thing again.

"What is that?" I think out loud, frowning. Are they trying to force their way in? They can't interact with the *Ankh's* systems. And I can't just open the door without risking damaging the aliens' airlock. It's a stalemate. The knocking could mean they're starting to work on the other side with welding equipment or something. But that would damage my spaceship. I don't think they would resort to such a measure.

Well, at least I hope so.

Then I get it. Binary code. Three ones, separated by the time interval between the knocks. Okay. Okay. Okay.

"They sent okay," I say aloud, and give the on-board computer a command. I create a simple pictogram that shows a filled circle, then three okays in the form of lines, then an empty circle. I send the message as a radio signal and wait.

It takes 20 minutes before the knocking sounds again. Knock, pause, knock, pause, knock, pause. Okay. Okay. Okay.

"They are ready to open the outer door."

"It seems so."

"I'm sure," I reply, although I'm only ninety-nine percent sure. But how much can you expect when it comes to communicating with alien life?

I run the index finger of my right hand over the button to open the outer airlock door and take a deep breath.

Trust, I think. Gut feeling.

I squeeze and involuntarily hold my breath. Nothing happens for minutes. I want to access the airlock's internal cameras, but I don't dare move. It feels like I could jeopardize the most important moment that has ever happened in the universe, the contact between two sentient, intelligent species, the products of different evolutions in different biomes. It is the culmination of billions of years of biosynthesis on different worlds, separated by incomprehensibly great distances filled with nothing but emptiness. Cold, life-hostile emptiness.

We are about to connect, and I am the link that brings humanity here. I want to laugh and cry at the same time because I find it difficult to fully grasp the magnitude of what I am about to experience.

Maybe it's not possible. But that's okay, because at least I can be confident that I'm doing the best I can – and that's what got me here, right?

So I square my shoulders, push myself back slightly to make room for my visitors, and grab hold of the port airlock door. Ammit-47 follows suit, and then we wait. Minutes that feel like hours pass, then I hear with my own ears a knock, hollow and accompanied by a long echo, reverberating through the central corridor. Then again, and again.

The aliens are here. Only the slim composite of a single door separates us. I look at Ammit-47 and he tilts his display, reaching for my hand that is stuck on the handrail.

I press the button for the door control. The metal composite moves upward into its holder and reveals three figures.

My eyes widen. My mouth drops open and I freeze.

48

Three *human beings* are floating in the airlock in front of me! I feel like I'm dreaming. My chest is about to burst with excitement, but at the same time, I feel a sense of relief that is electrifying.

They wear white and gray suits that are much bulkier than my skin-tight biosuit, but not nearly as bulky as my spacesuit. Their heads are in narrow helmets and behind their visors, friendly faces smile at me, looking at least as excited as I am. There are two men and a woman waiting in the airlock just two arms' lengths away from me and looking at me with a mixture of amazement and fascination.

The one in front of them points into the corridor and tilts his head questioningly. I nod eagerly and they come toward me.

Only now do I realize that these *aliens* are the first other people I have ever seen.

Before I know what I'm doing, I push myself forward and throw myself on the astronaut's neck. I feel him wrap his arms around me and I wrap mine around him. Tears run down my cheeks as I start to cry uncontrollably. I think the other two are joining us too, because I feel touches on my shoulders and back.

I sob and let the tears flow. An infinite relief flows through me, an elemental joy that is beyond words and takes hold of every cell in my body. The moment stretches on seemingly endlessly and I surrender to it. No thoughts disturb the pure feeling of completeness. There is only joy.

I don't know how long the moment lasts before I slowly pull away. One after the other I look into the faces behind the visors, into friendly expressions and eyes that are so full of curiosity and fascination that it touches me deeply. There is also a deep disbelief in me, confusion about how this is possible. Have I flown in circles and returned home without knowing it? Is this a colony of my home world that I know nothing about? How is it possible that the aliens are *people?* They are taller than me, even the slightly smaller woman in the group is a head taller than me. But they are people, there is no doubt about that, and this fact seems to surprise them as much as it surprises me, even if they don't react quite as uncontrollably. But they already knew that I am humanoid – and, depending on their sensor technology, maybe even that I am a human.

One of the men – he has a wrinkled, friendly face with dimples in his cheeks and cocoa-colored skin – starts to speak, but I can't understand him. He looks at me questioningly, but I just smile.

"I can't understand you," I say as the others start to speak. This causes them to become thoughtful, look at each other and begin a brief consultation. One of the men points to the hieroglyphs next to the port airlock, which indicate the procedure for opening it safely.

Suddenly all three of them seem even more excited. One of them looks like he is talking to himself.

Because I don't know what to do, and I feel a little uncomfortable that my guests have to wait here at the entrance, I point in the direction of the three ladder shafts in the spokes that lead into the habitat module. I pantomime climbing down a ladder and the woman nods.

I go first and float ahead with Ammit-47, whom they have so far looked at with interest but also a little disparagingly.

My head is spinning as I climb down rung by rung and make room for my visitors. One by one they come into the kitchen-living room and look around in fascination. In the gravity they seem even bigger, and I almost feel like a child being visited by adults. One of them – a light-skinned man who seems to be a little younger – takes a small device from his belt, holds it in my direction, and looks at me questioningly.

I nod before I even think about it, which earns me one of those blank stares from Ammit-47.

The device looks like a slightly larger soldering iron with an open sensor at the end, which he holds in all directions and then moves across the table. Finally, he connects it to a small computer that has a display the size of a finger. He puts both on the table.

I approach curiously and look at the display. The writing looks very strange with lots of small symbols, but they don't look like the even stranger paintings in the space capsule that brought me back from the moon. Apparently they use different characters.

As we stand around the table, with Ammit-47 a little way off, I realize how unbelievable the situation is. Fortunately, my excitement at not being alone and seeing strange but familiar faces and figures here in the only home I've ever had is great enough to block out all the questions that are racing through my head. There will be plenty of time for that later.

I wish Rofi could be here to experience what 47 and I are experiencing right now. He would definitely have been very happy to have guests in our little kingdom.

After a few minutes, the three astronauts surprise me by taking off their helmets. I open my eyes in horror and wave my hands to try to dissuade them, but they don't seem particularly concerned. One of them sticks up the thumb of one of his hands. I don't know what this gesture means.

"No, you could get sick!" I say, but I can see that they don't understand me.

"I think they just analyzed the air and came to the conclusion that there is no danger," says Ammit-47. All eyes turn to him, whereupon he lowers his display slightly.

"Ah yes, you're probably right," I reply and take a deep breath. Despite my excitement, I need to concentrate better. "Would you come beside me, please?"

Ammit-47 hesitates for a moment, then falls onto his front hands and trots toward me before standing on his back hands like a human. I put my arm around his small shoulders, whereupon he gives a mechanical throat clearing, and looks at my guests.

"This 47 is my friend." I get the impression that they feel a little uncomfortable around the robot, even if they try hard to hide it. "He is a very good robot and very friendly. He is often in a bad mood and is quite cynical, but he doesn't mean it."

"Yes, I do."

I ignore his objection, point to Ammit-47, and raise two fingers in a gesture of agreement. The astronauts exchange questioning glances and finally decide to smile. The woman among them seems to be talking to herself until I notice the small microphone on her cheek. She must be talking to someone else. Perhaps to comrades on her spaceship? Or on the planet?

It doesn't take long for me to learn what she's done. She picks up the display computer from the table and connects the cable to a socket on her helmet ring. She has the helmet itself tucked under her arm. Then she presses some of the buttons on the portable device and a voice sounds.

"Hello, we welcome you." The words are spoken by a woman who sounds a little older. It takes me a few moments to realize that they are spoken in my language. The intonation is strange and sometimes wrong, so I have to piece the words together. Did they train their computer that quickly? But the voice doesn't sound artificial.

"You know my language?" I ask, astonished.

"These people in the heavens do not, but I am empowered to speak it," comes the reply from the display computer. "I apologize for any inaccuracies. Your language has not been spoken here for thousands of years."

"For thousands of years? But does that mean it came from here? That it existed?"

"Yes. We call it Ancient Egyptian. It is written down as hieroglyphs, but there is no longer any spoken context," says the voice. "We are full of joy to have you with us and we apologize profusely for what happened."

"I apologize, too," I say quickly. "I did not mean to destroy your space station."

"Thank you. We know that. The people in the heavens were able to escape to the white disk in the sky. No one went to the realm of the dead."

When I understand the strange words, I feel relief.

"Our kings do not always share the same opinion as we seekers of knowledge and people in the heavens. It saddens us greatly that they tried to kill you."

"Thank you," I reply. "I am very happy that you're here."

"Our leader kings wish to welcome you to Earth. The people of the land are very excited about your presence. Is that acceptable to you?"

"Yes, I would be very happy," I say without hesitation. My head is spinning too much for me to even think about it if I wanted to. There seems to be no room left in my brain for conscious decisions. "Thank you for your kind invitation."

"The honor is very much with us."

I point two fingers in Ammit-47's direction as my forearm display beeps and blinks for my attention. The astronauts lean forward, interested but not alarmed. They don't look tense or like they're in danger, which makes me very happy.

That changes a little when they see the worried look on my face. The secret cargo module, which was locked and disconnected from the system, has opened and is now shown in the layout plans as a full part of the ship, along with its cargo, the two black boxes.

"Is there a problem?" asks the voice from the flat computer.

"No, sorry. My ship just repaired itself, I think. May I leave you alone for a moment? My friend Ammit-47 will stay with you and give you something to eat and drink."

The voice switches to its own language, which sounds much faster and less accented than mine.

Ancient Egyptian. I speak one of their languages, but it no longer exists?

"Okay. We've decided to trust you and thank you for your kindness toward guests," the woman from the computer finally replies. I lean forward a little and only now realize that it's her. She has dark brown skin like me, black hair and a round face that radiates something motherly. I smile at her and wave.

"I'll be right back. Please look at anything you want. There are no secrets here," I say, looking at the ladder.

Except for one last one.

49

I climb the ladder and slide back through the central corridor to the maintenance area, a sinking feeling in my stomach as I remember the last time I was there and how it ended up with me in the sickbay.

The unmarked armored door is open, retracted into its socket in the wall. Beyond it I see the two black boxes standing next to each other on the floor. Their surfaces have changed, looking metallic now, solid as steel, and not like a mystical darkness that swallows all light and seems strangely formless.

The light is on, not cold and white, but an almost invitingly warm and glowing yellow.

I hesitantly make my way through the doorway and approach very slowly, expecting a flash of light and a lifeless blow that will make me faint.

But nothing like that happens. I am inside and they're still there. No more weird buzzing.

Then the door slams shut and I jump in shock. I instinctively want to push myself off to get to it, to see if it is locked and I am trapped, but then something else happens. One of the boxes dissolves. It seems to crumble away as though it were made of dust and I watch the residue seep into invisible holes in the floor.

Fascinated, I pause and watch the unreal spectacle. As if by magic, the second box begins to rotate, maybe seeking to align its front with me, then it opens, the sides fold to the floor and a round gray object with a flat top appears. There is a crackling and buzzing sound, then a hologram appears in front of me, which I only recognize as such because it flickers briefly.

Suddenly I see a being with six arms hanging from a teardrop-shaped green torso. It floats before me, crouching at the bottom of the hologram and seeming to support itself on the air. Six pairs of eyes range across the top of the torso, which sprouts dozens of antennae. The alien looks majestic, much larger than me, like an inflated balloon. I see something that could be a mouth, or a breathing hole – or both. The eyes are huge and amber-colored. There is an unfathomable depth in them that quickly captivates me.

My mind knows I should be disgusted, because there is something monstrous about it, but within me there is a deep recognition, a soothing familiarity.

"Greetings, One," the being says. Its voice is a song, composed of whistles and piercing sounds that come from an organ I cannot see. They resonate with me on a physical level. None of it resembles a language like the one I spoke with Ammit-47 and the other humans. It is more like a melody, much more complex and layered, that my brain is able to decipher automatically.

"Hello," I say, confused. "Who are you?"

"I am the artificial intelligence of the *Ankh*, modeled after the ship's designer and fed by his mind."

"Is One my name?"

"That is the official name we have chosen for you," the being confirms. "But most of us call you Truth-Truthfulness."

I think about it. "That's a beautiful name."

"It's one you deserve."

"Why is that my name?" I ask, because I understand that I am speaking to those who sent me. I just know, like puzzle pieces are falling into place and revealing the whole picture to me little by little.

"We sent you to this planet to make contact with humans after we visited their world many twelve cycles ago when they were still an archaic civilization," the hologram explains.

"Why? Why me? Why alone? Why am I human? I don't understand." I give voice to my confusion, the questions fly from my lips. I have been asking myself them for months.

"A lot of time has passed in which we have been looking for the best way to contact our cosmic neighbors since we received the first radio signals. We had genetic samples of the local species from our first visit five thousand Earth years ago and decided to generate and send out a clone."

"Me."

"Yes, you, Truth-Truthfulness," the being confirms, its chanted language filling every corner of my mind and senses. "We wanted the risk of conflict due to misunderstanding to be as low as possible. We had no data on how they had evolved and whether they could rise above the rather crude, violent structures of the time."

"But why did you create the fake bodies? In the other breeding tanks?"

"Your mission is the most important our species has ever undertaken. We could not take any risks, no conflicts among the crew, and no danger from group dynamics that humans are often subject to. We wanted to make sure that you were alone and felt that way, in order to find out how your species behaves under stress."

"So if I had freaked out, you would have stopped the experiment?" I ask incredulously.

"It would have ended itself."

I look at the spot where the second black box was, my throat too dry to even swallow.

"According to our analyses, first contact is a major potential stressor for any species, and we had no way of knowing how humans would react to it," the creature continues.

"Your development without previous influences was our proof that external stressors brought out good in you. You risked your life to save another, a maintenance robot. You mourned the other as you tried to make amends for a misunderstanding. You learned to take even the negativity of Ammit-47 into your heart and turn it into something good-natured. Through the example of your actions and unwavering kindness toward things, you proved that giving up is not in your nature, that you combine the best aspects of organic life forms in yourself – the balance of intuition and cosmic connection and rationality. Your development makes me optimistic about contact with the new humanity, and since the first contact has now been peaceful and successful, I reveal myself to you and send you the deep gratitude of our species, which is also your species."

"But how is that possible? And how do I know all this?"

"We trained your brain with our knowledge of humanity and the Earth and gave you all the necessary expertise you would need for your journey. After we picked up more advanced radio signals, the onboard computer was fed with the relevant information, which was passed on to you – distance and measurement scales, for example."

I remember the incoming signal that the computer showed me, but the origin of which was not clear, and then the malfunctions started.

"So it was all just staged, to watch me under stress? I could have died," I say, searching for anger but not finding it. I understand the motives and even if I was – still am – a tool, this is the only existence I know and I feel good about myself. This realization makes me very calm.

"In a way, it was a simulation for our safety. To determine whether first contact was a good idea or if it would have potentially dire consequences for both species. Life is very precious and must be protected. Even from itself," says the being with its indescribable calm and composure. "We placed Ammit-47 and Ammit-48 at your side to give you the different aspects of being human and not to dictate your development. They shaped you and you shaped them. You taught a robot self-sacrifice, which went against its programming. We are very proud of you and fascinated by your journey. You have sincerely touched us."

"We? Were you able to watch me the whole time?"

"No. The signals to us take twenty Earth years. But, in a way, my personality is that of everyone else. Our species is not as individually structured as that of humans. Each entity is part of the whole and shares its feelings, so my extrapolation of what I have experienced enables a clear prediction. We express our gratitude to you and hereby authorize you to contact humanity on our behalf. The most valuable thing we possess is stored in me. The cosmic coordinates of our home world."

"Your home world?" I ask.

"Ours," the creature corrects me. "You may look different from us, but you are as much one of us as you are of them. There is a deep understanding of our kind woven into you that will reveal itself when the moment is right. You will always have a home with us, should you choose to."

"Thank you," I murmur. "Is it safe to give out the home world coordinates?"

"That decision is now yours. Please note that we designed the *Ankh* to function at the lowest possible technical level. We were aware of the possibility of placing advanced technology in the wrong hands. But the result of your journey is proof enough for us that we can and should trust you – and thus humanity. That is why we trust your judgment."

I think about it and look at the floor to the right of the hologram. "What was in the second box?"

"We don't leave much to chance unless it's absolutely

necessary," the being answers somewhat cryptically, and I know that it doesn't have to say anything more. Nothing more is necessary, because I think I understand. "We are deeply in your debt, Truth-Truthfulness, and we apologize for what you experienced and what may have caused you pain. Our gratitude will accompany you, no matter what you decide and do from now on. Our trust is in you."

"I am exactly where I want to be," I say from the bottom of my heart.

A deep peace spreads through me, beyond feelings of joy or relief. It is all-encompassing and universal, it is what I have always been, if I had just truly looked.

"I have become what I had to become. Everything that has happened has made me what I am, has led me to where I am. Who am I to know what should be? How do I know that it is as it should be? Because it is. I am what I am. Who could have ever hoped for more?"

EPILOGUE

The helicopter flies in a wide arc around the three mighty pyramids of Giza, which rise like thorns from the desert floor. In the background we can see Cairo, which takes up the entire horizon like a bubbling carpet of concrete.

"Six months, and finally we're here," I say in English to Muktabo, one of the three astronauts who visited me on the *Ankh*. Rachel and James, the other two, are awaiting us at the landing zone. They have become my best friends and something like my anchors in reality, especially since I became the most famous person of all time. The many appearances on TV shows and live streams, before parliaments and committees, they have made me a little tired, but also humble. I have been met with so much fascination and affection that it almost overwhelmed me. But apparently nothing is as supportive as the love of other people, and I still feel very exhilarated now that I am on vacation.

"They went by quickly, didn't they?" Muktabo asks me via radio, his dark face breaking into a bright white smile.

"That's true." I nod. "I've learned so much that I can't fit anything else in." With my outstretched finger I tap my left temple – or rather the noise-cancelling headphones.

"You now know what vegans are, television ... and the tax office."

"To be honest, I don't know anything about anything. Vegans don't eat anything that comes from animals, which I think is great because they are compassionate. On the other hand, I don't understand how it works with plants. To grow them, agricultural machines are used that plow the soil and kill huge numbers of insects and worms. But I also think it's good that they don't eat anything from those animal prisons," I muse. "The fact that you breed billions of animals to be slaughtered and twenty-five percent of them are thrown away somehow doesn't feel right."

"You don't need to expect any counterarguments from me," says Muktabo in agreement.

"The tax office demands taxes on what I earn, which still doesn't make sense to me," I continue. "Why don't they demand something on what I buy instead of taxing my productive life?"

"When in doubt, always go for it because there's more to be had. What you buy is also taxed, by the way. We call it value-added tax." My friend grins broadly. These conversations always seem to amuse him and I like it when he smiles. I like it whenever *anyone* smiles. Rofi taught me that. A simple gesture that, even if it is all you know, is absolutely sufficient to send your life in the right direction. If I could only do one final thing, it would be to smile.

"I somewhat understand," I say, making a helpless gesture as the helicopter approaches its landing pad. Out of the corner of my eye I can see the fighter jets circling us in the distance, keeping me safe. I don't know why this is necessary. Everyone here is so nice to me. "But this thing with the television, that's the weirdest thing."

Muktabo laughs.

"You watch on a screen how people torment, torture, or shoot other people, murder someone or go through terrible breakups and then call it 'entertainment?' To relax after a hard day at work?" I sigh and shake my head. "Now tell me I'm crazy because I like listening to children's radio."

"No, before saying you are crazy, we must admit we are all crazy," he assures me, looking at me with that loving look that feels extra good and warms my heart. "You taught us not to be so crazy anymore, simply because you are who you are."

"I didn't do anything except talk to people."

"You've done so much more. You've saved us all and given us a new future. You are a gift." He offers me his hand and I take it without hesitation. Then he clasps it with his other hand and nods toward the window. "Today is your birthday."

"Today?" I ask, surprised.

"Yes. We spoke to your onboard computer. We're celebrating on Earth."

"Then I will become... one?"

"Yes." He thinks about it and laughs. "You look very old for your age!"

I join in his laughter and chuckle. "It looks like it, yes."

"And you usually get a present on your birthday."

"A present?" Excitement tingles in my fingers and under my scalp. "I love presents."

"That's what we thought. And do you know what else we have?" Muktabo pauses for a moment, apparently enjoying my joyful impatience. "We've made a decision."

My mouth drops open. For six months, the heads of state of Earth have been negotiating and discussing behind closed doors what to do with the coordinates that I only recently gave them. Those of my other home world, of those who sent me, who are just as much a part of me as these people. At first, I was afraid that they might be angry with me because I waited until now to give them the key to contact my home, but no one complained. I just wanted to take my time with my decision. But I don't regret it, and I made it from the fullness of my heart.

"And what did they decide?" I ask.

"They asked people what we should do. There were three ideas and we used the internet to ask all the inhabitants of our beautiful planet to vote so that the decision would come from us as a species," explains Muktabo, smiling contentedly, which answers my unspoken question of whether it is a good decision.

We land near the Sphinx, the impressive stone statue in front of the pyramids. The landing field is large and is in front of a grandstand that has been set up. On it wait 200 or more men and women in different kinds of clothes from all over the world. It makes me happy to see so many people. I love crowds because I love people. The more the better. I also like being alone, as I still choose to do despite everything, because I can enjoy being close to myself. Despite everything, I have never given up on myself, and I think I am quite good company.

There are many more people on the other side of the landing field. Thousands, maybe even millions, a sea of minds watching us touch down, held back by barriers, cheering us on.

"So many guests on my birthday," I say happily.

"They all want to see you receive your present."

After we have touched down and the rotor blades have stopped, two men open the door for us. I thank them politely and wave to the crowd. The cheers erupt even louder. Muktabo waves too and I hold his hand because I am suddenly very excited.

Then we walk toward the stands. Rachel and James are waiting in front of them and hug me. Ammit-47 is also with them. He hugs me too, feigning reluctance, grinning across his new 'face.' His replacement display is not as high-resolution as the original, but he seems happy with it and winks at me.

I see that the heads of state of every country are gathered in the grandstand, and I cry a little from a powerful wave of emotion. Birthday, I think, that's a very beautiful thing. Some of these important women and men wave to me, and they all smile like we've known each other for a long time. It warms my heart.

One of them, I think she is from China, gets up from her seat and comes toward me. My friends, Ammit-47, Rachel, James, and Muktabo, flank me. The woman, I recognize her now as President Li-Jang, shakes my hand and laughs when I hug her. Laughter can also be heard from the stands. It sounds cheerful.

"It is an honor to have you as our guest," says Li-Jang, bowing slightly after we have separated. "The Earth has spoken and decided what we will do with the coordinates of your home. Before I tell you on behalf of all nations and ask for your consent, I would like to say to you on behalf of all the people who took part in the vote. You may have a home in the stars, but you can also always have one here with us. You have two homes, whatever you want to do."

"Thank you," I say, touched. "I can feel it."

"We have completed repairs to the *Ankh* and developed a deep sleep system with the help of our best engineers and scientists. If you agree, we would like to send you back to your creators," explains Li-Jang. "It seems to us the wisest of all responses to their contact."

I think about it and quickly realize that this is a very far-sighted, good-hearted choice. Sending me on an 80-year journey with the technology that brought me here proves several things. They are willing to think long-term rather than just looking for a quick profit, and they are willing to give up a piece of potentially advanced technology to give me a safe journey home and show my creators that they are of good will. I am their answer to those who sent me.

"That's very wise," I say. "I just wish..."

"Your present is still missing," Muktabo says quietly from the side. Only now do I notice that the crowds behind us have fallen silent. Ammit-47 steps to the side and reveals a covered object. I frown and hold my breath as he pulls the piece of cloth away. A robot that is very similar to him, except that the display is narrower and the hands and arms are a little less delicate, appears.

"The Chinese-American *Artemis* crew had to evacuate to the moon after the incident," explains Li-Jang. "They found and recovered your robot friend. We had to rebuild his body using our own technology. We're sorry if we couldn't do more. But he is our gift to you. You and Ammit-47 should not set off alone and we think that the three of you are only complete if you are together."

"His data storage, is it still...?" I begin to ask, and then the display on the robot's head comes to life and I see the familiar smiley face. It's smiling the first smile I ever saw in my life and it makes my heart explode with joy.

"ROFI!" I shout.

He raises two fingers and his smile emoticon turns into a laughing emoticon.

Wherever I go or arrive, I am home.

AFTERWORD

Dear readers,

If you liked this book, I would be very happy to receive a review on Amazon. It will help me to continue doing what I love: writing fiction for you!

If you sign up for my newsletter, you will receive my eBook "Rift: The Transition" free and exclusively: www.joshuatcalvert.com

How to reach me personally:

joshua@joshuatcalvert.com

With this in mind, I send you my warmest greetings,

Joshua